ELIZABETH'S Heart

O'CONNER PREQUEL

RHONDA BREWER

Acknowledgments

With so many people in my life to thank for making publishing this book possible, I could almost write another book on that alone. However, a simple thank you never seems enough to convey my gratitude, but I will try to do that the best I can with this acknowledgment.

First, thank you belongs to the many authors who have become both friends and mentors to me. Then there are the amazing ladies who help with editing and errors. A special thank you goes to Michelle Eriksen, Abbie Zanders, and Amabel Daniels for their constant support and keen eye. To my dedicated betas and dear friends, Jackie Dawe Ford, Nancy Arnold-Holloway, and Karie Deegan thank you so much for the support and constant encouragement. To my readers, you are the reason that I can continue to do this.

To my husband and children, I would never be able to do what I love without your love and support. You all mean the world to me, and I love you with all my heart.

Dedication

I've dedicated this book to my wonderful grandmother, Mary (Laura) Holwell. She's the inspiration for Nanny Betty that we all love and adore. She's one of the angels who sits on my shoulder.

Rhonda Brewer

Prologue

Elizabeth Power O'Connor, or Nanny Betty, as everyone knew her, never thought she would see the day she would marry again. Starting a new relationship didn't seem to be in the cards for her after she lost her beloved Jack. Especially not at eighty-five years old with three children, eleven grandchildren, and too many great-grandchildren to count.

Still, fate smiled upon her again, and her first love came back into her life. She first met Thomas Roberts when she was only seventeen years old when he was simply Tommy. He was the first boy she ever loved and the first one to break her heart. She didn't know at the time, but he didn't leave Newfoundland because he wanted to. Tommy didn't have a choice, but when he left, it shifted her life into another direction.

Elizabeth fell in love with Jack O'Connor, and for nearly fifty years, she was happily married. Their life wasn't always easy, and like everyone, they hit a few bumps in the road. She and Jack married young and worked together to become a strong couple. They never allowed anything to put a wedge between them.

Losing Jack had been the hardest loss of her life, and there were days she didn't know if she would survive the pain, especially when she was alone.

For the years after his death, she lived the way he would have wanted her to. Elizabeth didn't get lost in her grief; she used her strength to be there for her family.

The day that Tom walked back into her life was a shock and something she never expected. Tom wasn't the same boy she'd known all those years ago. He was a successful businessman who was featured in magazines over the years and was well-respected, not that Elizabeth cared about any of that. She was happy that he'd achieved so much success.

When Tom re-entered her life, she didn't think she would be able to open her heart to him again, but he was the same kind-hearted person he had been as a boy. Tom's persistence, kind heart, and generosity wore down her resistance. All of it made Elizabeth realize they could rekindle the love they had once shared.

Looking up into his eyes as they danced at her granddaughter's wedding, she knew Tom was her future. He'd proposed to her at her granddaughter Isabelle's wedding, and she'd accepted. They wanted to wait until the last of her grandchildren were married.

"Would you like to sit down for a bit, Betty?" Tom asked when the song ended.

"Yes, it gives me a chance to watch the youngsters dance," she answered as she linked into his arm, and he led her off the dancefloor.

She smiled as she watched each of the couples move around the floor. Her children, grandchildren, great-grandchildren, as well as men and women she considered her family were all full of smiles that made her heart so full. It made her happy to see her legacy.

"All of this started with you and Jack, my love," Tom whispered into her ear.

"Everything happens for a reason, and although it broke my heart when you left, I wouldn't have this wonderful family if you'd stayed." Elizabeth turned and met his blue eyes.

"Fate has a way of doing what's best for everyone," Tom responded.

A smile formed on her face as she turned back to the dancefloor. Love and happiness oozed from everyone around her, and all of it was there because she married a fisherman.

Chapter 1

The din faded into the background as she closed her eyes and listened to the crash of the waves on the shore. Elizabeth Power loved to be there when her father's fishing boat, *The Cora Lee*, sailed out of the harbor. At seventeen years old, she was old enough to go on the vessel with her father, but she was a girl, and that wouldn't be proper for Patrick Power's daughter.

According to her mother, her job was to help keep the house while the men were gone. Isabelle Power didn't believe ladies should wear anything but dresses and constantly nagged when Elizabeth would put on a pair of peddle pushers. Trying to explain that the three-quarter-length pants were the style would fall on deaf ears.

Since it was mid-March, all the fishing boats were back in the water and heading out to fish for cod. They'd start to pull the boats out of the water in November and dry dock them for the winter. Then as soon as March hit, they'd be back on the water.

"Is your fadder gone for the first run of the season, Elizabeth?" one of the older fishermen asked as she walked by one of the fish flakes where they would lay split cod to salt and dry.

"He'll be back a week from today," Elizabeth answered.

It was amusing to her whenever the family would go to St. John's. People would know she was from the Southern Shore because of her accent. She didn't think she had one since everyone in Cape Broyle spoke the same way. Some people had told her that she sounded like an Irishwoman, and she would smile and walk away. If she said what she wanted to say, she'd probably get the hard end of her mother's slipper.

"I think the other O'Connor boats are gone out today too," the man shouted as Elizabeth continued down the wharf.

The O'Connor family were well known around the community because they owned more than half the fishing boats that sailed out of Cape Broyle. Sean O'Connor and his two sons, Jack and Billy, went on another boat together and had several crew members with them. Sean hired her father as the Skipper of *The Cora Lee*, and both her brothers fished with him.

Kurt and Charles, or Charlie as everyone called him, were both older than Elizabeth and were the typical older brothers. They teased her, but they would give their life for her if she was in trouble. It was one of the reasons she put up with their overbearing ways. They were also charming, kind and attractive, although she would never tell them that. All their qualities made them popular with the girls around town.

The O'Connor boys were also very popular around the southern shore, mostly because they were considered by most to be a catch. Elizabeth didn't know them personally, but she understood why the girls wanted them. The young men were handsome, polite, and relatively wealthy.

From the rumors around Cape Broyle, Billy knew how to use his assets, and the talk was he had a girl in every community around the Southern Shore. Elizabeth hadn't heard any rumors about Jack, but she was sure he wasn't an angel.

It didn't matter to her because the only boy who turned her head was Tommy Roberts. He came from just outside of Cape Broyle, but a lot of people were wary of him because of his older brothers. Eddie was the oldest of the three brothers and had been in and out of jail since he was sixteen. Melvin was the middle brother and had his own trouble with the law.

Tommy's father, Big Ed, was a farmer, and his mother Darla was a seamstress like Elizabeth's mother. Tommy worked with his father on the farm and managed to keep himself on the straight and narrow. Although he worked long hours, Tommy always found time for her. She was deeply in love with him and couldn't wait until she turned eighteen. Tommy told her he would ask her father for his blessing to marry her as soon as she did.

Elizabeth already knew how that conversation would go. Her father had warned her more than once to stay away from Tommy. He believed Tommy would end up like his brothers, but her dad didn't know that Tommy was her destiny.

Tommy was motivated, intelligent, and had plans for the future. He was saving to go to university and dreamed of owning his own company. He wanted people to respect him and not judge him because of his brothers. After all, Tommy's parents were good people. Elizabeth had so much faith in him and couldn't wait to follow him wherever he went.

Elizabeth made her way to the cliffs above her family home, where she could see from one end of the community to the other. She could also see into the next town and the outskirts of the Roberts' farm.

There was plenty of snow around, but her father and brothers had built a tiny shelter at the top of the cliff for her when she was a little girl. She loved to watch the boats sail out to sea, and they'd often find her up there shivering. She managed to keep the shelter standing for the last few years, and she loved to go there to think as well. For the most part, it would stay free of snow.

Inside the structure, her father had put a bench that she could stretch out on and would often go there to read in the summer when she wanted to get away from everyone. It was also a safe place where she could escape with Tommy without anyone knowing.

"Hey, darling."

Elizabeth glanced up as she got to the top of the cliffs where she could watch her father's boat make its way out to sea.

"Tommy," she exclaimed as she leaped into his arms.

"I got away early today and thought I might find you here." He smiled as he placed her back on the ground.

"Fadder's boat just left." She took his hand and tugged him toward the shelter.

"I sent off my application for university today." Tommy grinned as they sat on the large bench.

"That's simply wonderful." She stared into his eyes. "I just know you're going to get in."

"Fadder isn't happy about it." Tommy leaned back on his elbow.

"Honey, he doesn't understand. That generation doesn't know anything but farming and fishing. They don't understand how important education is." Elizabeth lay back and turned on her side to face him.

"I know, but I wish I could make him understand that I want to do more." Tommy met her eyes.

"I understand," she whispered.

"It's why I love you." Tommy moved forward and brushed his lips against hers.

Like every time their lips met, her heart pounded, and she'd feel that tingle between her thighs that told her she wanted so much more than a kiss. They both did, but trying to make that happen when they lived in such a small, nosey town was close to impossible.

"Every time I kiss you, I wish the rest of the world would vanish," Tommy whispered against her lips.

"Me too." She sighed as he pushed her back and deepened the kiss.

His hands hardly ever went places they weren't supposed to, but as his tongue thrust inside her mouth, his hand slowly slipped under her coat and sweater. Elizabeth trembled as his cool fingers skimmed the skin below her breast, and his leg moved between her thighs.

It was the only area where they felt safe enough to make out and not get caught. It was part of the Powers' private land, and the only people who went there were Elizabeth and her brothers. Since they were on the boat, she could relax and enjoy being with Tommy. At that moment, she was more than thankful, especially when his hand covered her breast and he gently squeezed.

He was hard against her hip, and it only made her want more, but Tommy would never go beyond that point. It frustrated her. Elizabeth wanted to take their relationship to the next level. After all, they were going to be together forever.

"Elizabeth, you make me so hard," he murmured as he moved his lips to the front of her sweater and nipped gently.

"I want you." She moaned.

"I know. I want the same, but not here." He flopped onto his back and groaned.

"When and where?" Elizabeth rolled over and rested her chin on his chest.

"Your fadder is gone for a week, right?" Tommy twirled her hair around his finger.

"Yes." Elizabeth held her breath as she waited for his idea.

"Your mudder goes to her sister's house on Wednesdays, right?" Tommy smirked as he tugged her closer.

"Yes, she's usually gone until midnight." Elizabeth closed her eyes as he spoke into her ear.

"I'll come over after she leaves," he whispered.

"Tommy," Elizabeth breathed his name as his hand cupped her breast on top of her sweater.

"I know. I can't wait, either," Tommy murmured as he placed soft kisses around the edge of her ear.

She wanted so much to go all the way with him, and she knew the risks. Elizabeth wasn't naïve. Taking that step with Tommy was what she wanted, and to her, it didn't matter if she ended up with his child because he was her future. It also meant her father couldn't turn Tommy down when he asked to marry Elizabeth.

Chapter 2

Wednesday seemed to take a thousand days to arrive, and when it did, the minutes ticked by like hours. After supper, her mother began to prepare to spend the evening with Elizabeth's aunt and a couple of other ladies. Elizabeth's heart thundered in her chest as she paced the room, waiting for her mother to leave.

To her relief, she only asked Elizabeth once if she wanted to join them. It was as if her mother was relieved when Elizabeth declined. It wasn't often she would join the Wednesday ladies' night with her mom, mostly because it was boring.

"Elizabeth, would you be uneasy here if I didn't return until morning? Jean hasn't been feeling well the last few days, and I'd like to stay with her to make sure she's taking care of herself." Her mother always worried about her older sister.

Jean Ryan lived on her own and had never been married and still lived in her childhood home. Jean had always been sick as a child and spent the majority of her life in and out of the hospital. Elizabeth didn't know what was wrong with her aunt, but she always seemed happy when they went to visit her.

"I'll be fine, Mudder." Elizabeth smiled.

If her mother was going for the night, that meant Tommy didn't have to leave before midnight. He was waiting up at the shelter until her mother left. Her body hummed with excitement at the thought of making love to Tommy for the first time.

"If you want, I can have Mrs. O'Driscoll send her daughter over to spend the night with you." Her mother turned as she headed out of the house.

"Mudder, Maureen O'Driscoll is the last person I'd want to spend an hour with, let alone an entire night." Elizabeth rolled her eyes.

"She's a lovely girl." Her mother appeared shocked at Elizabeth's reaction.

"Mudder, she's lovely to you, but you never went to school or sock hops with her. Thank you for worrying about me, I love you for that, but I'll be fine." Elizabeth walked out on the front porch as her mother stopped at the bottom of the steps.

"Okay, but if you need me to come home, call me at Aunt Jean's house," her mother shouted as she scurried down the road.

"Have a good evening, Mudder. Don't worry about me." Elizabeth shivered with excitement as she backed into the house.

"Okay, you should probably bring some wood up to your room for the night. It's supposed to be cold," her mother shouted and then she disappeared as she turned on to the next road.

13

As evening fell, Elizabeth sat on the sofa with her foot tapping nervously while she waited for Tommy to sneak up to the back door. Cape Broyle wasn't a place where you wanted the boyfriend that was spending the night to come to the front door.

The clock on the wall didn't seem to move as she waited for Tommy to arrive. She returned to the kitchen window several times to look out, and a few times, she thought she'd heard a knock, but when she opened the back door, he wasn't there.

After what seemed like forever, Elizabeth started to think he'd changed his mind. She was about to give up and go to her room when she heard a soft tap on the back door. Elizabeth jumped to her feet and practically ran to the door, only stopping herself for a moment to calm her erratic heart.

"Hi." She smiled when she opened the door.

"Hi," he murmured and stepped into the house quickly.

"You look freezing." She tugged him into the living room next to the woodstove.

"I'm fine." He slipped out of his jacket and rubbed his hands together over the top of the stove.

"I have good news." Elizabeth closed and locked the door.

"What's that?" Tommy turned when she entered the living room.

"Mudder is gone until the morning." Elizabeth folded her hands in front of her and peeped at him under her lowered lashes.

"That's wonderful." Tommy grasped her hands in his and gently pulled her toward him.

"Are you hungry?" Elizabeth blurted out, suddenly more nervous than she'd ever been in her life.

"Relax, darling. I'm not going to jump on you right here and now." Tommy chuckled as he linked his fingers with hers.

"Sorry, I'm just, nervous." She could feel the heat rise in her cheeks.

"Me too," he replied.

For several minutes, they stood in the middle of the living room holding hands. Elizabeth could feel her pulse race as he took a tiny step toward her, and she held her breath when he lowered his head closer to hers. He lightly brushed his lips against the corner of her mouth in barely a whisper of a kiss. Elizabeth's nerves got the better of her, and she tensed.

"Elizabeth, I understand if you've changed your mind. We can just sit and talk or listen to some music." Tommy raised his hand to push a stray piece of hair behind her ear.

"I haven't changed my mind, Tommy," she whispered.

With every ounce of courage she had, she reached up and cupped her hand on the back of Tommy's head. She pulled him down, and her lips met his in a slow passionate kiss. Tommy wrapped his arms around her and deepened the kiss while Elizabeth pressed her trembling body against his.

It was obvious Tommy was aroused by the kiss as much as she was. His hands slipped around her, and he pulled her tightly against his body as his tongue slipped inside her mouth. Elizabeth breathlessly pulled her lips from his and grabbed his hand.

"Elizabeth, are you sure?" Tommy hesitated when they were halfway up the stairs.

"I'm sure, Tommy," she replied and tugged him to her room.

She stopped just inside the door of her bedroom and waited for him to enter. Tommy was almost a foot taller than her, but when he stood in her room, he appeared even taller because of the lower ceilings on the second floor of her house. At six feet tall, he was only an inch or two from the light fixture in the middle of the room. When he glanced up above his head, he smiled.

"Good thing I'm not as tall as the O'Connors." Tommy chuckled.

"You're not exactly short, Tommy." Elizabeth sat down on her bed and tried to appear relaxed.

"This room is the perfect size for you." Tommy knelt in front of her and braced his hands on either side of her hips.

"You're perfect for me," Elizabeth whispered as she held his face between her hands.

"I love you, Elizabeth." Tommy gazed into her eyes, and her heart soared with joy.

"I love you too." Elizabeth couldn't imagine loving anyone more.

Tommy leaned closer and pressed his lips lightly against hers, but he still seemed to be hesitant. When she tried to deepen the kiss, he pulled back and took a deep breath.

"If we cross this line, Elizabeth, you're mine. Forever." Tommy's voice was soft and seductive.

"I'm yours," Elizabeth whispered.

With those words, Tommy kissed her again and lowered her back on her bed. All her nerves and doubts disappeared because Tommy was part of her. Body, mind, and soul.

Elizabeth woke when the bed dipped next to her. She opened her eyes to Tommy's smile, and she watched while he buttoned his shirt. They made love several times during the night, and although the first time was awkward, the other times had been better.

"Go back to sleep, darling," Tommy whispered.

"What time is it?" Elizabeth sat up, making sure to keep her quilt wrapped around her naked breasts.

"It's a little before five. I want to make sure I get out of here before the fisherman start heading to the pier." Tommy sat next to her.

"I can't wait for the day that we can be like this every night." Elizabeth ran her hand down his cheek.

"Me too," Tommy whispered and brushed his lips against hers.

"When can I see you again?" she asked.

"I've got to help the old man with some stuff today, but I should be able to meet you on the peak after supper." Tommy gave her a soft kiss.

"I'll be there." Elizabeth smiled as he backed away from the bed.

"I love you." He blew her a kiss and quietly opened her bedroom door.

"I love you too." She couldn't wipe the smile off her face if she tried.

"Go back to sleep." Tommy grinned and closed the door behind him.

Elizabeth fell back on the bed and sighed. There was no way she'd be able to go back to sleep with everything that was running through her head. After she tossed and turned for almost a half-hour, she got out of bed and made her way to the mirror.

Elizabeth scanned her reflection and tried to see if she looked any different. Would someone be able to look at her and know what happened between her and Tommy?

"Elizabeth, don't be so foolish," she mumbled to herself. "How in heaven's name would someone know by looking at you?"

She did have to change her bed and take a bath. She was a little sore, and from what she'd heard, it was normal after the first time. Even with all that, she was so happy that the boy she'd spend the rest of her life with would be her one and only.

Elizabeth had more energy than she knew what to do with after her bath. She cleaned the entire house and while she hung several loads of laundry on the clothesline, she got several odd looks from the fishermen who were on the way to the wharf. The March temperatures weren't the best for drying clothes.

A little after seven that morning, she finished her breakfast and headed out on the front step to drink her tea. A dark cloud of smoke rose from the west end of town. It was unusual for a forest fire during the winter since there was so much snow around.

"How's she gettin' on, Elizabeth?" One of the older fishermen hobbled down toward the harbor with his cane.

If anyone outside Newfoundland heard what he asked, they would have no idea what the man meant, but it was merely a way of asking someone how they were.

"I'm doing good, Mr. Colbert." Elizabeth smiled at the man.

Gerald Colbert was one of the oldest residents of Cape Broyle, but Elizabeth wasn't sure of his age. She assumed he was at least in his mid-seventies. She remembered her father telling her once that Gerald taught him how to drive a boat after Elizabeth's grandfather died.

"Looks like something is gone up in smoke over there." He pointed toward the dark plume.

"Strange time for a forest fire." Elizabeth nodded.

"Isn't that the Roberts' farm over that way?" Gerald stopped and held his hand over his eyes as if it would help him see clearer.

Elizabeth's heart felt as if it stopped in her chest at Gerald's words, he was right. The smoke was definitely rising from where the farm stood. She ran down the front steps and sped toward the peak where she could see better.

"Don't go too close to that fire, Elizabeth," Gerald shouted.

She waved behind her as she ran to the top of the hill, tripping several times and even falling once because she didn't pay attention to the rocks or twigs. It didn't matter that blood trickled down her leg as she climbed to the top of the peak. Elizabeth was determined to see where the smoke was coming from. She stopped at the top where she could see not only the harbor but out to the farm as well.

Elizabeth gasped in horror at the sight of the black smoke swirling up from the direction of Tommy's house. Large red flames were licking around the tiny home, and dark smoke engulfed the shed next to it. What happened? Tommy left no more than two hours earlier.

Elizabeth wasn't sure what she should do, and she didn't even realize tears started to run down her cheeks at the horrible sight in front of her. As the flames licked around the farmhouse, Elizabeth stood frozen in fear. She could see the fire engines next to the property, but they didn't seem to be doing anything.

Elizabeth ran as fast as she could off the peak and headed toward her Aunt Jean's house. Her mother probably already knew about the fire because news spread as quickly as the flames did, but she needed to be with someone in her family. Someone who would tell her everything would be okay.

Halfway up the road, she met her mother and her aunt, hurrying toward her with Anne and Maureen O'Driscoll. She ran right into her mother's arms and sobbed as she tried to tell her mother how terrible the fire looked.

"Oh, ducky, don't you worry. I'm sure Tommy is fine," her mother whispered in her ear.

"Mudder, the house… it's awful…" Elizabeth sobbed.

"Probably one of those Roberts boys playing with fire," Anne said in her usual snarky tone.

"Anne, you shouldn't say something like that," Jean chastised the woman.

"Why not? Those boys are nothing but trouble," Anne snapped.

"They are handsome, though." Maureen sighed.

"Maureen, you stay away from those boys. They're trouble," Anne pointed her finger at her daughter.

"Mrs. O'Driscoll, you don't even know them. Not all of them are trouble," Elizabeth snapped at the snooty lady.

Anne looked at Elizabeth in shock, but it was the smirk on Maureen's face that made her want to slap the girl. Elizabeth knew for a fact that Maureen had spent time with at least one of Tommy's brothers. She bragged about it at a dance one evening.

"Elizabeth, don't be rude." Her mother said the words, but Elizabeth knew that she was only saying it for Anne's sake.

Her mother had a distinctive look when she was serious. She would give what Elizabeth and her brothers would refer to as the *devil's glare*. When her mother narrowed her eyes and pressed her lips together, they knew better than to push it.

Elizabeth didn't say another word to the nasty woman, more for her mother's sake than anything. She didn't care what the old bat thought, because Elizabeth knew the truth.

"Mudder, you've got to bring me over there. I need to see if Tommy is okay," Elizabeth begged.

"I'll go with you." Maureen sounded excited about going to the farm.

"You will not." Anne grabbed Maureen by the arm. "We are going home, and you'll be helping me cook lunch for your fadder when he comes home."

With that, Maureen and Anne walked away back to their house, and Elizabeth felt a sense of relief that they were gone. Why they had come with her mother and Jean, she didn't know, but she was glad they were gone.

"I've got the keys to your fadder's truck. Aunt Jean is going to drive." Her mother nodded as they hurried back home.

Jean was one of very few women in the community who could drive a vehicle. Elizabeth had always wanted to learn, and both her brothers had offered to teach her, but her father had rejected the idea.

The truck bounced as they drove over the gravel road that led to the farm. Elizabeth had only been to Tommy's house a handful of times, and she would feel sick every time she'd drive over the terrible road. This time she was ill for a different reason. She was worried.

They didn't get very far when members of the Royal Canadian Mounted Police stopped them. The RCMP weren't in the area often, and when they were, it was terrible. If the police were at the fire, then something was really bad. That alone terrified Elizabeth. She jumped out of the truck when her aunt stopped and ran toward one of the uniformed men.

"I'm looking for Tommy." Elizabeth grabbed the man by the arm.

"I'm sorry, young lady. You can't go any further," the man shook his head.

"My boyfriend lives there with his family. Are they okay?" Elizabeth tried to sound calm, but her voice cracked.

"I'm sorry to tell you this, but it looks like none of the family were able to get out of the house," the officer said coldly.

"What?" Elizabeth staggered back, and she didn't recognize her own voice as she stared at the police officer.

"The fire is too intense for the firefighters to get closer. I'm sorry. We only have one of the family, and he's at the station," the officer explained.

"Who is it, and why did you bring him to the station?" Elizabeth felt ill.

Was it possible that Anne was right, and one of Tommy's brothers started the fire? It also meant that the boy she loved was gone. Elizabeth shook her head because she didn't want to believe what she heard.

"He's suspected of starting the fire. He was the only one not in the house when it started at around four this morning." The officer looked back over his shoulder.

"Who did you take to the station?" Elizabeth demanded.

"Young lady, not that it will make a difference, but the boy's name is Tommy," the man grumbled.

The world around Elizabeth started to spin, and she staggered back. There was no way Tommy could have started the fire. He'd been with her all night, and he didn't leave until almost five. If the fire started at four. Tommy didn't do it.

She didn't know what to do as she glanced back at the truck. Her mother's brow furrowed, and she had concern written all over her face. Elizabeth swallowed the lump in her throat and turned back to the police officer. Elizabeth straightened her shoulders and composed herself.

"Would I be able to see him, or is he arrested?" Elizabeth asked.

"Right now, he's just being held for questioning. I'm sure if you ask at the station, they'll let you speak to him." The officer nodded.

Elizabeth didn't wait for him to say another word. She hurried back to the truck and told them what the police officer said. They didn't even ask if she wanted to see Tommy. Jean spun the truck around, and they made their way toward the police station the next town over.

Chapter 3

The Ferryland Detachment of the RCMP was only fifteen minutes from Tommy's family farm. It was a small building close to the main road and didn't look like what you would believe to be a police station.

Elizabeth walked into the building and frantically scanned the area for someone. An older woman sat at a desk tapping keys on a typewriter and only looked up when the telephone rang. When she finished with the call, she went back to her typing.

"Excuse me." Elizabeth walked up to the desk.

"Can I help you?" The older woman turned and smiled at her.

"My boyfriend was brought here from his family's farm. There was a fire, and he's here to answer some questions. The officer I spoke to said I could come here and talk to him because his whole…" Elizabeth stopped when the woman held up her hand.

"Ducky, I know we talk fast in Newfoundland, but good heaven's you should be an auctioneer." The woman chuckled.

"I'm sorry. I'm just really worried." Elizabeth sighed.

"Let me check. What's your boyfriend's name?" The woman stood up.

"Tommy Roberts," Elizabeth replied.

The woman stared at her for a moment and then nodded. She walked through the door behind her and returned a few minutes later. The woman gave her a soft smile and stepped around the desk next to Elizabeth.

"He's in with one of the officers at the moment, but he shouldn't be too much longer." The receptionist led Elizabeth to a chair on the other side of the room. "You can wait here."

For what seemed like hours, the older woman continued to glance at her with pity. It upset Elizabeth, and she wanted to yell at the woman to tell her Tommy didn't do anything, but how could she say what she knew with her mother sitting next to her?

Elizabeth would never believe that Tommy could do anything to hurt his family or anyone. Even if he hadn't spent the night with her, she still wouldn't believe it.

"What's taking so long?" Elizabeth murmured mostly to herself.

It got harder for her to sit still the longer she waited. Elizabeth began to pace the small reception area and continued to glance at the door, praying for Tommy to come through and tell her it was all a mistake.

"Elizabeth, maybe we should go and come back in the morning," her mother suggested.

"Mudder, you don't think they're going to keep him here overnight? He didn't do anything." Elizabeth's heart raced at the thought of Tommy locked behind bars.

Before her mother responded, the door opened, and an older officer appeared. He whispered something to the secretary before he turned his attention to Elizabeth.

"Hello, I'm Sergeant Harold Doyle. I understand you're Tommy's girlfriend." The man reached out to shake Elizabeth's hand.

"Yes. Can I see him?" Elizabeth hated to sound like she was begging, but she was desperate.

"I'll let you in for a few minutes if it's okay with your parents," Harold said.

"That's my mudder." Elizabeth pointed to where her mother sat.

"Is this okay with you, ma'am?" The officer turned his attention to her mom.

"Yes." Her mother nodded.

The officer hesitated for a moment, then motioned for Elizabeth to follow him. The door behind her clicked, and the sound echoed through the small area. As they walked down the narrow hallway, Elizabeth felt closed in and wondered how anyone would survive in the building if they had to work there.

"He's in here, Miss." Harold pushed open the door, and Elizabeth peeked inside.

She gasped when she saw Tommy behind a table with his hands folded in front of him. When he saw her, he immediately stood up, but the look that he gave Harold made her uneasy.

"I'll leave you alone, but I'll be back in a few minutes." Harold closed the door leaving Elizabeth alone with the boy she loved.

She started toward Tommy, but he held up his hand. Elizabeth stared at him for a few seconds as she tried to read the unusual expression on his face. He scowled at her and then he spoke.

"Elizabeth, what are you doing here?" Tommy asked with a coldness she'd never heard from him ever before.

"I came to tell them you couldn't possibly have started that fire," she replied and slowly lowered herself into the chair across from him.

"No." Tommy practically yelled but then took a deep breath and continued. "You don't tell them anything."

"But, Tommy…" Elizabeth was interrupted when he shot to his feet and raised his voice.

"I. Said. No." He leaned over and stared directly into her eyes.

Elizabeth swallowed the lump that formed in her throat and tried to blink back the tears in her eyes. This wasn't her Tommy. He was cold, scary, and angry.

"I don't want you to tell them anything. The last thing I need is for the entire town to find out what happened last night. I didn't start the fire, and they'll figure that out, but there is no way you are going to be my alibi. Got it?" Tommy dropped back down into the chair and took one of her hands in his.

"Yes," she choked out.

"I'm sorry, darling. I didn't mean to speak to you like that. I'm still trying to deal with the fact that my parents and my brothers are gone." Tommy dropped his head, and Elizabeth saw a tear drop to the table.

"I can't believe it." Elizabeth cupped his cheek in her hand.

"You need to go home. I'll come and see you as soon as I deal with this. I promise." Tommy pulled her hand up to his lips and kissed her palm.

"I love you, Tommy." She sobbed as she stood up and walked around the table to wrap her arms around him.

"I love you too." Tommy pulled her into his arms.

Elizabeth didn't hear the door open, but she turned when she heard Harold clear his throat. Tommy kissed the side of her face and whispered in her ear that she needed to keep their night together a secret from everyone.

"I'll see you soon," Tommy said as he released her.

"Okay." She kissed his cheek and then left the room.

The police would find out that he didn't hurt his family. Tommy would be back in Cape Broyle before she knew it. She didn't know where he would go. Elizabeth knew her father would never agree to give Tommy a place to stay, even if he was in a terrible situation.

Her father didn't like Tommy, and no tragedy would change that. The only other person who would help would be her Aunt Jean. It would do her some good to have someone stay with her. Elizabeth knew Jean wouldn't hesitate to give him a safe place to live.

On the drive home, Elizabeth didn't say a word, but she tried to think positive and prayed that God would bring Tommy back to her. There was no way God would let a good person go to jail for something they didn't do, right?

Chapter 4

It had been almost a year since she'd left Tommy at the station, eight months, to be exact. Nobody knew where he went or what happened to him. For the first couple of months, she thought she would die of heartbreak and only came out of her room to sit for supper with her family and to help her mother with chores.

By the third month, Elizabeth was angry. Furious, in fact. She blamed the police for accusing Tommy of setting the fire. She was upset that her father continued to talk critically of Tommy, and he believed "that Roberts boy" was guilty of something, but the one person she was angry with the most was Tommy.

He didn't come to see her as he promised. He didn't call or even send a letter, he simply disappeared. Kurt did find out the police released Tommy without charges, but nobody seemed to know where he had gone.

Elizabeth gave up on him at that point and put all her energy into helping her mother around the house. She'd even started spending a lot of time with Jean and perfecting her seamstress skills as well as her cooking skills.

One day while she was in the middle of making a quilt for her brother's birthday, Jean came to sit next to her. She didn't speak at first and only helped Elizabeth fix a couple of things with the material she was sewing together. Then she turned to Elizabeth and cupped her cheek.

"I know what you feel, ducky. Nobody knows as well as I do, but if Tommy is your future, fate will bring you back together. It might be a week, a year, or maybe longer, but if God wants you together, it will happen." Jean kissed her cheek and then stood up. "Everything happens for a reason." Jean believed that was true.

Elizabeth's current problem was her father had decided he was a matchmaker for her. He'd continuously talk to her about what great young men Jack and Billy were and how she should get to know the brothers.

It was why she was so annoyed when he invited them to supper that evening. Her father said it was because they were going to pull the fishing boats on the dry dock until March, but she wasn't a fool. Even her brothers sensed he was up to something.

Winter had hit early, and there was already almost a foot of snow on the ground. Her father had predicted a terrible winter because of the number of dogberries growing on the trees around the town. It was usually a sign of a long, hard winter, but that wasn't uncommon in Newfoundland.

Elizabeth stood at the kitchen sink peeling potatoes and dropping them into the water. When her father clomped in wearing his fishing boots, her mother slapped her hands down on the table where she was kneading bread and blew out an irritated groan. Elizabeth turned back to the sink and stifled a snicker.

"Lard dine, Jesus, Paddy, can you not drag the snow in all over my clean floor?" her mother complained.

"I wiped them on the rug by the front door." Her father shrugged and glanced behind him.

Her mother motioned to the wet footprints her father had left behind him. It was as if he didn't see them as he turned around and continued out to the back porch. He and her brothers were storing the fishing gear in the large shed in their back yard.

"Why can't you just pass the equipment over the fence? At least I wouldn't have to mop up the floor every five minutes," her mother grumbled as she swiped the mop over the floor.

"I'm sorry, darling," her father shouted as he shoved through the back door. "I'll tell the boys to pass it over the fence if that makes you happy."

"Yes, it does." Her mother shook her head.

"Elizabeth, I want to see you dressed properly for supper. We have company coming, and I want you looking like the lady you are, not like the girls from town," her father shouted before the door slammed behind him.

34

"What's wrong with what I'm wearing?" Elizabeth looked down at herself.

"You don't look ladylike in those," her mother explained.

"Mudder, these are called cigarette pants, and they're all the rage. For heaven's sake, it's the nineteen fifties." Elizabeth dropped another potato into the sink.

"Just do as your fadder says, young lady," her mother ordered.

"Who is he trying to impress? The O'Connor boys? If he saw the way that Billy O'Connor acts with the girls at the town dances, Fadder would think twice about me wearing a dress around that boy," Elizabeth grumbled.

"Jack is coming too, and that poor boy is probably heartbroken. His fiancé ran off to the mainland and gave him back his ring a couple of months ago." Her mother shoved more wood into the stove.

"From what I heard, he didn't want to marry her." Elizabeth shrugged as she wiped her hands off.

"Mudder," Charlie yelled as he came into the house.

"Why do those boys have to shout like savages?" Her mother scurried off to see why Charlie bellowed to her.

"Why should I care what I wear in front of anyone?" Elizabeth mumbled as she glanced out through the window to see Billy hand a net to her father over the fence.

"Because Fadder said so." Kurt chuckled behind her.

"You better not let Mudder see you with your boots on." Elizabeth ignored her brother's statement and pointed to his wet footwear.

"I wasn't even here." Kurt took a large step and ran out through the back door, but not before her mother caught him.

"I'm going to burn those bloody boots," her mom shouted after him.

"Sorry, Mudder," Kurt yelled.

"You'll be sorry when I make you scrub the floors, Kurt," her mother grumbled.

Elizabeth made her way upstairs to her room. She hadn't exactly been easy to live with over the last several months because she still missed Tommy. Anytime Elizabeth brought up Tommy's name, her father would get angry and remind her that he'd warned her about "that Roberts boy." She figured it was better to make her parents happy for a change.

She grabbed a blue, full-skirted swing dress that she hardly wore anymore. It zipped up in the back and was form-fitting to her upper body. It showed off her figure more than the pants and blouse did. Elizabeth checked herself out in the mirror as she tied her hair back with a blue ribbon.

"Fadder, this is the best you're getting," Elizabeth mumbled to herself as she left her bedroom.

Elizabeth sat between Kurt and Charlie at the dining table and remained quiet as her father discussed the best way to get the boats hoisted on to the dry dock. She glanced at her mother, who seemed equally as bored with the conversation and tried to hide her smile when her mother rolled her eyes for the third time.

At one point, when Elizabeth glanced up from her plate, she caught Jack staring at her. When she met his eyes, he gave her a small smile that made his dimples look deeper. She had to admit the boy was probably one of the best-looking young men in town.

It was probably the most she'd ever associated with Billy and Jack. They went to the boys' Catholic school with her brothers and played on some of the same sports teams with Kurt and Charlie, but she wouldn't consider them friends. The O'Connors tended to travel in a different circle than Elizabeth and her family.

Jack and Billy had girls hovering around them like flies to honey, but Elizabeth wasn't the kind of girl who fawned over men. She would sit back and observe what was going on around her, but if a young man approached her, then she would talk to them.

For the last couple of years, she hadn't gone to many of the events held in the town for the younger people. She would rather spend time with Tommy, and most of the people who went to the dances looked down on him because of his family. After Tommy left, she couldn't bring herself to go anywhere.

"You look lovely this evening, Elizabeth," Jack interrupted her thoughts.

"Thank you." She returned his smile then quickly went back to the supper she didn't want.

"She always looks lovely when she dresses like a young lady," her father interjected.

Elizabeth had to fight the urge to roll her eyes at her father's blatant hatred for the clothes she wore. He was old fashioned and hated when women wore pants. To him, a lady dressed as such and pants made them look like men.

"She's all right for an annoying sister, I guess." Kurt nudged her with his elbow.

"Why didn't you give them away at birth, Mudder?" Elizabeth sighed.

"I say that to my mudder all the time about Billy." Jack chuckled.

The conversation was a little more inclusive, as her father finally dropped the boat talk. By the time her mother served the blueberry Bundt cake, the conversation had turned to the fire and how terrible it was. She had to bite her tongue when her father gave his opinion about Tommy and how he should be in jail. Elizabeth had just about had her fill when her mother spoke.

"Paddy, that's enough," her mother ordered.

Her mother had obviously picked up that he was upsetting Elizabeth. Any talk of Tommy being guilty always upset her. It didn't matter how angry she was with Tommy for leaving her, she wouldn't allow anyone to tarnish his reputation, not even her father.

"What? The lad was nothing but trouble." Her father went on.

Elizabeth glanced around the table and saw quickly how uncomfortable everyone seemed, including her. She was about a second away from jumping to her feet and telling her father how she knew for sure that Tommy didn't set the fire.

"I just thank the good Lord that Elizabeth stopped seeing him," her father continued, and Elizabeth couldn't hold her tongue anymore.

"That's it," Elizabeth said louder than was polite as she shot to her feet.

"Sit down, young lady." Her father pointed to the chair.

"No, Fadder. I won't. I'm so tired of you degrading Tommy every chance you get. You never gave him a chance, and that's where you missed out. He's one of the nicest people I ever knew, and I know for a fact he didn't have anything to do with that fire, Fadder. Do you know how I know that?" Elizabeth braced her hands on the table as she leaned over and glared at her father.

"Just how would you know that?" he snapped.

"Because he was with me. The whole night," she shouted.

The room was so quiet if a feather hit the floor, they would have heard it. Elizabeth didn't turn away from her father, even when his face turned scarlet red with anger.

"Elizabeth, I hope you aren't telling me what I think you are." Her father's voice was low but filled with rage.

"Yes, Fadder. I am. I loved him, and I would have married him, but they sent him away. For all I know, you're probably the reason he didn't come back." With those words, she spun around, grabbed her coat, and stomped out of the house.

Her father's bellowing could probably be heard three towns away, but she didn't even acknowledge that she heard him. Elizabeth didn't care as she clomped through the snow to get to the cliff and her shelter. The cold didn't even bother her as she got to the top.

The icy wind whipped around her legs, painful against her skin. It didn't hurt as much as her heart. Elizabeth finally admitted that he wasn't coming back. Tommy left her and broke his promise to come for her. She thought the pain of losing him had gotten less, but it hit her like a sledgehammer.

Elizabeth curled up on the bench as she sobbed for her loss and wondered if any of the stories spreading around Cape Broyle were true. She didn't know what to believe. Some were saying he was sent away to prison, others said he ran off with another girl, and then there was the story that they sent him away because he'd fooled around with someone in Witless Bay.

The only thing she knew was her heart shattered once more, and she didn't know if anyone could ever put it back together again. She could feel the tears freezing against her cheeks as others continued to fall.

"Elizabeth?" Kurt's voice startled her as he stepped inside the shelter.

"Go away." She quickly wiped her face.

"It's hard for Fadder." Kurt pulled her up into his big arms.

"Oh, yes, really hard. Fadder has no problems saying awful things about Tommy." Elizabeth tucked her face into her brother's jacket.

"You're his little girl. When we're out on the water, me and Charlie have to listen to how much he worries about you and how he doesn't want you ending up with someone who isn't going to treat you the way you deserve." Kurt kissed the top of her head.

"Shouldn't that be my decision?" Elizabeth sighed.

"Yes, but it's not going to make him worry any less or us either for that matter. You've been different since he left, and we want our sassy little sister back." Kurt ducked his head so she could see his smirk.

"I miss him. That's all. I want to hate him for not coming back, but I can't, and anytime someone talks about him, the pain comes back again." She wiped the tears away and looked up at her older brother.

As much as they teased her, she knew they always looked out for her. They would die for her and she for them. The problem was, neither of them had ever been in love or at least not for long. It didn't seem as if either of her brothers would ever settle down.

"I know this isn't what you want to hear, but things happen for a reason. Isn't that what Mudder and Aunt Jean always say?" Kurt sat back on the bench while she lay her head on his shoulder.

If things always happened for a reason, then what was the reason she had to have her heart broke? Why did Tommy's family have to die, and why did he have to go away? It didn't matter why any of it happened. None of it eased her pain.

Still, God didn't give her what she couldn't handle. Everything in her life had made her the girl she was, and God would never give her something she wasn't able to survive.

Chapter 5

Spring was finally in the air, and Elizabeth was helping her mother plant vegetables in the garden. She'd turned nineteen the previous week and had been teased again by her brothers because her birthday was on April Fool's day.

"I think we need to plant more this year. We were pretty close to running out this winter," her mother said as she dug out the vegetable garden.

"Maybe if the boys didn't eat so much, we would be fine." Elizabeth laughed.

"I don't know where they put all the food they eat." Her mother chuckled.

Elizabeth kept herself busy over the winter. She helped her Aunt Jean with housework and errands. Her aunt wanted to clear out one of her rooms and get rid of things she didn't need. She told Elizabeth there was no need to have something she didn't use.

One evening, Elizabeth mentioned that Jean was getting rid of a lot of her possessions. Jean had herself convinced she was dying and didn't want to leave a burden for her family. To Elizabeth, Jean seemed better than she had in years.

Jean had made it through the winter and started walking every day. She finally realized the reason she was feeling so poorly was that she didn't get much exercise. Jean also took it upon herself to teach Elizabeth how to drive, and when she got her driver's license, Jean gave Elizabeth her car.

Her father hadn't been happy, but there wasn't much he could do about it, especially when her mother told him he had no say in the matter. It took several months for her and her father to get over the blow-up at the table that night. She'd apologized for her outburst and told him she didn't want to talk about Tommy. He agreed and said he didn't want to hear about it again.

That was his way of saying he didn't want to know exactly what happened between her and Tommy. As far as he was concerned, none of it ever happened, and things between them went back to normal.

Her father and brothers were due in from a fishing trip, and Elizabeth couldn't wait to see them. They had been gone over a week because Sean O'Connor had given up fishing himself to deal with the business part of his fishing fleet.

Jack and Billy moved to the same ship with her father and brothers. Sean told her father that of all the skippers in his crews, he felt the most comfortable sending his boys with Elizabeth's father.

Since that day, her dad seemed to be inviting the O'Connor family to their house frequently. Her parents and the O'Connors had become close over the winter, which was strange to her because they hadn't run in the same circles before.

"I hope they get in before dark," her mother said as she stood up and pressed her hand against the center of her back.

"I'm sure they will be. Mudder, let me do that." Elizabeth took the shovel from her mother.

"I'm quite capable of digging, ducky." Her mother reached for the shovel.

"Mudder, your back has been bothering you for weeks. Go inside and rest a bit." Elizabeth linked into her mother's arm and guided her toward the house.

"Listen, here, young lady. I'm perfectly fine to do my garden." Her mother tapped Elizabeth's hand.

"I know, Mudder, but let me take over. You take a bath or something. Get yourself all fresh and clean for Fadder when he comes home." Elizabeth shook her head in amusement as her mother grumbled all the way into the house.

By the time Elizabeth finished the rest of the planting, it was a little after four. She was putting the gardening tools away when she heard the loud, boisterous laughter of her brothers coming up from the pier. Elizabeth ran out of the garden and down over the hill to the road to meet them.

"Jesus, were you playing in the mud?" Kurt chuckled as she jumped into his arms.

"I've been digging the garden for Mudder." She slapped his arm and turned to embrace Charlie.

"What's wrong with your mudder?" her father's smile disappeared, and he was suddenly concerned.

"She's fine. Her back is bothering her again," Elizabeth explained as she hugged her father.

"That woman is going to see Dr. Connolly, and I'll have no arguing about it." Her father clomped up the steps to the front porch.

"Good luck with that, Fadder. All she does is grumble at me when I mention the doctor." Elizabeth rolled her eyes.

"She'll go, and that's all there is to it." He nodded as he entered the house, yelling out to her mother.

"Hello, Elizabeth." Jack's voice caused her to spin and meet his blue eyes.

"Hi, Jack. How was the trip?" She smiled.

"Rough." He sighed.

"Really?" She glanced at her brothers.

"Waves were a little high, but nothing new." Kurt shrugged, but it was the warning glare he gave Jack that worried her.

"I still think it's too early to be out fishing. The ocean is unpredictable on the best days," Elizabeth complained.

At least once or twice a year, a fishing boat got lost or destroyed during the spring. It was a way of life for the town, but it didn't stop her from worrying about the men who went out, especially her father and brothers.

"We're a hardy bunch. We can handle it." Jack winked at her, and her stomach felt like a thousand butterflies started to flutter around.

"A stubborn bunch, maybe," Elizabeth returned with the usual sassy tone she reserved for her brothers.

Her recent reactions to Jack made her uneasy when he was close by, and she did her best to hide it. The fact that he seemed to be around more and made a point of talking to her. He'd often drop in at her house randomly and would spend most of his time chatting with her.

"I heard there's going to be a dance at the town hall this weekend." Kurt glanced at her as he lit a cigarette.

"Yes, I'm sure Maureen will be hunting you down for a spin on the dance floor." Elizabeth smirked.

"She hunts him down for more than that." Charlie winked.

"You're such a dipstick." Elizabeth laughed.

"Will you be going to the dance, Elizabeth?" Kurt glanced over her shoulder toward Jack and Billy.

Elizabeth turned around in confusion. Billy grinned, but Jack suddenly seemed in a hurry to leave. She turned back to her brother and narrowed her eyes, giving him her own version of the devil's glare.

"Catch you later, Kurt, Charlie. Nice to see you again, Elizabeth." Jack turned and quickly walked away.

"What was that all about?" Elizabeth turned back to her brother and rested her fists on her hips.

"Come on, Elizabeth. You should feel flattered that O'Connor has the hots for you." Charlie laughed.

"I'm not interested in Billy. He's a philanderer." Elizabeth shivered with disgust.

"Not Billy. He's talking about Jack." Kurt raised an eyebrow.

"You're so full of it." Elizabeth slapped his arm.

"I just spent almost two weeks on a boat with him, Elizabeth. Trust me, Jack is interested." Kurt tossed his cigarette on the ground and stepped on it.

She stood stunned as her brothers walked away and disappeared into the house. Elizabeth glanced behind her to see Jack and Billy had made their way home. She could still see them in the distance, and she felt that familiar flutter when Jack glanced back at her.

That evening, Elizabeth sat at the supper table with her family. Her brothers talked about the few days of rough seas they encountered and how they almost capsized when a rogue wave hit them.

"Only for Jack I would've fallen off the boat at one point," Charlie said as he shoved a forkful of food into his mouth.

"That O'Connor boy almost lost his own life, grabbing you," her father agreed.

"Dear God, can we stop talking about how we could have lost you all and just enjoy that you're all home safe." Her mother was distressed whenever they discussed the dangers of fishing.

Her mom wasn't much older than Elizabeth when she lost her father. A sudden storm had hit hard and smashed against the cliffs around the shore. It was why her mother hardly slept when the men were out to sea.

"I'm sorry, darling. The good news is we're back for two weeks, and you'll have me all to yourself this Saturday night." Her father winked at her mother.

"Why is that?" Her mother smiled.

"The boys have plans to go to the dance at the community hall." Her father replied.

"Okay, but in case you forgot, I still live here." Elizabeth laughed.

"I'm pretty sure you'll have plans." Her father grinned as he sipped his tea.

"I don't have any plans, Fadder. Sorry," Elizabeth replied.

Before her father could respond, there was a soft knock on the door. Usually, her father or brothers would immediately go to answer the door, but for some reason, they sat grinning like idiots.

"Elizabeth, would you mind getting that?" Her father pointed his fork toward the door.

Elizabeth studied them suspiciously as she slowly made her way to the front door. When she pulled it open, she saw a freshly shaven Jack O'Connor.

"Hi." Jack smiled, causing his dimples to show.

"Hello," Elizabeth responded.

She waited for him to say something as she stood in the doorway. Jack shoved his hands into his jeans pockets and glanced behind him, then turned back to her.

"For Jesus' sake, Elizabeth, invite the boy inside," her father shouted from the dining room.

Elizabeth glanced behind her and narrowed her eyes at her father's sly grin before she finally motioned for Jack to enter. He pulled his hands from his pockets and stepped just inside enough for her to close the door.

"Come in, Jack, my boy," her father shouted.

"How did my father know you were at the door?" Elizabeth whispered.

"I told him I'd be dropping by to ask…" Jack dropped his head and seemed overly interested in his boots.

"To ask what?" Elizabeth's heart jumped in her chest when he lifted his head and met her eyes.

"I wanted to…I was wondering if I could escort you to the dance Saturday night?" Jack smiled.

"Me?" Elizabeth breathed in surprise.

"Yeah, you. I'm not here to ask Kurt." Jack smirked.

"I don't think he's available anyway," Elizabeth returned.

"Thank God." Jack gazed into her eyes.

Elizabeth stared at him for several seconds. For some reason, her stomach tightened, and an overwhelming feeling of guilt came over her. She hadn't even agreed to go with Jack, but the thought of it made her feel as if she was cheating on Tommy.

"I asked your fadder if I could ask you, if that's what you're concerned about." Jack's smile faltered.

"No, it's not that. I...It's just I wasn't expecting...I didn't know." Elizabeth pressed her lips together and took a deep intake of breath.

"It's okay if you don't want to go with me, Elizabeth. It's just I like you. A lot." Jack sounded defeated as he dropped his head.

"I'd like to go with you," Elizabeth blurted out before she gave herself another second to think.

Jack lifted his eyes to meet hers, and a smile slowly formed on his handsome face. His shoulders relaxed, and he adjusted his jacket as he turned to leave.

"Good, I'll pick you up at six," Jack told her.

"Can you stay for dessert?" Elizabeth asked.

"Of course, he can stay for dessert." Her father's voice sounded closer than the kitchen, and when Elizabeth turned, she saw him quickly make his way back to the table.

"I don't think we will have to tell them we're going to the dance together." Elizabeth rolled her eyes as she and Jack walked into the kitchen.

"I think you may be right." Jack smiled, and Elizabeth had to bite back a sigh.

Elizabeth was a little scared at how a simple smile from Jack could make her heart flutter. The only boy to ever quicken her heartbeat was Tommy, but the more she got to know Jack, the more attracted she became.

Tommy's kiss would make her weak in the knees, and she would crave more. As she sat across the table from Jack, she wondered what it would be like to have him hold her and kiss her the same way Tommy did.

"Are you okay, Elizabeth? Your cheeks are flushed." Charlie grinned.

"It's hot here." She glared at her brother.

"It is a little warm in here." Her mother fanned herself as she stood up and opened one of the windows.

"Isabelle, are you trying to freeze us all out of the kitchen?" her father complained.

"I'm just having a moment, hush." Her mother stood in front of the window and allowed the cool wind to blow in her face.

Elizabeth was glad for the distraction as she wondered how was it possible for Jack to cause her to react the way she did? Her heart belonged to Tommy. Didn't it?

Chapter 6

Elizabeth couldn't hide the smile on her face as she walked into the community hall on the arm of one of the most handsome men in the town. Elizabeth smirked as she and Jack walked by Maureen and received a cold glare.

"Kurt and Billy said they would save us a seat at the table." Jack motioned to where his brother waved at them

Seeing Billy and Jack dressed up for the dance, it was clear why the girls around swooned over the brothers. Her own brothers were no slouches either and turned a few heads themselves.

Billy, Kurt, and Charlie all had dates for the dance as well. Elizabeth knew all three women and knew Charlie's date was deeply in love with her brother, but he didn't seem to want to settle down.

Geraldine Melvin grew up a few roads away from Elizabeth and her brothers. Geraldine dated Charlie on and off for a long time, and once she'd caught her brother and Geraldine behind the shed doing a lot more than kissing. Still, Charlie seemed reluctant to make it official.

"There's my favorite sister." Kurt pulled out a chair next to his date, Irene Vokey.

"I'm your only sister." Elizabeth laughed.

"That's why you're my favorite." Kurt winked.

Elizabeth scanned the hall as people continued to fill the area. Cape Broyle wasn't a large town, but the dances usually brought young people from surrounding communities. She couldn't hide the smile as Jack sat next to her and draped his arm over the back of her chair.

The music started, and the floor quickly filled with dancing young adults. She was excited when Jack leaned in and asked her to dance, but before they made it to the dance floor, Elizabeth saw Maureen headed toward their table with her eyes locked on Jack. He didn't seem to notice, but Elizabeth sensed trouble.

"Well, look who I found at the lower-class table." Maureen placed her hands on her hips and pushed out her small breasts.

"It's the best table around," Charlie responded as he stepped next to Elizabeth.

"I can't believe none of you stood up when I came up to the table. I guess all the gentlemen are on the other side of the room." Maureen smirked.

"They do when a lady comes to the table." Linda Comerford stood behind Elizabeth.

Linda was Billy's date, and she used to be a good friend of Maureen at one time. When they were in high school, Maureen slept with Linda's boyfriend, and they had a huge argument.

"What am I?" Maureen spun around and winked at Jack.

"A tramp, slut, there are more words, but I'm pretty sure everyone here knows what you are," Linda replied.

"If that's not the pot calling the kettle black." Maureen sneered at her former friend.

"Did you come over here for a reason?" Billy wrapped his arm around Linda.

"I wanted to let Jack know that I'll leave a dance spot open for him." She winked at Jack.

"Sorry, all my dances are saved for Elizabeth." Jack pulled Elizabeth closer to his side.

"I can't believe you're going to forget she used to go out with a guy who killed his family." Maureen sneered.

Elizabeth narrowed her eyes and took several steps toward Maureen. She knew that the girl was trying to bait her but bringing up Tommy was low. Elizabeth was no more than two inches from Maureen and leaned closer so that she was nose to nose with the one girl who always pushed her buttons.

"Elizabeth," Charlie said in a warning tone.

"No, leave her alone. Let her show Jack that she's no different than Tommy Roberts." Maureen smirked and crossed her arms over her chest.

"You're a piece of work, aren't you? You go around spreading lies and rumors about people. For one, Tommy didn't have anything to do with that fire, and for two, Linda is right, you're no lady. The only reason I haven't given you a black eye is that my mudder raised me right." Elizabeth turned her back to Maureen, but before she could walk away, Maureen grabbed her by the hair.

Elizabeth gasped as Maureen dragged her down to the floor and jumped on top of her. Maureen slapped Elizabeth across the face, but before Elizabeth could strike back, someone pulled Maureen off her, and Jack helped Elizabeth to her feet.

Maureen screamed at Elizabeth as Charlie wrapped his arm around the out-of-control woman and lifted her off the floor. He carried her out of the hall while she continued to shriek at Elizabeth. Geraldine followed behind them, shaking her head.

"I'm not giving her a chance to accuse Charlie of doing something," Geraldine shouted behind her as she disappeared out of the hall.

"Are you okay?" Jack gently touched her stinging cheek.

"I'm furious, but I'm fine." Elizabeth flinched as Jack ran his hand down the side of her face.

"I'll get a cold cloth." Linda ran toward the ladies' room.

"I'm fine." Elizabeth sighed as Jack pulled out a chair and helped her sit.

"Your face is scratched." Jack cupped her chin as he turned her face to the side.

"That girl is out of her mind." Irene crouched next to Elizabeth.

"She is always looking to cause a fight with someone." Linda handed a wet cloth to Jack when she returned.

The coolness of the cloth felt good against her injured cheek. Jack was gentle and had concern written all over his handsome face. When she glanced up over his head, Kurt and Billy had a different expression on their faces. They looked ready to kill someone.

"This isn't turning out to be a very good first date." Jack forced a smile.

"I think it's perfect." Elizabeth returned his smile.

"You know if a man hit you like that, I'd pound him into the floor, but what can I do to that… girl." Jack sighed.

"You can put down the cloth and ask me to dance." Elizabeth covered his hand where it lay against the cloth on her cheek.

She stared into his blue eyes, and at that moment, she knew they were right where they were supposed to be. Jack stood up, held out his hand, and she smiled as she placed her hand in his.

"Would you dance with me, Ms. Power?" Jack grinned.

"I'd love to." Elizabeth stood up.

Jack led her to the dance floor as the song, "Only You" by The Platters, began to play. It was a new song and very popular on the radio. They didn't get the up-to-date music very often, but the disc jockey seemed to have a lot of the newer stuff.

While she danced with Jack, he gazed into her eyes, and she could hardly breathe. The sky blue of his eyes hypnotized her as everyone around her disappeared. It was their first date, but she could feel the connection with Jack, and for the first time in a long time, she started to see happiness in her future.

"You're so beautiful," Jack whispered.

"Thank you." Elizabeth felt the heat rise in her cheeks, and she lowered her eyes.

"Elizabeth, don't look away when I tell you how lovely you are." Jack put his finger under her chin, and she raised her eyes to meet his again.

"You could have any girl in this room. Half of the single girls in this town are in love with you." She watched for his reaction.

"The only girl I see is you," Jack replied.

"Jack." She smiled.

"I know your heart is healing, and part of it will probably always belong to Tommy, but maybe there's a little room for someone else. Someone like me?" Jack ran a finger down her uninjured cheek.

What could she say to that? If she could look away from Jack at that moment, she probably would have seen half the females stare at her with envy because she was in his arms. Could she open her heart again? Tommy wasn't coming back, and she couldn't pine away for him for the rest of her life.

Jack was a good man, and he was the kind of man her father approved of, but could she fall for him? When Jack smiled at her, Elizabeth knew the answer.

"I think you've already stolen a piece of my heart, Jack O'Connor." Elizabeth stood up on her toes as the song ended and pressed her lips against his cheek.

"I'll be happy with a piece of your heart right now, but trust me, Elizabeth, once I have all your heart, I'm going to marry you." Jack gazed into her eyes as his words stole her breath away.

Chapter 7

Elizabeth hummed to herself as she helped her mother bottle some of the beets that they'd picked that morning from the garden. She and Jack had been courting for almost three months, and she was looking forward to him returning from this last fishing trip.

He'd told her when he came back, he'd take her to the drive-in theater in St. John's. Of course, he had to approve that with her father, which only pissed Elizabeth off, but Jack was old-fashioned. He had great respect for Elizabeth's parents, and she really couldn't be angry about that.

"I think I hear the boys coming." Her mother wiped her hands and headed for the front door.

Elizabeth's heart picked up speed as she sealed the last of the mason jars and hurried to the front door. She stopped short on the top of the steps when she saw the anxious expressions on her father's and brothers' faces.

Her stomach tightened as she glanced behind them for Jack. She didn't see Jack or Billy, and she turned her attention back to her father.

61

"Where's Jack?" Elizabeth asked frantically.

"I don't want you to worry." Her father held up his hand.

"Fadder, if you don't want me to worry, that's not the way to start an explanation." Elizabeth crossed her arms over her stomach.

"Okay, sorry. Jack's fine, but we had to send him to the hospital," her father began.

"What? If he's fine, why did he have to go to the hospital?" Elizabeth practically shouted.

"He had a little fall when a wave crashed over the deck. It's why we're in early," her father explained.

"Pretty sure he broke his leg," Kurt interjected.

"Oh, dear. Poor Jack." Her mother shook her head.

"He's hard as nails. He'll be fine," her father said as he gave Elizabeth and her mother a hug.

"The rest of us are fine, though." Charlie smirked.

"Of course, we're happy you're all back safe." Her mother hugged both Elizabeth's brothers.

"Charlie, can you take me to the hospital?" Elizabeth asked.

She was so worried about Jack that she didn't even see how exhausted they looked. Still, with a grin on his face, Charlie nodded, and they headed for his truck.

St. John's wasn't a short drive from Cape Broyle, and most of the roads were gravel until just before entering the city. Still, Charlie didn't hesitate to drive her the hour-drive to Newfoundland's capital city.

"You really like him, don't you?" Charlie said as they drove.

"Yes," Elizabeth returned.

"I'm glad you were able to move on. I was a little worried about you for a while after the other fella left." Charlie clenched his teeth.

Her oldest brother didn't like how Tommy had left without a word to her. Charlie had told her a couple of days after her first date with Jack that he thought Tommy was a coward for not coming back to face her.

Elizabeth was at the point that she hardly thought about Tommy. She knew two things for sure. Tommy wouldn't hurt his family, and if he decided to leave, it was for a good reason. Still, she didn't know if she could ever forgive him for leaving her.

At the hospital, she found Billy asleep in one of the chairs outside the emergency room. She hated to wake him, but she needed to find out about Jack. If Billy was asleep, that meant Jack wasn't in bad shape.

"Billy?" Elizabeth gently touched his arm.

Billy's eyes snapped open, and he sat up straight as if someone had just electrocuted him. He looked around in confusion for a few seconds before he finally noticed Elizabeth and Charlie in front of him.

"Jesus, I must have dozed off." Billy wiped his hands down over his face.

"Sorry, I wanted to know if you heard anything on Jack." Elizabeth sat next to Billy.

"They said they'd come to get me when he was out of surgery." Billy yawned.

"Surgery?" Elizabeth gasped as she dropped in the chair next to Billy.

"Relax, woman. They've got to do something with the bone in his leg. He's probably going to have to stay for a bit." Billy stood up.

"Really?" Elizabeth began to think there was more wrong with Jack than she thought.

"Depends on what happens with the surgery. Dumb bastard thought he could walk across an icy deck covered in saltwater." Billy shook his head and stood up.

"He'll be okay, though?" Elizabeth felt as if she was about to burst into tears.

"Yeah, don't worry, Betty." Billy winked.

Jack started calling her Betty after the dance. He said because her eyes reminded him of Betty Davis, the actress. The name caught on quickly, and almost everyone called her by the nickname.

"Betty was a little worried about her man." Charlie smirked as he flopped down on one of the chairs.

Charlie was right. Elizabeth was worried about Jack. Fishing was his livelihood, and if he couldn't go back on the boat, he would have to find another job. In Cape Broyle, there wasn't much else to do besides fishing. He could go to work at a processing plant, but that meant he would need to work outside the small town.

"I called Mudder and Fadder to let them know what was going on. Mudder made it sound like I told her he lost his leg, and I had to get Fadder on the phone to tell him what happened." Billy rolled his eyes. "God forbid something happen to her precious Jack."

"She's your mudder, and she worries about both of you." Elizabeth tried to make Billy feel better.

The truth was the entire town knew that Louise O'Connor favored Jack. Maybe because he was her firstborn, but Elizabeth heard several people say, according to Louise, he could do no wrong. A rumor spread that Louise was part of the reason that Jack's engagement had ended. Not that Elizabeth wasn't thankful for that part.

Elizabeth had asked Jack about it in passing, and he denied his mother had any hand in the breakup. Jack explained that his ex-fiancé wanted to leave the province, and he didn't. He also admitted that he only proposed to his ex because everyone expected him to do it. He said that he knew deep in his heart it would be a mistake to marry the woman. That night he told Elizabeth he always felt drawn to her and only kept his distance because of Tommy.

"Are your parents coming to the hospital?" Elizabeth asked and secretly hoped Jack's mother wouldn't show up and cause a scene.

"No, I told them to stay put." Billy twisted his waist as if to stretch out stiff muscles.

They seemed to be waiting for hours before someone came to talk to Billy. Elizabeth waited quietly while the doctor explained that he repaired Jack's leg, and he'd been placed in traction to keep the leg immobile. Jack would stay in the hospital for a week before he would be allowed to go home. She knew Jack wouldn't be happy about being stuck in the hospital. The only thing she wanted at that point was to see with her own eyes that he was okay.

"Can we see him, Doc?" Billy asked.

"We gave him some strong pain medication, but you can go in for a few minutes," the doctor replied.

Charlie waited in the lobby while Elizabeth and Billy followed the doctor to Jack's room. Elizabeth moved back so Billy could go in ahead of her, but he laughed and pushed her in front of him.

"Who do you think my brother would rather see, you, or me?" Billy winked.

Elizabeth walked into the small area, and her eyes immediately found Jack's sleeping form. He was propped up a little with his leg suspended from a contraption above the bed. It didn't look comfortable.

Her attention was drawn away from his dangling leg to his naked chest. She could feel the heat rise in her cheeks as she allowed her gaze to travel down his muscled chest and to his abdominals. A light dusting of auburn hair a shade lighter than the hair on his head covered his chest. She and Jack had only kissed up to that point, but she wanted more.

"He's gonna be pissed when he wakes up." Billy chuckled.

"Why?" Elizabeth ambled toward the bed.

"Looks like they shaved his leg." Billy leaned over Jack's leg.

"The hair will grow back." Elizabeth rolled her eyes.

"Yeah, but I'll get to tease him about shaving his legs for a long time." Billy motioned for Elizabeth to sit in the chair next to Jack's bedside.

"I'm sure he has a few things to poke fun at you too." Elizabeth chuckled.

Billy sat in a chair on the other side of Jack's bed. Elizabeth saw his eyes flutter closed as his head dropped, and he drifted off to sleep. Charlie had fallen asleep in the waiting room and told her to wake him when she was ready to go back home. The problem was she didn't know if she wanted to leave.

Elizabeth rested her elbow on the bed and cradled her chin in her hand while she watched Jack sleep peacefully. He winced a few times but didn't wake up for several hours. She allowed her gaze to take in his body and her eyes scanned down over his torso. It was the first time she noticed the tattoo on the right side of his chest.

Elizabeth stood up and leaned closer to inspect the colorful artwork. It was a crest, and the ribbon on the bottom of it had Jack's last name written across it. It was beautiful. She never thought she would think that about a tattoo, but Jack's was stunning.

"It's my family crest." Jack's voice sounded raspy, and it startled her.

"I hope I didn't wake you," Elizabeth whispered.

"No, the pain did." Jack shifted in the bed and winced when his leg moved.

"I'll get the nurse." Elizabeth turned, but Jack grasped her hand.

"I'll be fine, Betty. Waking up to your beautiful face is the best medicine I could have." He brought her hand up to his lips and kissed it tenderly.

Elizabeth eased down on the side of the bed, making sure she was careful not to jostle his leg. He pressed her hand against the tattoo on his chest and cupped her cheek with his other. For several minutes, he gazed into her eyes as he caressed her cheek.

"You know what I was thinking about when I was lying in the bunk as we were coming back in?" Jack asked.

"What?" Elizabeth covered his hand where it lay against her cheek.

"How I'm not going to be able to take you to the dance this week?" Jack whispered.

"Jack." She smiled.

"I've taken you to a dance every time I'm on land since the middle of April," Jack said.

"I think I'll be fine with missing a few dances. As long as you're okay." Elizabeth turned her head and kissed the palm of his hand.

"Betty, when I'm out on the water, you're all I think about." Jack gently squeezed her hand.

"You should be thinking about being safe," Elizabeth chastised.

"I'm falling in love with you, Betty. No, that's not true. I'm already head-over-heels in love with you." Jack tugged her closer.

"Jack, I think you're a little loopy." Elizabeth giggled.

"No, I wanted to tell you before I left this last time, but I chickened out." He smiled.

"You're such an incredible man." She cupped his cheek when he released her hand from his chest.

"I know you're probably wary about falling in love again, but I swear, Betty, I'm not going anywhere, and I'll wait as long as you need." Jack tugged her down until her lips were a hair away from his.

"Jack, you don't need to wait. I've already fallen for you." Elizabeth brushed her lips against his.

Jack cupped the back of her head and kissed her tenderly. It was a kiss that told her he meant everything he said. He loved her, and she had fallen completely for him. She finally knew why Tommy needed to leave. Jack was her future.

Chapter 8

Jack didn't deal well with his recuperation. He had to stay in the hospital for a couple of weeks and was home for over a month. Although the doctor told him he was healing well, it would still be a few weeks before the doctor would clear him to go back on the boat.

What made it worse was Elizabeth's father, her brothers and Billy were heading out the following morning. It was early September, which meant the weather could be unpredictable. Jack wasn't happy about being what he called grounded. When Jack told his father he was going anyway, his father put his foot down and forbid it.

"This is bullshit," Jack complained as he limped out of his house.

"Jack, he wants to make sure you don't get hurt again." Elizabeth stepped in front of him and wrapped her arms around his waist.

"The only good thing about not working is I get to spend all my time with my beautiful sweetheart." Jack pressed his forehead against hers.

"I kind of like that as well." Elizabeth smiled.

"Are you trying to get me out of my bad mood?" He narrowed his eyes.

"Is it working?" She brushed her nose against his.

"Yes." Jack gave her a quick kiss on the lips.

"Your birthday is coming up this week." Elizabeth smiled as they strolled down toward where the boats were getting ready to sail.

"I know. Your man is getting old." Jack feigned a sigh.

"You're going to be twenty-two, not ninety-two." Elizabeth chuckled.

"I'm not too old for you?" He held his cane in the other and her hand in the other.

"Never." She rested her head against his chest as they stopped at the edge of the wharf.

Jack got quiet as several of his father's fishing boats pushed off from the dock. Jack loved to sail on the water, and she couldn't blame him. She loved it as well, but Sean and the doctor were right in keeping Jack off the water to take a little more time to heal.

"You'll get out there again," Elizabeth assured him.

"I know, but Fadder asked me how I'd feel about taking some of the paperwork off his shoulders." Jack sighed.

"He does have a lot of boats now, and maybe he feels overwhelmed by it all," Elizabeth returned.

Sean O'Connor had ten fishing boats with six crew and a skipper on each vessel. Sean did all the payroll, bill payments, and other business decisions himself. He was getting older and probably wanted to take some of the burden off his shoulders.

"I love the water. I don't know if I want to sit behind a desk." Jack shrugged.

"You don't have to stay off the water forever. You can go out for fun," Elizabeth told him.

"True. Maybe I can take you out to Gull Island for a picnic." He winked.

"Jack, I love you, but I'm not going to Gull Island for a picnic. You do realize why they call that Gull Island, right?" Elizabeth cringed.

"Okay, maybe we'll just sail around the Island." Jack chuckled.

If she got to be on the water and be with Jack, she'd take it. To have her two favorite things together would be heaven. It amazed her sometimes how much her relationship with Jack had blossomed in such a short few months.

Later that evening, Jack invited Elizabeth and her mother to his family home for supper. It was the first time Elizabeth felt comfortable with Louise. It was unusual for her to be so friendly because anytime

Elizabeth's mother wasn't around, Louise would rarely speak to Elizabeth.

"I don't sleep well when they go out to sea," Louise said as she served tea.

"I don't either." Elizabeth's mother sighed.

"Thankfully, Jack didn't have to go out this time." Louise smiled.

"Billy is still out there, Mudder." Jack rolled his eyes.

"Oh, I know that." Louise didn't even seem to be concerned about her youngest child.

"I don't worry about Billy when he's out with Paddy." Sean winked at Elizabeth.

"Fadder's a good skipper." Elizabeth smiled.

"He's had to fish his whole life. Billy doesn't need to. He just does it until he figures out what he wants to do with his life." Louise picked up her cup and sipped her tea as if she was at tea with the Queen.

It didn't make any sense for Louise to look down on Elizabeth's father because he was a fisherman. Especially since she was married to a man who was a fisherman. It didn't matter that he owned several boats, Sean saw himself the same as every other man that risked their lives fishing.

"Paddy is more than a fisherman," Elizabeth's mother snapped.

"I didn't mean anything by that, Isabelle. All I'm saying is he comes from that background." Louise gave Elizabeth's mother a look that told Elizabeth she meant exactly what she said.

"As do I, Louise," Sean said through gritted teeth.

"Why are you getting upset with me? I'm just having a conversation." Louise sounded as if she would burst into tears.

"Just drop it," Sean ordered.

The rest of the evening was relatively uncomfortable, and Jack seemed to sense Elizabeth's discomfort. He offered to walk Elizabeth and her mother home but not without resistance from his mother.

"Jack, I don't like you walking back alone with your bad leg. I'm sure Elizabeth and her mother can get home fine," Louise complained.

"Louise, let the boy walk his girl and her mother home. He's trying to be the gentleman we raised him to be." Sean sounded annoyed.

By the time they got back to her house, her mother seemed ready to fall asleep. Elizabeth noticed her mother had been getting tired quickly over the last few months, and she was getting worried about her.

"I'm going to call it a night. Thanks for walking us home, Jack." Her mother smiled and made her way up the stairs.

"Is your mother ill?" Jack asked when they were alone.

"She says she isn't, but I think something is wrong." Elizabeth took Jack's hand, and they went into the living room.

"I feel strange being in your house without one of your parents in the same room." Jack chuckled.

"Mudder must trust you." Elizabeth smiled as they settled on the sofa.

"I don't know if she should." Jack raised an eyebrow and leaned in to give her a quick kiss.

Elizabeth smiled as she moved closer to him, and Jack deepened the kiss. He cradled her head in his hand as he slipped his tongue into her mouth, making the kiss sensual, and her body heated. Jack dropped his hand on her knee as he eased her back to the sofa. Jack's kisses could make her forget that her mother was one floor above them.

"You make me forget I need to be a gentleman." Jack moaned against her lips.

"But you are a gentleman." She shifted, and his obvious arousal pressed against her leg.

"Do I have to be?" Jack whispered.

"I'm not ready, Jack." Elizabeth was terrified to go too far with him.

The last time she did that, the boy she loved went away and never returned. No matter how much she wanted him, it wasn't easy to take that next step again. She knew in her head that Jack would never leave her, but it was her heart she had to convince.

"I'd never push you to do anything you weren't ready for." He cupped her cheek and gazed into her eyes.

"I know." She smiled as he gave her a soft kiss.

Jack sat up and pulled Elizabeth with him. For a few minutes, they sat listening to the radio and holding each other. Her father told them when he returned from this last trip, he would buy a television for the house. It was exciting since only a few people in the town had one.

Jack's family had a small one, but it didn't excite her. Elizabeth would rather spend an evening reading, listening to music, or play a game of cards.

"I really should head home," Jack said shortly before midnight.

Jack held out his hand, and she placed hers in his. He pulled her to her feet, and they walked to the front door. As he lowered his mouth to meet hers, his hands rested on her hips. Elizabeth slipped her arms around his neck, and Jack deepened the kiss as he backed her against the door.

"Goodnight, Jack," Elizabeth whispered against his lips.

"You're killing me, Betty." Jack sighed.

"I love you," she murmured against his cheek.

"I love you, darling" Jack kissed her cheek and pulled away from her.

Jack stepped outside and turned to face her again. He grasped her hand and brought it up to his lips. For several minutes they just gazed into each other's eyes. Then he spoke.

"I'd feel better if you make sure your doors are locked when I leave." Jack tugged on her fingers.

"We never lock the door." Elizabeth laughed.

"I know, but I'd feel better if you did. I don't like leaving you and your mom alone." Jack's concern only made her love him more.

"Okay, I'll lock them if it makes you feel better." Elizabeth smiled.

She knew he waited until she closed and locked the door because when she made her way to the window, he had just started to descend the steps. She watched him as he limped down the road to his house.

Elizabeth sighed as she turned off the lights and made her way upstairs to her room. Something made her stop in front of her mother's bedroom, and she opened the door. She found her mother in bed with a book in her hand. Elizabeth walked into the room and sat on the bed.

"Mudder, are you okay?" Elizabeth asked.

"I'm fine. I always find it hard to settle the first few nights your father leaves." She smiled at Elizabeth and gently patted her leg.

"Are you sure that's all it is?" Elizabeth was uneasy with her mother's answer.

"Yes, Elizabeth, or do I start calling you Betty now?" Her mother smirked and raised an eyebrow.

"Elizabeth is fine, Mudder." She laughed as she stood up.

"Why does he call you that?" her mother asked.

"He says my eyes remind him of Betty Davis." Elizabeth fluttered her eyes.

"Oh, he's a smooth one, he is." Her mother laughed.

"I know." Elizabeth headed out of her mother's room. "Goodnight, Mudder."

Elizabeth stepped into her room and casually got ready for bed. She couldn't stop smiling as thoughts of Jack floated through her mind. It was still a surprise at how much he'd come to mean to her. Elizabeth never thought she would feel that way again. How could she fall in love with Jack when she was still getting over Tommy? She didn't know the answer to that. The only thing she knew was she loved Jack.

Chapter 9

It was heading into her second Christmas with Jack, and she couldn't believe how fast the time had gone. Since the winter months were usually leaner than the rest of the year, Elizabeth made Christmas presents for her family and Jack.

Elizabeth had learned to knit when she was young, and like her mother, she would always knit socks, mittens, and hats for her brothers and father. Elizabeth made blankets and sweaters for them as well. That was what she made for Jack, a warm sweater for him to wear when he was out on the boat.

Since they were spending Christmas dinner at the O'Connor's home, she made something for Jack's parents and Billy. She wasn't nervous about Jack, Billy or Sean but she did worry about the lace shawl she'd made for Louise. Jack's mother hadn't become any friendlier with Elizabeth.

What was worse, Louise seemed as if she wanted to put a wedge between Jack and Elizabeth. She'd often invite Maureen over for tea or supper and would make a point to let Elizabeth know about it. Maureen also didn't hesitate to let everyone know that she still wanted Jack and would do anything to get him.

"Elizabeth, I picked up that surprise for Jack today." Her mother grinned as she and Elizabeth's father returned from the city.

"Thanks, Mudder. I'd like to see it." Elizabeth was so happy to know her father had suggested they pick up a Christmas tree ornament for Jack.

Her family had a tradition that went back to her father's grandfather. Every member of the family had their own ornament, and it would be hung on the tree every year. Whenever someone new came into the family, they received something with their name on it.

Her mother opened the small box and pulled out a wooden fishing boat that was handmade by her father's friend. On the side of the boat was Jack's name written in black letters.

"Mudder, it's wonderful." Elizabeth smiled.

"I got one for Billy, Louise, and Sean as well. I hope they like them." Her mother seemed excited about it.

Elizabeth wasn't sure if Jack's mother would care about the Power family tradition. Louise didn't seem the type to be impressed by anything her family considered endearing. Elizabeth didn't understand why Jack's mother looked down on her family, but it seemed the longer Elizabeth and Jack were together, the more direct she became.

Jack met them at the door as they arrived on the front porch of the O'Connor home. His smile was inviting, and he quickly hustled

Elizabeth and her family into the house. Of course, when they arrived, Maureen and her parents were in the living room with Sean, Louise, and Billy.

Elizabeth had to press her lips together to keep from laughing as Billy quickly stood up to get away from where Maureen was practically sitting on his lap. For a girl who had her eyes set on Jack, it was surprising how she flirted with Billy.

"Look, it's the Skipper and his family." Billy never called her father by his name, probably because it was how they referred to her father on the boats.

"Hope we're not late." Her father shook hands with Billy and Jack's father.

"Not at all, Paddy. Would you like a bit of spirit before we have dinner?" Sean asked as he picked up a bottle of dark rum.

"I won't say no to that." Her father chuckled.

"That's not surprising," Louise muttered as she stood up and went to the kitchen.

Elizabeth glanced at her mother to see if she'd heard Louise's snarky comment, but thankfully, Anne had Elizabeth's mother engaged in conversation. Maureen's mother was a little more tolerable than her daughter, but that was probably because she didn't know how nasty Maureen could be.

Elizabeth smiled as Jack relieved her of the packages and placed them under the tree. He then took her hand and led her to the small couch across the room from where Maureen sat glaring.

"Merry Christmas, Darling." Jack kissed her cheek as he linked his fingers with hers.

"Merry Christmas to you too." She gazed into his bright eyes.

"Was Santa good to you?" Jack asked.

"He was. How about you?" Elizabeth grinned.

"He was, but the best present just arrived." He pressed his forehead against hers.

"Elizabeth, have you seen the new dress I got for Christmas?" Maureen bragged.

Elizabeth wasn't going to let the girl ruin her holiday with Jack and her family. She put on a fake smile and turned to where Maureen spun around, showing off the beautiful red dress with white trim.

"It's lovely." Elizabeth nodded and turned back to Jack.

"It is, and Jack said I looked incredible in it," Maureen cooed.

"You do." Elizabeth smirked when Jack rolled his eyes.

"If you'll excuse us, Maureen, I'd like to show Betty the tree in our dining room." Jack stood up and held out his hand.

"I haven't seen it either." Maureen started to follow them, but Kurt stood in front of her.

"I think they want to be alone," Kurt said with a smug smile.

Elizabeth didn't bother to glance back to see Maureen's reaction as Jack showed her into the large dining room. The dinner table looked elegantly decorated, and a sizeable evergreen tree stood in the corner decorated with bright lights and store-bought ornaments. Elizabeth had never seen a tree look so lovely.

"It's beautiful, Jack." She stared at it in awe.

"Mudder seems to get more and more extravagant every year. I swear the old man is going to blow his top one of these years because he says it's a waste of money." Jack wrapped his arm around her waist.

"Did I tell you last year about our family Christmas tradition?" Elizabeth looked up at him nervously.

"Not that I remember." Jack turned to face her.

"Everyone in our family has a special ornament. All are usually handmade, and they go on our tree every year. We have them going back at least three generations," Elizabeth said proudly.

She ran back to the living room and grabbed the package she'd brought for Jack. When she returned to the dining room, she handed it to him. As he opened it, she nervously linked her hands together in front of her. The whole time he tore at the paper, she prayed he would like it.

"Betty, this is incredible." Jack held up the small boat with his name on it.

"Fadder wanted you to have one." Elizabeth looked up at him, and he lifted his eyes from the ornament to meet hers.

"I'm so honored." Jack held the small boat like it was a piece of gold.

"I think he might like you a little." Elizabeth grinned.

"Can I hang it on this tree, or does it have to go on the tree at your house?" Jack asked.

"It's yours. You can hang it where you want." Elizabeth shrugged.

As Jack was reaching to hang the boat on their tree, Louise scurried into the room carrying a large platter. She gasped as Jack hung the ornament on the tree.

"Heavens, Jack, get that off the tree," she spat as she placed the platter on the dining table.

"Mudder, it's an ornament that Betty gave me," Jack returned.

"Well… it's nice, but it's not the right type for that tree. Maybe you can put it in your room." With those words, Louise spun around and left the dining room.

"You can come over and put it on our tree later." Elizabeth went to remove it, but Jack stopped her.

"That's staying there, and I don't care what Mudder says." Jack held her hand as they went back to the living room.

The meal was delicious, and for the most part, Louise was polite. The only hiccup was when Maureen tried to put herself between Elizabeth and Jack. Luckily, Sean put a stop to that and made the girl sit across the table from Elizabeth.

Sean seemed to like Elizabeth and her family and never treated them any different than he did anyone else. He'd even made a big deal about the ornaments her mother gave them and did the same as Jack had, placing each of the homemade wooden ornaments on the beautiful tree in the dining room. Much to Louise's dismay.

Louise did seem to like the shawl Elizabeth made for her. Jack's mother kept the wrap over her shoulders while they had dessert and tea. It made Elizabeth proud that someone like Louise wore something she made.

"I need you to show me how you knit this, Elizabeth. It's beautiful," Anne said as she looked at the intricate pattern.

"Elizabeth creates her own patterns," her mother said proudly.

"It's lovely." Louise sat back in the chair and looked very comfortable with her new shawl.

Elizabeth couldn't help but feel relief that Louise didn't look down on her gift. Jack's mother still wasn't happy about the ornaments on her tree, but Elizabeth felt as if she pulled out a win for once.

"Now that we are all fed. I want to give Betty her present." Jack stood up and stepped in front of her.

Elizabeth glanced around the room. Her parents were beaming, and her brothers and Billy were grinning, as was Sean. The only one who seemed confused besides Maureen and her parents was Jack's mother. When Jack got down on one knee in front of Elizabeth, Louise gasped.

"Jack, what are you doing?" Louise sat up straight.

"Hush, Louise," Sean warned.

"Betty, I knew the first time I kissed you that there was no other girl for me. I fell in love with you and thanked my lucky stars that fate brought us together. Elizabeth Ann Power, would you make me the happiest man in Cape Broyle by saying yes? Betty, will you marry me?" Jack held up a dainty gold band with a diamond solitaire.

For a moment, she stared down at him in shock. She never expected a proposal for Christmas, but the man she loved was in front of her down on one knee, asking her to say yes. What else could she do?

"Yes," Elizabeth whispered because she couldn't get her voice to go any louder.

"Yes?" Jack grinned.

"Definitely, yes." Elizabeth's hand shook as he slipped the ring on her finger and pulled her into his arms.

"Looks like we'll have many more holidays together," Billy shouted.

"The Powers and the O'Connors joining together, God help Cape Broyle." Kurt laughed.

"Don't you think this is a little fast?" Louise's voice sounded as if she was about to burst into tears.

"Mudder, they've been courting for almost two years." Billy snorted. "Most couples would be married with a youngster on the way by now."

"We were married and had Jack seven months later." Sean chuckled.

"Sean," Louise gasped.

"Wait, that means Mudder was already on the nest when you two got married." Billy laughed.

"Billy, hush," Jack's mother snapped and quickly left the living room.

"It was only a matter of time before that came out." Sean scoffed. "How many seven-month babies were over nine pounds?"

"I don't think that was something she wanted to be known by everyone, Sean," Elizabeth's mother chastised.

"It's not like I didn't marry her." Sean shrugged.

"Fadder, I don't think that's the point." Jack sighed.

Elizabeth left the living room and made her way to the kitchen. Louise was frantically wiping down the counter, and it was obvious she was trying to hide her humiliation. Elizabeth's heart went out to Jack's mother.

"Mrs. O'Connor, are you okay?" Elizabeth asked.

"I'm fine. I guess you think I was a hussy to get pregnant before I was married." Louise didn't turn around.

"Not at all. When you love someone, sometimes it's not easy to wait until marriage." Elizabeth didn't have any right to look down on Jack's mother.

She and Jack had not made love but had come close several times. Elizabeth was still wary of taking that huge step again, and Jack didn't push it. That made her love him even more.

"Sean should never have said that." Louise's voice cracked.

"Mrs. O'Connor, it doesn't matter. You ended up with two incredible sons, and you're married to a wonderful man." Elizabeth stepped further into the kitchen.

"I know." Louise turned around and met Elizabeth's eyes. "You better not break his heart the way that other one did."

"I won't." Elizabeth smiled.

"What about if Tommy Roberts returns?" Louise snapped.

Before Elizabeth could answer, she heard Jack growl behind her. He stepped into the kitchen and walked straight to his mother, and it wasn't difficult to see the anger in his expression.

"Jack," Elizabeth said with a warning tone.

"Mudder, Betty and I love each other, and no matter who comes or goes, who you put in front of me every chance you get, or who comes back to town, we're staying together. We're getting married." Jack looked straight into his mother's eyes.

"I don't want you to get hurt." She sobbed.

"I'm a big boy, and I know Betty is the only woman for me. I can feel it in here." Jack slapped his hand against his chest.

"What about her? Is she going to stay with you if the Roberts boy comes back for her?" Louise pointed to Elizabeth.

"Mrs. O'Connor, I love Jack, and Tommy is no longer part of my life. If he did return, it wouldn't matter." Elizabeth wrapped her arm around Jack's waist.

Louise stared at her for a few minutes before she turned back to Jack. Elizabeth clenched her teeth together as she waited for whatever Louise was about to say.

"Then why can't you wait another year or two before you get married?" Louise asked.

"Because I love her, Mudder. Waiting a month, a year, or ten years is not going to change how I feel. I want to be Betty's husband and have her as my wife. I want to start a family with her. I know you may be having a difficult time understanding that, but it's not going to stop me from doing it." Jack hugged Elizabeth into his side.

Elizabeth closed her eyes to blink back the tears of happiness as she listened to Jack's conversation with his mother. If he was so sure about their relationship, how could anyone else doubt it, including her?

Chapter 10

Elizabeth blew out a shaky breath as she stared at herself in the mirror of the church's bride room. How was it possible that in less than an hour, she would walk down the aisle in the same church where she'd attended all her life?

She didn't recognize herself in the ivory and lace, ballerina-length, wedding dress. It had a sweetheart neckline that modestly covered the cleavage of her full breasts. It clung to her torso, then the skirt flared out at the bottom.

Her veil stopped at her shoulder and was attached to a thick white headband that held back her hair. Her shoes were plain white pumps that made her look about two inches taller than her five feet. Her mother gave her a pair of white satin gloves, and as Elizabeth slipped them on, she wondered if it was all real.

"You look so beautiful." Irene fawned over her.

She'd asked Irene, Linda, and Geraldine to be her attendants with Geraldine being her maid of honor. Jack had asked both her brothers to stand with him, and Billy was his best man.

"Jack is going to pop a button when he sees you." Linda laughed.

"I hope I don't faint before I get there." Elizabeth sighed.

"Nervous?" Geraldine asked.

"I keep dreaming that Mrs. O'Connor stands up and stops the wedding, then Maureen marries Jack," Elizabeth admitted.

"If I see her standing up, I'll knock her down." Linda winked.

Elizabeth laughed and hugged Billy's girlfriend. It seemed since she and Jack had become a thing, both her brothers and Billy had decided to enter relationships. It was great because they would all do things together, and Charlie had even told her he was going to propose to Geraldine the following weekend.

"Elizabeth, it's time." Her father's voice sounded strained.

Elizabeth turned around and smiled at her father. He was dressed in a black pinstriped suit and tugged at his tie when he entered the room. Seeing her father all dressed up, it was evident where her brothers got their looks.

"We'll see you outside." Linda winked as the three women left the bride's room.

"I can't believe you're getting married before your brothers." Her father chuckled as he walked toward her.

"I don't think you'll be waiting very long for another wedding, Fadder." Elizabeth smiled.

"So I've heard." Her father cupped her face in his hands.

"Don't you dare make me cry," she warned, but the tears were already forming.

"I know I was hard on you when you were with the other fella, but I knew he wasn't the one for you. Jack was always the one I saw you with." Her father smiled.

"What do you mean?" Elizabeth asked.

"I knew young Jack was your future. I knew that from the day I saw him running down the road after his fadder when he was just a boy." Her father kissed her forehead.

"How would you know that, Fadder?" Elizabeth scoffed.

"I just knew." He held out his arm. "Although I don't know if I'm ready to give you away."

"I love you, Fadder." She stood up on her toes and kissed her dad's cheek.

"I know I don't say it often, but I love you too, more than I could ever tell you. You'll always be my little girl. All I've ever wanted was for you to be happy." Her father smiled as a lone tear ran down his cheek.

"I am happy. Jack is the best thing that has ever happened to me." Elizabeth reached up and wiped the tear from her father's cheek.

"He's a good man." Her father nodded.

"Let's get me married." Elizabeth linked into her father's arm, and they walked out of the bride's room.

Elizabeth stood at the back of the church with her father as "Here Comes the Bride" echoed through the church. The two large oak doors opened, and everyone stood, but Elizabeth's eyes went immediately to the front where Jack stood with a huge smile and looking perfect.

"Last chance. We can make a run for it." Her father smirked.

"Fadder." Elizabeth chuckled as they started the long walk toward her future.

Elizabeth hardly remembered any of the ceremony because once she stood next to Jack, the only thing she could do was stare into his eyes. She held her breath when Father Murphy asked if anyone was against the marriage, and when nobody spoke, Jack chuckled as Elizabeth blew out a nervous breath.

The one thing she did remember was her confusion when the priest referred to Jack by his given name. She wasn't used to the name John and didn't know anyone that called him that.

"I'm John, in case you didn't know," Jack whispered in her ear.

The rest of the ceremony, she focused on him. It was hard to keep her attention on what Father Murphy was saying when Jack smiled at her.

"Here they are for the first time as husband and wife, Mr. and Mrs. John O'Connor," Father Murphy said as Jack and Elizabeth turned to face the congregation.

As everyone applauded, she and Jack practically ran to the back of the church. Before they made their way outside, Jack pulled her into his arms and kissed her full on the lips. It wasn't like the kiss they'd had after the ceremony, although he did take her breath away with that kiss.

"How do you feel, Mrs. O'Connor?" Jack whispered as he pulled his lips from hers.

"Sweet Jesus, don't call me that. I'll be looking around for your mother." Elizabeth laughed as they made their way out of the church and headed to the car.

"Wait for your driver, you two," Billy shouted as he ran down the steps toward them.

"Well, hurry the hell up so we can get to the party," Jack yelled.

"Yeah, you just want to get the party over with so you two can be alone." Billy winked at Elizabeth.

"You're just jealous." Jack chuckled as he helped Elizabeth into the car.

"Damn right." Billy started the car, and they pulled out onto the road.

Since they had to wait for the guests to arrive before they entered the hall, Elizabeth and Jack stayed in the small room outside of the hall. Jack kissed her more times than she could count, and at one point, she thought they were going to make love right there.

Jack pulled away, panting, and gazed into her eyes. Her heart thudded in her chest, and her body tingled all over. She couldn't wait to go to the cottage where they were spending their honeymoon. It was a small house that his family owned in St. Mary's Bay.

The house was right on the beach, and there wasn't another around for miles. Jack told her it used to be his mother's parents' house, but when they died, his mother kept it as a summer home.

"How long do we have to stay here?" Jack groaned.

"I think we should stay for a few hours." Elizabeth wrapped her arms around his waist and pressed her lips against his.

"Betty, you're killing me." He moaned as she nibbled his lower lip.

"Think of it this way, after we leave here, you have me all to yourself for seven days." She grinned.

"I can't wait." He sighed against her mouth.

The reception was fun, but Elizabeth cried more than once, especially when she danced with her father and brothers. Louise sobbed as she danced with Jack.

The only thing irritating her was when she watched Maureen sidle up to Jack and whisper something to him. Jack had stepped back and said something before he turned and walked away from the woman. After the tenth time she spotted Maureen harassing Jack, Elizabeth made her way to her husband and wrapped her arms around his waist. Maureen smirked as she dropped her hand from where she had it placed against Jack's chest.

"I'm ready to leave when you are, Darling." Elizabeth gazed into his eyes.

"Me too, my love," Jack replied with a grin.

"So soon, but I never got a chance to dance with the groom or give him a kiss," Maureen complained.

"The only one that kisses my husband is me," Elizabeth interjected as she and Jack walked away, leaving Maureen fuming.

Elizabeth changed into a pale-yellow skirt with a matching jacket and placed a pillbox hat on her head. They had their last dance to "You Are My Special Angel" by her favorite artist Bobby Helms. and as soon as the song ended, they were hustled out to the car. They drove away in his father's Oldsmobile. Of course, her brothers and Billy tied tin cans to the back of the vehicle and placed a huge sign on the back window that said *just married*.

The cottage was tiny with two bedrooms, a bathroom, a small kitchen, and a sitting room. The large bedroom had a queen-sized bed made with a beautiful homemade quilt, and a fire burned in the woodstove by the time they arrived late that night.

"Fadder had one of the neighbors up the road make sure the house was warm before we got here. It's still a little cold in the evenings," Jack said softly as he placed their suitcases at the foot of the bed.

"You would think it would be warmer in June," Elizabeth said as she tried to calm her nerves.

"It is Newfoundland, Darling." Jack shrugged out of his suit jacket and loosened his tie.

"True." She walked to the window and gazed out into the darkness.

It was after midnight by the time they arrived at the cottage, but she was too nervous to be tired, although she had no idea why. It wasn't like this would be her first time, but it would be her first time with Jack. They'd talked about past experiences, and he wasn't a virgin either, but that didn't calm her butterflies.

"When the sun comes up, you can see the beach through this window." Jack stepped behind her and wrapped his arms around her waist.

"Sounds lovely," Elizabeth leaned back against him.

"There's no rush, Betty. I'm nervous too," he whispered into her ear.

Elizabeth turned into his arms and rested her head against his chest. His heart pounded under her ear, and she smiled. It was obvious by the erratic beat of his heart that he wasn't lying about being nervous.

"I'm going to go change." She tipped her head back and gazed up at him.

His Adam's apple bobbed, and he stepped back for her to make her way to the bathroom. As she grabbed her valise, she struggled with her thoughts. She wanted to show him she was ready to be intimate with him, but undressing in front of him felt strange.

"I have a bottle of wine in the icebox, would you like a glass?" Jack asked as she placed her coat and hat on top of the dresser.

"I would, thank you." She glanced over her shoulder and caught Jack staring at her ass.

"Good. Okay." He hurried out of the bedroom as she entered the bathroom.

Geraldine had given her a long white nightgown with a cover-up to go over it. It was silk, and as she looked at herself in the mirror, she thought it made her look both sexy and virginal. She brushed her teeth for the second time and then her hair. She took a deep breath and pulled open the door.

The only light in the room was the flicker of the fireplace and the small oil lamp on the bedside table. The bedroom was warm, and Elizabeth halted when she saw the blankets of the bed pulled down.

Jack stood next to the window shirtless, and he turned around when she walked further into the room.

"You're so damn beautiful." Jack moved toward her and held out a glass.

"Thank you." She smiled and sipped from the glass.

Elizabeth wasn't a huge wine fan, but at that moment, she wasn't sure what to do. Jack took her hand, and they walked toward the bed. He sat down and tugged her down next to him.

"If you're not ready, we can just hold each other tonight," Jack whispered.

Elizabeth placed her glass on the nightstand and took his from him. After she placed it next to hers, she put her hand against his cheek and turned his face, so he had to look at her.

"I'm ready, Jack. I love you, and I want tonight to be perfect. I'm your wife, and I want to make love with you," Elizabeth whispered.

"I love you, Betty," Jack murmured and held her face between his hands as he kissed her the way a man kisses his wife.

Chapter 11

"Mrs. O'Connor, I'm quite capable of making drapes for the windows. I don't feel it's necessary to waste money on store-bought things that I can make myself." Elizabeth tried not to roll her eyes as they walked through the department store.

Her mother-in-law of four months seemed to want to take over all the decoration of the house she and Jack bought a couple of weeks after their honeymoon. She was so glad that they only had to spend twelve days in the same house as Jack's parents.

They had the most amazing seven days at the cottage, and she hated to leave when it was time to get back to real life. Jack was gentle and passionate, and she never thought having sex could be so incredible, but Jack brought her to heights of ecstasy she never thought possible.

Growing up Catholic, she learned that sex was for procreation, but she and Jack made love every night and morning. They had been married for a little over three months, and she couldn't get enough of him.

Jack had also returned to fishing on the boats, and he had left two days earlier. Elizabeth didn't want him to go, but he only went out when one of the boats were short-handed. He still did most of the paperwork for his father. With him gone, she was alone in her house, or at least she was supposed to be.

Louise decided it wasn't proper for Jack's wife to be alone while he was out to sea. She'd given Jack a whole speech on a wife being vulnerable when the husband was away. Elizabeth wasn't alone, of course, because her mother stayed with her until the men returned.

"Why go through all that trouble when we can buy ones much better than you could make?" Louise picked up several drapes and tossed them in the basket.

"I'm a very good seamstress." Elizabeth tried not to feel offended.

Elizabeth glanced at her mother, who only rolled her eyes and browsed through the fabric that Elizabeth had mentioned would make great bedroom curtains.

"She's right, Louise. Elizabeth is a talented seamstress." Her mother placed a bolt of fabric in the basket.

"I don't see why you can't have both store-bought and the homemade drapes. You can put the good ones up when company comes over." Louise continued to browse through the drapes.

Elizabeth tipped her head back and asked God for the patience to get through the rest of their shopping trip. By the time they finally returned to Cape Broyle from St. John's, Elizabeth went directly to Louise's house and dropped Jack's mother off. It took a few minutes for Louise to finally get out of the car because she wanted to help Elizabeth put up the new drapes. She told her mother-in-law that she wasn't doing anything that night and would be heading to bed early.

The truth was she and her mother wanted to have a quiet night at home and watch a little television. Jack bought it for Elizabeth with the hope it would help the time not seem so long while the men were out to sea.

"That woman is going to drive me to drink." Elizabeth sighed as she and her mother walked into the house.

"She's trying to be helpful." Her mother eased down on the couch.

"She's trying to take over my life," Elizabeth complained.

"She's a mother-in-law." Her mother chuckled.

"So, will I warn Geraldine to expect the same from you?" Elizabeth laughed.

"Of course," her mother teased.

"Mudder, you couldn't be that intrusive if you tried." Elizabeth sat down and wrapped her arms around her mother.

When her mother winced, Elizabeth noticed it right away. Over the last few years, her mother was becoming less and less active due to her back issues. The doctors had assured them that it was the result of so much physical work over her mother's lifetime, but Elizabeth worried that it was more.

"Mudder, did you want an aspirin?" Elizabeth placed a homemade quilt over her mother's legs.

"I'll take one before I go to bed for the night, but right now, I'm just glad to sit down." Her mother lay back against the couch.

"I'll get some tea, and we'll turn on the television. I think *Bonanza* is on at eight." Elizabeth hurried to the kitchen and prepared a pot of tea.

Before the end of the show, her mother had fallen asleep on the sofa. Elizabeth covered her up and turned off the television. She was cleaning up the kitchen when she heard a soft knock on the door.

It was a little after nine in the evening, and although she didn't usually go to bed before ten, it was strange to have company so late. She dried her hands and made her way to the door.

"Hi." Geraldine smiled when Elizabeth opened the door.

"Come in. I wasn't expecting to see you tonight." Elizabeth hugged her future sister-in-law.

"I had an argument with my mudder and was wondering if I could stay here tonight?" Geraldine asked.

"Of course. Mudder is asleep on the sofa, but you can take the guest room." Elizabeth motioned for Geraldine to follow her.

"That's fine." It wasn't unusual for Geraldine to disagree with her mother, but for her to walk out was rare.

"Want to talk about it?" Elizabeth made another pot of tea.

"I told Mudder that I was pregnant." Geraldine sighed.

"You are?" Elizabeth asked.

"Yes, I found out today." Geraldine couldn't hold back the tears.

"Honey, don't cry. You're engaged to Charlie. It's not like he's going to abandon you." Elizabeth covered Geraldine's hand with hers.

"I know, but Mudder doesn't want me to tell anyone until after the wedding. I mean, people aren't stupid." Geraldine rolled her eyes.

"You're welcome to stay here until Charlie comes back in from fishing." Elizabeth hugged Geraldine.

"Thanks." Geraldine smiled and wiped the tears away.

By the time Elizabeth got to bed, it was after midnight, and she was exhausted. She was excited to find out she would be an aunt, but she and Jack were also trying to have a baby. Elizabeth was concerned that it was taking longer than she expected.

Her mother told her that the more she worried about it, the more stress she'd put on herself, and it would make it challenging to get pregnant. That was easier said than done, especially since she had a constant fear that children weren't in her future.

By the new year, Elizabeth was deeply involved with helping to prepare for Charlie and Geraldine's wedding. They moved the date up to late January so they could be married before Geraldine started to show.

When Geraldine told Charlie about the baby, he became so excited that he began to jump around the kitchen. Elizabeth couldn't remember seeing him so thrilled about anything.

While in the middle of the plans, Elizabeth came down with a bad case of the flu. Jack was in the off-fishing season and took care of her until she was well. After a week in bed, she'd had enough, but the flu had drained all her energy.

"Betty, maybe you should go see Dr. Connolly," her mother suggested one evening.

"Mudder, it's the flu." Elizabeth sighed as she curled up on the sofa.

"It's hanging on too long," Jack sat next to her.

"Fine, I'll go in the morning." Elizabeth sighed.

"No need. He's coming up the steps." Her mother smiled.

"You knew this, didn't you?" Elizabeth glared at Jack.

"I have no idea what you mean." Jack kissed her cheek.

By the time Dr. Connolly left, he'd taken blood, gave her orders to stay in bed for another few days, and drink plenty of fluids. Like she hadn't already been doing that for over a week.

"I don't want to stay in bed all day, again," Elizabeth complained the next morning.

"It's Sunday. I'll stay in bed with you." Jack smiled as he placed a tray of eggs, toast, and tea in front of her.

Elizabeth glanced down at the plate, and it looked wonderful, but the smell of the eggs made her stomach lurch. She practically jumped out of bed and ran for the bathroom. She barely made it before she started to vomit.

"That's it. I'm calling Dr. Connolly again." Jack didn't give her a chance to respond.

An hour later, she sat on her bed as Dr. Connolly examined her. He didn't seem the least bit worried about her illness and seemed to concentrate on her stomach.

"I think you might have to expect this for another few months." He smiled down at Elizabeth.

"Months?" Elizabeth gasped.

"What's wrong with her?" Jack sat next to her.

"The first term of pregnancy is the roughest." Dr. Connolly grinned. "Dry crackers will help with the nausea."

"I'm having a baby?" Elizabeth asked.

"You're having a baby. If my calculations are correct, you'll have a wee bundle by Labor Day," the doctor told them.

"We're having a baby," Jack whispered.

"You're having a baby," Dr. Connolly repeated and nodded as he left the room.

For several minutes they sat on the bed and stared at each other. It was almost as if they didn't believe it, but when a smile crept on Jack's face, he jumped to his feet and shouted.

"We're having a baby," Jack yelled.

"We're going to be parents." Elizabeth stood up and wrapped her arms around Jack.

It was still hard to believe that she and Jack were going to get the baby they so desperately wanted. Her mother and father would be even more excited since they were going to have two grandchildren by the end of the year.

"Shit," Jack grumbled.

"What?" Elizabeth tilted her head and stared at him.

"Mudder is going to drive you crazy." Jack smirked.

"I can handle her." Elizabeth had learned pretty quickly that negotiation with Louise was the only way to deal with her.

"You handle her like nobody else I know." Jack pressed his lips against her forehead.

"I love you, Jack." She wrapped her arms around him and pressed her cheek against his chest.

"I love you too, Betty. More than I could ever tell you." Jack tipped her head up, and he covered her lips with his. "So, let me show you." And he did.

Chapter 12

Months flew by but not without heartache. Geraldine had to be rushed to the hospital because she started bleeding. The baby didn't survive, and Geraldine had to have an emergency hysterectomy. The couple were devastated, and Geraldine tried to push Charlie away. He wouldn't have any of it and stood by his wife.

Her mother's health had deteriorated to the point she had to walk with a cane, and her father was worried sick. When it was time for them to go out on the water, her mother would come to stay with Elizabeth, and Geraldine would stay with her parents.

Jack's mother was as expected, and Elizabeth was close to the brink of insanity because of her mother-in-law. Louise tried to take over the decoration of the baby's room, but Sean quickly put a stop to that. Jack made arrangements to be home for the last two weeks of August and the first two weeks of September. He wanted to make sure he was home when the baby arrived, and Elizabeth was elated to have him close.

"You should set up the cradle at least, Betty," Louise said as they ate supper.

"We can do that when the baby comes," Elizabeth repeated for what seemed like the hundredth time.

"You won't have time," Louise pushed.

"Louise, leave the girl alone," Sean interjected. "Jack will be here, and he'll help."

"That's not a man's job," Louise insisted.

"No, it's a parent's job, and we're both parents." Elizabeth leaned back in the chair and pressed her hand against her swollen belly as the baby gave her a hard kick.

Elizabeth was sure the baby was a boy, and although Jack believed her, he refused to get excited until the baby was born. If the baby was a boy, they already had the first name. Since it was a tradition in Jack's family to name the first boy after the paternal father, the baby would be Sean.

Jack also had a suggestion for the middle name, but Elizabeth didn't know how comfortable she felt about it. Her mother's father's name was Thomas, and although that wasn't the reason Jack suggested the name, she knew it would be a point of contention with Jack's mother.

Jack wanted to use Tommy's name because he was part of the reason she and Jack were able to start a life together. If Tommy hadn't left, then she never would have fallen in love with Jack.

Jack also made plans for them to go to the cottage to have some time alone before the baby came. She only had to wait two days for him to return from the last trip. She was sure her mother and Jack's mother wouldn't be happy about them going because there were no hospitals or midwives in that area, but it didn't matter, they were going.

"Oh come now, Betty, you don't expect your husband to take care of the baby, do you?" Louise laughed.

"Why not? Paddy did his share of taking care of the youngsters when they were little," her mother retorted.

"Goodness, I wouldn't expect a hard-working man to do that." Louise seemed utterly shocked by the idea.

"It's because you wouldn't let me," Sean grumbled.

"Your job was to teach the boys to be men. I cared for them until then." Louise narrowed her eyes at her husband.

Elizabeth glanced at the clock on the wall and prayed for time to fly by so Louise and Sean would head home. She'd invited them to supper after church, and at that moment, wished she hadn't because Louise started her nitpicking the minute she walked into the house. She didn't take kindly to Elizabeth not attending mass every Sunday, but Elizabeth didn't feel going to church every week was necessary. She prayed anytime she felt the need, and she would argue the bible said, "Keep Sunday the sabbath," not go to church every Sunday.

Her only reprieve was when Louise disappeared into the kitchen to clean up after supper. Her mother-in-law felt Elizabeth needed to put her feet up and relax to keep the baby healthy. The older generation always thought a pregnant woman was delicate. Dr. Connolly had assured Elizabeth she could do everyday things but to make sure she did get an adequate amount of rest.

"I'm sorry, Betty. She means well." Sean winked as he sipped his coffee.

"I know, Mr. O'Connor." Elizabeth liked Jack's father.

He reminded Elizabeth a lot of Jack in his looks and his demeanor. Sean had a way of staying calm, even when everything around him was chaos.

"Trust me, she thinks the world of you," Sean assured her.

Elizabeth wasn't sure if her father-in-law was right, but she did notice that Louise had not mentioned Maureen as often, and she called every day when Jack was gone to make sure Elizabeth and her mother didn't need anything. Still, it was hard to get close to the woman when she was consistently critical.

Later that night, Elizabeth lay in her bed wearing one of Jack's shirts. She missed him when he was gone, and the only way she could sleep was to wear something he had worn before he left. Elizabeth knew her mother still did the same thing.

Elizabeth closed her eyes and tried to imagine what her baby would look like when it came. She pictured Jack and her father teaching their child to fish, because in her mind, she knew the baby was a boy.

Elizabeth woke up when someone touched her arm. She turned over and stared before she realized what she was seeing. Jack stood next to the bed with a huge grin on his handsome face.

"Jack, what…when…" Elizabeth sat up, and he knelt next to the bed.

"We had an amazing catch yesterday, and the boat was full. We had to come in and offload." Jack grinned.

"So, you're going out again today?" Elizabeth hated to feel disappointed, but she didn't want him to go so soon.

"Actually, no. Your fadder won't let me go out for the rest of the summer, and my fadder is dropping off the paperwork for me to take over until the new year." Jack wrapped his arms around her or as much as her huge belly would allow.

"Can you do that, financially, I mean?" Elizabeth knew they weren't poor, but they were a young couple starting their life together, and the house had depleted Jack's nest egg a great deal.

"We'll be fine." Jack kissed her forehead and placed his large hand on her belly. "Has he been a good boy?"

"He or she has been kicking a lot." Elizabeth smirked at the way Jack referred to the baby as a boy.

"That's my boy." Jack crouched and kissed her belly.

"Yes, Jack, I'm pretty sure it's your boy." Elizabeth giggled.

"So, it is a boy?" Jack looked up with a hopeful expression.

"I guess we'll find out in a couple of months," Elizabeth teased.

Her house was a buzz of activity with the return of the men. Her father, Kurt, and Billy headed back out the next day, but Charlie decided to stay in and take his wife on a little trip to St. John's. He'd hoped it would help her out of her depression.

Elizabeth and Jack took their trip to the cottage, and when they returned, she felt relaxed, and if it was possible, even more in love with her husband. They'd set up a small office area in their house for Jack to take over his father's duties.

The weeks flew, and by the time the end of August came, Elizabeth thought she would explode if she got any bigger. Jack was a nervous wreck, and if she whimpered, he was on his feet, wondering if he had to call the doctor.

Her father, brothers, and Billy were due in that evening. She was excited to see them, but she was extremely uncomfortable as she tried to shift in the chair. She blew out an exasperated breath as she tried to stand up.

"Jack," she shouted.

"What? Is it time?" Jack ran into the living room.

"Yes, it's time for me to pee again," Elizabeth snapped but winced as soon as the words were out of her mouth.

She didn't mean to be so cranky, but it was hard to be pleasant when she couldn't stand up on her own, she felt as big as a house, and her mother-in-law hovered to let her know what she could and couldn't do.

Jack was an angel with her and didn't complain any time she became frustrated or cranky. He helped her to her feet and gave her a quick kiss. She took two steps and stopped when something began to run down her legs.

"Uh-oh." Elizabeth glanced down as water pooled on the floor.

"What's that?" Jack stepped back but kept hold of her hands.

"I think it's time." She glanced up at him with a smile.

"For the baby?" Jack grinned.

"Yes, call the doctor." Elizabeth waved him off as she made her way to the bathroom and prayed that the pain wouldn't be as bad as she expected.

Chapter 13

"It's a boy." Jack's voice echoed through the house.

Elizabeth gazed down at the tiny bundle in her arms, and every minute of her sixteen hours of labor faded as she looked at her son. Sean Thomas O'Connor was over nine pounds with a full head of auburn hair. He had a cleft in his chin like his father, and he had her nose.

"You are going to be so loved," Elizabeth whispered to the sleeping baby.

The doctor and midwives helped her clean up after Sean was born, and when she was back in the bed, Jack was permitted into their bedroom to see his son. His eyes filled with tears as he nervously accepted the baby from the midwife. Jack gazed down at the baby as he softly spoke to his son. Elizabeth smiled as she watched her husband fall in love with their child.

"Are you up for some visitors?" Kurt asked as he returned to the room.

"Sure." She smiled.

Kurt pushed open the bedroom door to reveal their family. It wasn't hard to see how excited everyone was to see the baby, especially her mother and mother-in-law.

"Oh, my goodness, he's so beautiful." Her mother sobbed.

"Have you picked a name?" Kurt asked.

Elizabeth glanced up at Jack and nodded to let him know she was okay with the name he picked. He took the baby from Elizabeth and walked over to where his father and Elizabeth's mother stood.

"We're carrying on with the family tradition. His first name is Sean." Jack smiled at his father.

"What about his middle name?" Louise gazed at the baby in Jack's arms.

"Mudder, we're naming him after your late fadder." Elizabeth smiled as her mother's mouth dropped open.

"You're calling him Sean Thomas?" Louise gasped.

"Yes." Jack turned and placed the baby in Elizabeth's mother's arms.

"Isn't that a little embarrassing to my son?" Louise glared at Elizabeth.

"Why would naming my son after his great-grandfather be embarrassing to me, Mudder?" Jack narrowed his eyes.

"Because of…you know?" Louise stammered over her words.

"Mudder, just because it's the same name as Tommy Roberts doesn't mean it's going to embarrass me. Now I don't want to hear another word about the name I picked for our son." Jack's voice was stern as he turned back to where her mother sat rocking baby Sean.

"I hope that's okay with you, Mrs. Power." Jack crouched in front of her mother.

"It's more than okay. Thank you so much. My fadder would be so proud." Her mother had tears streaming down her cheeks.

"I think we should all let Elizabeth and the baby rest." Charlie bent over the bed and kissed Elizabeth's head. "Congratulations."

Charlie left the room quickly, but she didn't miss the tears in his eyes. Her brother and Geraldine were having a tough time since the loss of the baby. Geraldine had not returned to the home she shared with Charlie, and over the last week, she refused to see him. It was killing Charlie.

"Your brother is right. Get some rest, and if you need anything, call." Her father kissed her cheek and the top of the baby's head.

By the time everyone left, the only people left in the house were her mother and Jack. Her mother stayed to help with the baby until Elizabeth was back on her feet, although she didn't see why she needed to stay in bed.

"Do you want to try and feed the baby now?" her mother asked.

"I'll go make some tea while you do that." Jack kissed her cheek and left the room.

"Are you sure you're okay with the middle name Thomas, Elizabeth?" her mother asked after Jack left them alone.

"Yes, Mudder. I am." Elizabeth smiled.

Three weeks later, they celebrated Sean's baptism, and everyone gathered at their house later to celebrate. Elizabeth was on her way to the kitchen when she overheard two neighbors whisper about the baby's name.

Apparently, they heard a rumor that baby Sean wasn't Jack's son, but he agreed to accept the baby as long as Elizabeth refused to see Tommy again. It angered her, and she immediately stopped to confront the women.

"Let's stop this rumor before it gets out of control, ladies. Our son, meaning Jack's and mine, was named after Mr. O'Connor and my mother's father. Do you remember my grandfather, Mrs. Budgell? His name was Thomas Ryan. They used to call him Tom."

"Betty, we…didn't…" Ida Budgell stammered when she realized that Elizabeth had overheard her.

"No need to be embarrassed. I'm sure Mrs. Hynes was about to tell you that the rumor wasn't true. Weren't you, Mrs. Hynes?" Elizabeth turned to the other woman whose face was red as beets.

"Oh, of course, I was just about to say…" Iris Hynes suddenly found the hem of her skirt very interesting.

"So, why don't we stop this little story here and now before it goes any further? I know who started it, but it's going to end with you, right, ladies?" Elizabeth gave the women a smile that said they should probably agree.

"Oh, of course, my dear." Ida nodded.

"Yes, no need for it to continue," Iris agreed.

"Good, thanks for coming." Elizabeth smiled and walked away from the women.

Elizabeth had an idea of where the rumor started, but she wasn't about to play Maureen's game and confront her. Besides, the woman would never admit to spreading the false story. The only thing to do was to ignore her.

A week later, her father and brothers dropped by before they headed out for the last fishing trip of the season. Jack seemed sad that he wasn't going, but baby Sean changed his mood pretty quickly.

"Mudder is going to be so happy after they get in this time. The seas have been rough this year," Elizabeth said as she bathed Sean a couple of days later.

"Billy told me they had a couple of close calls on the last trip." Jack leaned against the counter and sipped his coffee.

"The joys of being a fisherman." Elizabeth chuckled as the baby grinned up at Jack.

"I want more for him. I know it's a noble profession, but I'd rather not worry about my son being out on that water." Jack allowed Sean to grab his finger.

"You and me, both." Elizabeth smiled as Jack leaned over and pressed his lips against hers. "I love you."

"I love you too, Darling." Jack ran a finger down her cheek.

"And we both love you, little man." Elizabeth lifted the baby out of the sink and wrapped him in a towel.

While she got him dressed, she thought about the coming holidays. It would be Sean's first one, and her mother already had someone working on his ornament to add to their family Christmas tree. She was excited.

The next morning, Elizabeth was woken to the sound of something hitting the bedroom window. A violent storm had rolled in unexpectedly overnight with high winds and driving rain. As Elizabeth stood in the bedroom staring out the window, she could see high waves crash against the rocks on the beach.

She couldn't calm her frayed nerves as she thought about her father, brothers, and brother-in-law on the open water. She had an uneasy feeling and hadn't been able to relax since she woke at five that morning.

Baby Sean was asleep, but Jack was in the kitchen, trying to make tea for both of them quietly. She could tell he was concerned, but he tried not to show her. Her father was a great skipper and had ridden out nasty storms in the past, but Mother Nature could be a tough adversary.

Elizabeth hadn't heard her mother stir, so she hoped the storm didn't wake her. Her mom would worry herself sick until she knew *The Cora Lee* was safe at the dock.

They were supposed to be out for another few days, but with the bad weather, her father would look at the safety of the crew. She just hoped he was able to make it in before it got worse. If that was possible.

"Here you go, Darling," Jack whispered as he handed her a teacup.

"Thank you." She kissed his cheek as she wrapped her hands around the china cup.

"Your mudder is still sleeping. I checked on her." Jack glanced back to where the baby grunted.

"Jack, I'm so worried." Elizabeth sighed.

"I know, but if I know your father, he's on his way back as we speak." Jack wrapped his arm around her shoulder, and they stared out at the entrance of the harbor.

Every second she prayed to see a boat come through. Of course, her father wasn't the only one out there. There were at least twenty fishing boats that had gone out over the few days prior. As far as she knew, none of them had returned before the storm.

"There are a couple of coves they can hold up in until the storm passes. We had to do that a few times," Jack whispered as he kissed the side of her head.

Elizabeth silently prayed for God to bring all the boats back into the harbor safely. They didn't need another tragedy like they had seen far too many times. The fishermen that went down with their vessels in the Atlantic Ocean didn't always come home to their families. Many of them become part of the sea.

By supper time, Elizabeth was doing her best to keep her mother from having a nervous breakdown. Her mother woke up to see the storm and wanted to call the Coast Guard. It wasn't like they hadn't faced similar days over the years, but for some reason, her mother seemed unusually scared. Elizabeth didn't like it and wondered if her mother sensed something that she wasn't saying.

When Elizabeth's grandfather died, he'd come to her mother in a dream the same night his boat went down. Elizabeth worried that maybe her mother had a nightmare about her father and brothers.

Jack and his father had made their way to the dock as some of the boats finally started to return to the harbor. Elizabeth didn't know if her father's boat had returned, but since the storm had calmed, she didn't feel as on edge.

Louise was doing her best to distract Elizabeth's mother, but it wasn't working for either of the women. Her mom kept going to the window, probably hoping to see the men returning, and Louise would continue to pull out her prayer beads.

By late evening all the boats returned except for two. Her father's and another of the O'Connor fishing boats. The Coast Guard was searching for them, and several of the fishermen had also made their way back out to search.

Her mother had become hysterical when Sean returned to the house to let them know that there were still two boats that haven't returned. Dr. Connolly had come to give her mother something to calm her down. It frightened Elizabeth to see her mother so out of control because she'd never seen her like it ever before.

Jack's parents sat at the table, and both looked ready to burst into tears. Elizabeth couldn't rid herself of the sense of dread she felt as she glanced around at everyone.

"Darling, why don't you go lay down while the baby is sleeping?" Jack wrapped his arms around her and pulled her into him.

"I won't sleep." She tried to swallow the lump in her throat.

She'd already tried to get some rest earlier, but every time she closed her eyes, she saw her father and brothers fighting for their lives in the water. It scared her.

Geraldine, Linda, and Irene arrived later in the evening. They had come to support the family and each other. Geraldine hadn't seen Charlie before he left, and she was terrified she would never see her husband again.

"Why hasn't anyone called?" Louise murmured.

"It's a big ocean out there, honey." Sean held her hand.

"They might not ever find them." Geraldine sobbed as she entered the kitchen.

"Don't say that, Geraldine," Irene snapped.

"Well, isn't that what we're all thinking?" Linda sat next to Louise.

"Why don't we all just pray they come home safe?" Jack interjected as he hugged Elizabeth tightly in his arms.

Jack was scared. Elizabeth could hear the pounding of his heart where her head rested against his chest. His younger brother was the only sibling he had. They were as close as two brothers could be. Exactly the way Charlie and Kurt were.

A soft knock on the door had them all turning toward it as if a bomb was about to go off. Jack hurried to the door and opened it. He blew out a breath when he reached for whoever was on the other side of the door.

Elizabeth held her breath as she waited for the person to appear. When she saw Charlie step into the house, she practically launched herself into his arms.

"Oh, Charlie," Geraldine shouted and wrapped her arms around her husband and Elizabeth.

"Where's Billy?" Louise sobbed.

"I don't know." Charlie choked out the words.

"What do you mean you don't know?" Sean asked.

"I wasn't on their boat. I went out with Skipper Barnes." Charlie replied.

"Why?" Elizabeth pulled back to look up at her brother.

"He was short-handed, and Fadder told me Skipper Barnes needed the extra hand." Charlie held Geraldine in his arms.

"I didn't know." Sean shook his head.

"It was last minute. One of the crew showed up at the dock, drunk," Charlie explained.

"Who?" Sean growled.

"Peter," Charlie told him.

Skipper Claude Barnes was another of the captains on the O'Connor boats. He was a good man, but his son Peter had a terrible drinking problem, and Sean removed the young man from several fishing trips over the season. As far as Elizabeth knew, Sean was ready to fire him permanently because of it.

"Jesus, Mary, and Joseph," Sean grumbled through gritted teeth.

"Where's Mudder?" Charlie asked.

"She was hysterical. Dr. Connolly gave her something to help her sleep," Elizabeth told her brother.

"Good." He met Elizabeth's eyes.

"Have you heard anything?" Jack asked.

"No, but we were the last boat to come in. I didn't even know Fadder's boat hadn't returned until I was on the dock." Charlie shrugged out of his coat.

"Let me get you a cup of tea." Louise jumped to her feet, obviously thankful for something to do.

"Thanks, Mrs. O'Connor." Charlie cupped Geraldine's cheeks in his hands and looked into her eyes. "I'm okay, sweetheart."

"I know. I see you, but I was scared that the last words you heard from me were that I needed space." Geraldine sobbed.

"You know what I want to hear now?" Charlie smiled.

"What?" She sniffed.

"You love me, and you're coming back home," Charlie whispered.

Geraldine didn't say a word, she just nodded and threw herself into his arms. Charlie hugged her tightly to him, and Elizabeth tugged Jack into the kitchen to give her brother a little privacy.

By the next morning, there was still no word on *The Cora Lee*. Her mother had been relieved to see Charlie, but she was still worried about the rest.

The Coast Guard had sent a message to the family to let them know they were still searching along with some of the fishermen around the community. Elizabeth didn't say it out loud, but she knew after such a long time searching, chances were things were not going to end well.

Elizabeth had a bad feeling in the pit of her stomach that her father, Kurt, Billy, and the rest of the crew were not going to return. After such a long time with no sign of them, it was difficult to keep hope alive. If they were okay, someone would have found them. Especially with all the boats that had joined the search party. She hoped she was wrong.

Chapter 14

After three long days of searching, the Coast Guard still had not found *The Cora Lee* or any of the crew. Charlie did his best to be strong for their mother, but as a fisherman, he knew as well as Elizabeth did that the longer they were missing, the less chance there was of finding them alive or at all.

While Elizabeth remained strong around her mother, at night she'd sob in Jack's arms. They prayed frantically for their family and the crew to come home safely, but with each passing hour, their hope faded.

Sean and Louise had taken over one of the extra bedrooms while her mother stayed in the other. Charlie and Geraldine stayed in their own home but returned in the mornings.

Elizabeth didn't sleep much, and when she did, dreams of her father and brother screaming for help would wake her, or she'd see them slip beneath the waves as they struggled against the cold Atlantic Ocean. Elizabeth would wake up in tears.

Her only solace was baby Sean. Holding him calmed her, and she tried not to think about how he would probably never get to know his grandfather or Kurt or Billy. He'd miss out on the great people they were.

"I'm going to head out with Skipper Barnes and help search," Sean said as he entered the kitchen.

"Absolutely not." Louise shot to her feet, and her voice echoed through the house.

"Darling, I've got to do something. I can't sit around and do nothing anymore. Our son is out there somewhere. My friend and his son and five other young men who are like sons to me." Sean's voice cracked.

"Fadder, I think it's better if you stay here. I'll go," Jack interjected.

"No," Elizabeth gasped, and for the first time, let tears fall in front of her family.

"Betty, I'll be okay." Jack immediately pulled her into his arms, and he tried to soothe her as she cried hysterically.

Elizabeth clung to him and let out all the frustration and fear she'd been holding in while she was in front of everyone. Logically she knew that the more people who searched, the better chance they had of finding something.

"No, Jack. You can't go," Elizabeth croaked through her tears.

Everyone was quiet in the kitchen with only the soft sobs of Elizabeth, her mother, and Louise, the only sound in the house. Jack held her tightly in his arms, and she buried her face in his chest.

An hour later, Elizabeth asked Jack to take a walk with her. She needed to get out of the house, and the only place she could think to go was the shelter her father had built for her on the top of the cliff.

She sat next to Jack on the bench and scanned the horizon in front of her. They were out there somewhere, and she prayed for something to come out of the sky and point to where to find them.

"That water is so cold this time of year," Elizabeth murmured. "They'll never survive in it."

"Betty, don't do this to yourself." Jack wrapped his arm around her.

"Jack, it's been four days. There hasn't been any sign of the boat or them. Out there somewhere are eight men and a boat, but nobody knows where." Elizabeth rested her head on Jack's shoulder.

"The Coast Guard is still searching," Jack whispered against her temple.

"For how much longer, Jack? You know as well as I do they can't look forever." Elizabeth closed her eyes.

The search would have to end at some point. The Coast Guard only searched for so long before they would end it. Elizabeth saw it more times than she could count. When a boat didn't return, they would investigate the coast and inlets, but after a week, there was little hope, and the search ended.

The Atlantic Ocean didn't give up what it claimed most of the time. Although a body would wash up on the shore, days, weeks, and sometimes months after they vanished. It was usually a grisly discovery, and most of the time, identification was difficult because of the state of the remains.

"Darling, I wish I could say something that would make you feel better, but the truth is, I'm just as lost." Jack sniffed.

Elizabeth lifted her head and looked up into Jack's face. It was only the second time he's shed a tear in the last four days. His brother was missing too, and Elizabeth tried hard to remember that he was scared.

"I should have been with them," Jack whispered.

"What good would that have done?" Elizabeth cupped his face in her hands.

"Maybe I could have done something." Jack shrugged.

"Or they would be out there looking for you too, and Sean would probably end up losing his father as well as his uncles and grandfather." Elizabeth didn't bother to hold back the tears.

"I want to fix this." Jack sighed.

"Jack, nobody can fix this. No matter what happens, we'll get through this. Together." She gazed into Jack's blue eyes.

"I love you, Betty." Jack pulled her into his arms and buried his face in the crook of her neck.

"I love you too," she whispered.

For a long while, they stayed in the little shelter holding each other. They needed the connection and to be away from everyone. She didn't know how her mother or Jack's mother would handle what was coming, but Elizabeth had come to terms with the fact that her father and Kurt were gone. She could feel it, and once that realization set in, she knew she had to help the rest of the family face it as well.

The next morning Elizabeth got up a little after seven in the morning. The house was quiet, except for Sean's hungry whimper. She fed him while she gazed out at the clouds that passed overhead. Jack had gone to the dock to see if there was any news, but she made him promise not to go out on the water.

After she fed the baby, she put him in his playpen while she made a pot of tea to have ready when everyone started to get up for the day. She was pouring herself a cup when she noticed Jack headed toward the house with Charlie and another man she didn't recognize.

Elizabeth pulled open the door as the three men came up the front steps to the front porch. When she glanced at the man, she realized who he was. He was one of the Coast Guards who had been to the house on the first day of the search.

Elizabeth stepped back when she met Jack's eyes and started to shake her head. She continued to back away as Jack reached for her, and she knew from his expression precisely what they were about to say. She pushed Jack away as if she could stop the news from coming if he didn't touch her.

"No." Elizabeth whispered.

"They found pieces of the boat." Charlie's words came out raspy.

"No," Elizabeth shook her head.

"It's possible the boat smashed against the side of the cliffs," Charlie continued.

"Why don't we get the rest of the family and I'll explain," the Coast Guard said softly.

Elizabeth couldn't remember his name, and at that point, she didn't care. A destroyed boat meant everyone on board was gone. A rogue wave could come out of nowhere, and if it was strong enough to slam the boat against the cliffs, no human could survive that.

It took about thirty minutes to gather everyone in the living room, and from their expressions, Elizabeth could tell they all knew what was coming. No matter how hopeful everyone had been over the few days, somewhere deep down, they knew the truth.

"I'd like to start by saying I know how hard this has all been for your family and the families of the rest of the men that were on *The Cora Lee*. We've confirmed that the remnants we found were definitely pieces of *The Cora Lee*," the man explained.

"So, you aren't going to search anymore?" Louise wailed.

"With the waves and the tides, it's highly unlikely that we'll find any of the men who were on the boat. I'm sorry." The man looked pained to tell them.

"But they have to be so cold." Louise sobbed.

"They aren't feeling cold where they are," Elizabeth's mother cried. "They're gone. My God, they're gone."

Elizabeth turned into Jack's arms and tried to compose herself as she listened to her mother and Louise crying hysterically. She wanted to do the same, but she had to stay strong for her family.

"I'm so sorry," the man said as he stepped next to Jack.

"Thank you for all your time searching." Jack shook the man's hand.

"We'll search for another couple of days, but as I said, it doesn't look promising." The man kept his voice low.

"I think we should probably call Dr. Connolly," Charlie whispered to Elizabeth.

"I'll call him." Elizabeth stepped away from Jack and went to make the call.

By the time Dr. Connolly arrived, Louise and her mother were inconsolable. He gave both women an injection, then Sean and Charlie settled the women in bed. Elizabeth wasn't sure what would happen when they woke up, but hopefully, the worst of their despair would be over.

"What can I do?" Geraldine asked as she put a cup of tea in front of Irene and Linda.

Elizabeth's heart went out to the two women as well. They'd been dating Kurt and Billy for a long time. This tragedy would hit the women as hard as it did the family. It would be a massive blow for the tiny town with the loss of eight of their residents. The amount of grief felt throughout Cape Broyle would be enormous.

"We'll have to have a service," Irene spoke low.

"I'll call Father Murphy later today," Jack murmured as he stared out through the window.

"How are we supposed to have a funeral? They haven't found any of them." Charlie sighed as he eased down on one of the kitchen chairs.

"When Grandda Ryan died, they had a memorial service, then Mudder and the rest of the family released wreaths into the ocean." Elizabeth remembered the story her mother had told her.

Unfortunately, it wasn't uncommon for fishermen's families to have funerals without someone to bury. When the Atlantic Ocean took a sailor, it didn't give them up easily.

Father Murphy and several of the church staff put together a memorial service for the fisherman six days later. On an overturned dory at the front of the church were eight photos of the smiling men who went down with *The Cora Lee*. The pictures of her father, Kurt, and Billy were all taken at Elizabeth's and Jack's wedding, so they were all dressed up in the photos.

The people from and around Cape Broyle filled The Immaculate Conception Roman Catholic Church. The front pews of the church contained the families of all the men lost on *The Cora Lee*. Elizabeth and Jack's family filled one full bench seat.

Jack stood next to Elizabeth with his mother on the other side of him. Next to Louise was Sean and Linda. Next to Elizabeth was her mother, Charlie, Geraldine, and Irene. Baby Sean was at home with one of Irene's younger sisters because Elizabeth didn't want the baby around so much grief.

As Father Murphy went through the service, Elizabeth tried to concentrate on the words he spoke. Her eyes kept flicking back to the photos of her father and Kurt, and she could almost hear them laughing and joking at her wedding. Even Billy's picture showed the joy they all felt that day.

"Lord, please welcome our brothers home with open arms, Patrick John Power, fifty-three, Kurt Nicholas Power, twenty-seven, William Jacob O'Connor, twenty-four, Ronald George Welsh, twenty-eight, Leonard Edward Kearsey, twenty-six, Gordan Alfred Dillon, thirty-five, Austin Cyril Cooper, thirty-six, and Donald Wilfred May, twenty. May they find peace in your house…" the priest went on, but Elizabeth had stopped listening.

Her eyes filled with tears as the names and ages of all the men echoed through the church. The older men had families, and the young ones had barely begun to live. She focused on the picture of her father and tried to pull strength from his love to get through the service.

Charlie's eyes glistened with unshed tears as he laid a comforting hand on her mother's shoulder. Elizabeth knew he felt enormous guilt for not going with his father that day, and no matter what anyone said to him, it still didn't ease the belief that he should have been with them.

Jack felt the same. It had been his father's idea for him to stay on land to help Elizabeth with the baby and take over some of the paperwork. Then there was Sean. He seemed to believe he was at fault because he never dry-docked the boats sooner. No matter who you talked to in the community, everyone had a different idea of who was at fault.

There was even some gossip going around that Elizabeth's father should have come in sooner. The problem was the storm came out of nowhere, and many of the fishermen who were on the water that day said they were lucky they made it into the dock.

If anyone was at fault for the tragedy, it was Mother Nature, and Elizabeth even started to blame God. It was why she felt like such a hypocrite being in the church when she was so angry at the Lord.

"Amen. We're all going to meet at the wharf where we'll launch the wreaths for each of our lost brothers," Father Murphy said when he ended the service.

Several of the fishermen hoisted the dory onto their shoulders and led the procession to the pier. Inside the dory, each of the wreaths had a photo tucked inside. One family member for each man would tie a rope to the wreath and lower it into the water. The lines were attached to a fishing boat, and after a short prayer, the wreaths were towed out to sea.

It was a beautiful tribute to the lost fishermen, but it didn't lessen the grief for Elizabeth, her family, or the rest of the people mourning their loved ones. It did help with closure and gave them a way to say goodbye.

Although, when Elizabeth glanced at her mother, she wasn't sure that moving on would be possible. She'd never seen such a forlorn expression on her mother's face. Over the next couple of days, her mother hardly spoke. Her mother not only lost her husband and son to the rage of the Atlantic Ocean, but it took her father as well. It was doubtful the woman that raised her would ever be the same.

Elizabeth knew she would never be able to relax when it came time for Jack and Charlie to go back out to sea. The thought of them returning to fishing in the spring terrified her. Thankfully, the boats were dry-docked for the winter, and she had four months before she had to worry about that.

Chapter 15

In the two years that followed the tragedy, Elizabeth watched her mother sink into a shell of her former self. Her health deteriorated to the point she would no longer go out anywhere unless it was the church, the doctor, Jean's house, or Charlie's house.

Her mother had not been able to return to the family home she shared with Elizabeth's father. She told them that she couldn't go back there when she knew her husband was never coming back. Charlie convinced her to sell the house, and the money was put away for her mother's care. Since she didn't want to live alone, she split her time between Elizabeth's and Charlie's homes.

Baby Sean was no longer a baby. He was a smiling happy toddler who could steal the heart of anyone who spent time with him. The only time Elizabeth saw her mother smile anymore was when Sean would climb into her arms.

Jack had cut down his time on the water since the tragedy and was building a fish processing plant so the fish could be handled locally. It would create employment for the people of the town and people like Charlie, who couldn't bring himself to step onto a boat again.

Jack's mother was dealing better with the loss of her son, but she'd become colder to Elizabeth. Jack's father also had some health issues and spent a lot of time in St. John's for medical appointments. He was diagnosed with a heart condition and told to reduce stress as much as possible.

"I don't know what this Christmas is going to be like," Elizabeth said casually to Geraldine as they prepared some blueberry preserves.

"Louise has been more of a witch than normal," Geraldine agreed.

Geraldine spent a great deal of time with Elizabeth when Charlie would go to work in town. He'd gotten a job with a road crew and would stay in town during the week and return on the weekends. He worked hard, but he couldn't wait for the processing plant to open because he could stay close to home.

"She hates me, and I've resigned myself to that. I still sleep at night." Elizabeth smirked.

"It's nice that you don't lose sleep over it." Geraldine laughed.

"She's not going to change, so I'm not going to stress over it." Elizabeth shrugged.

"Oh, I got a letter from Linda yesterday." Geraldine wiped her hands and pulled an envelope from her pocket.

143

Linda had left Newfoundland to go to the mainland a few months after the tragedy. She couldn't stay because there were too many memories. She wanted to start a new life where she didn't have to be reminded every day by the sadness.

"How is she?" Elizabeth asked.

"She's doing well, and she's working for a bank." Geraldine smiled.

"Good for her." Elizabeth was happy for her friend and hoped the same good fortune for everyone.

"I heard Irene is getting married too. She met the man when she moved to St. John's," Geraldine went on.

"Seems like we're the only ones staying here." Elizabeth laughed.

"I'm not going anywhere." Geraldine chuckled.

It was a hard time of the year for everyone since it was the anniversary of the tragedy, but Elizabeth had been feeling horrible for a few days. She thought she might be pregnant, but she hadn't had time to see Dr. Connolly.

"If I tell you something, do you promise not to say anything until I know for sure, and please don't be sad?" Elizabeth asked.

"You're pregnant." Geraldine smiled.

"I think so, but I haven't had time to see the doctor." Elizabeth sighed.

"No time like the present. I'll watch Sean, and you go see Dr. Connolly." Geraldine held up Elizabeth's coat.

"Maybe it will give us all some happy memories for this time of the year." Elizabeth pulled on her jacket, hugged her son, and headed out.

Dr. Connolly's office was practically empty by the time she walked to his large house. The doctor had turned a room in his family home to an office so he could see patients from the community and surrounding towns since he was the only doctor in the area.

She was glad there weren't a lot of people in the room because she wouldn't need to wait long. The only downside was Maureen was sat in the room and gave her a smug smile when Elizabeth went to the other side of the waiting room.

It didn't matter that Elizabeth and Jack were married, Maureen had not given up her attempts to put herself in the middle of the couple. She flirted with Jack incessantly and seemed to make it her life's goal to go to bed with Jack.

"Hi, Elizabeth," Maureen cooed in her usually annoying voice.

"Hello, Maureen." Elizabeth nodded as she sat down and grabbed a book from the table.

"How's the family?" Maureen's smirked.

Elizabeth held the urge to slap the woman. As much as she wanted to, Elizabeth had to remain calm and controlled. Maureen would love nothing more than to run back to Louise with dirt on

Elizabeth. Maureen would use anything to put a larger wedge between Elizabeth and her mother-in-law.

"They're wonderful." Elizabeth glanced up and then went back to her book.

"I've noticed Jack spends a lot of time at the new plant," Maureen continued.

"Yes, it will be opening soon." Elizabeth tried not to sigh with irritation.

"I know. I'll be working there. Didn't Jack tell you?" Maureen raised an eyebrow.

"No, when he's home, we like to spend time together. We don't talk about business." Elizabeth didn't even bother to look up to see Maureen's expression.

"I'm sure it must be hard with a child around. You know a man has needs, and with your mother there as well, it must be difficult for him," Maureen pushed.

"Trust me. Jack gets all he needs and much more." Elizabeth raised her eyes and smirked at Maureen. "Does that answer your not-so-subtle questions about the state of my marriage?"

"I wasn't insinuating that your marriage was in trouble." Maureen's attempt at feigning shock wasn't her best acting.

"No, of course not, but just in case you were wondering, we're very happy and satisfied." Elizabeth stared at Maureen for a second then went back to her book.

Dr. Connolly walked out of his private office with Maureen's mother and immediately stopped when he saw Elizabeth. The doctor wasn't stupid and knew there was no love lost between her and Maureen.

"Elizabeth, I didn't know you had an appointment." Dr. Connolly took her hand and gave it a friendly squeeze.

"I don't. I was wondering if I could talk to you for a few minutes?" Elizabeth asked.

"I hope everything is okay." Anne's fake concern only irritated Elizabeth.

"Of course. It's nothing serious." Elizabeth smiled at Anne.

She wouldn't dare say anything to either of the women. One word from her, and they would spread it around the town before Elizabeth left the office.

"Good. Thanks so much, Richard. I'll give what you said a try." Anne linked into Maureen's arm and both women slowly left the office.

"Come on in. I'm sure those two are trying to listen outside." Dr. Connolly rolled his eyes.

"You may be right." Elizabeth chuckled.

As they stepped inside the examination room, Elizabeth glanced around at the office she'd visited since she was a child. She wondered if he would ever change the décor.

"So what can I do for you?" Dr. Connolly asked.

"I'm almost sure I'm pregnant," Elizabeth told him.

"That's wonderful." The doctor smiled.

"I need to make sure. That's where you come in." Elizabeth pointed at the doctor.

Dr. Connolly smiled and started the examination. He took blood and examined Elizabeth's stomach. She knew it would be a couple of days before the results of the blood would come back, but she hoped he'd be able to at least tell by feeling her stomach. He smiled at Elizabeth and motioned for her to sit up.

"As you know, I have to wait for the blood results to be sure, but from the feel of your belly, it appears you're right." Dr. Connolly grinned. "Congratulations."

"Thank you." Elizabeth stood up and turned to leave.

"I'll call to tell you for sure in a couple of days, but as I said, you show all the signs." Dr. Connolly walked with her out of the examination room and out to the exit.

"Thanks, Dr. Connolly." Elizabeth waved as she made her way out to the road.

She wasn't surprised to see Anne and Maureen across the street at the small grocery store. They were probably waiting to see how long it would take for her to leave the doctor's office. Elizabeth didn't even acknowledge that she saw them as she hummed to herself on her way home.

Elizabeth didn't say anything to Geraldine when she got home because she wanted Jack to know first. Her sister-in-law wasn't stupid and figured it out almost as soon as Elizabeth walked in through the door.

Jack arrived home a little after five that evening, and as he always did, he made his way into the kitchen to kiss her hello. He'd then keep Sean busy while Elizabeth prepared supper.

Since Geraldine had invited Elizabeth's mother to her house for a few days, it gave Elizabeth, Jack, and Sean some rare family time with just the three of them. Jack talked about how well things were going with the build and how he had a list of staff ready to start when it opened.

"I heard about the staff. I hear Maureen is on that list." Elizabeth raised a brow as she met her husband's eyes.

"Betty, I didn't put her on that list. She was looking for a job and signed up," Jack explained.

"I know, but I had to hear from Maureen that she would be working at the fish plant. Close to you just like she wants." Elizabeth smirked when Jack almost choked on his tea.

149

"I'm not working at that plant. I'll be working from my office here," Jack said when he was able to speak.

"I'm just teasing, darling." Elizabeth laughed.

"Good. I know that woman rubs you the wrong way." He winked. "But I want you to be sure that the only woman I think about is you."

"I don't want to think about her or anyone else. I've got news." She glanced at him as she casually pushed the food around her plate.

"Yeah, what is it?" he asked.

"How would you feel about having another houseguest?" Elizabeth asked.

Jack stared at her for a moment and then dropped his fork on the plate. He leaned back in the chair and plowed his fingers through his thick hair as his blue eyes met hers.

"How long will this guest be staying?" Jack asked.

"Probably a very long time." Elizabeth kept her expression serious.

"Betty, I love your family, and I love my family, but I also love it when it's only the three of us." Jack sighed and dropped his hands on the table.

"It's only one little guest." Elizabeth pushed as she stood up and walked around the table.

"I also love it when our boy here goes down for the night, and I get you all to myself." Jack pulled her onto his lap.

"There's nothing I can do about it now. This little guest will be here by July if my calculations are correct." Elizabeth played with the hair at the back of Jack's neck.

"July?" Jack stared at her in confusion.

"Yes, it's going to take that long for this guest to arrive." Elizabeth smiled and gazed into his eyes.

"Where is this guest coming from?" Jack asked.

Elizabeth took his hand and placed it on her belly. For a second, Jack didn't pay attention as he stared at her, but after a few seconds, he glanced down at his hand. She knew the very second he figured out what she meant.

"We're having another baby?" Jack whispered.

"I went to see Dr. Connolly today, and he's pretty sure. To be positive, he has to wait for the blood results, but I know for sure." Elizabeth smiled.

Jack ran his hand around her stomach and then slowly moved it up as he gazed into her eyes. She could feel his growing arousal under her as he cupped her breast through her blouse.

"Are they sore again?" Jack pressed his forehead against hers.

"Not too much." Elizabeth brushed her lips against his.

"I love you," Jack whispered against her mouth.

"I love you too," she returned.

Elizabeth glanced up at Sean in his highchair. He stared at them with the funniest expression she'd ever seen. His head tilted to the right, and his lips pursed. It was almost as if he wanted to know the subject of their conversation.

"I think Sean is confused." Elizabeth chuckled.

Jack turned to Sean and started to laugh. When the little boy saw both his parents laughing, Sean giggled hysterically, which only made Elizabeth and Jack laugh more.

"Guess what, buddy?" Jack picked the little boy up and sat him on the table.

"Daddy funny." Sean giggled.

"Yeah, but you're going to be a big brother," Jack told their son.

"No." Sean shook his head.

"I'm afraid so, honey," Elizabeth told her son.

"No," he repeated.

"This is not a good sign." Jack chuckled.

"I'm sure he'll get used to it." Elizabeth stood up and gazed down at the two men in her life.

She couldn't love anyone more than she loved Jack and Sean. She was suddenly a little nervous because it was hard to believe that she could love another child as much as she loved Sean. She couldn't wait to see if the baby was a boy or a girl, not that it mattered. This baby would only bring more happiness to their family.

Chapter 16

Elizabeth held another sweet baby boy in her arms. He was over eight pounds and came faster than Dr. Connolly had expected. She'd only had six hours of labor, and Kurt Patrick O'Connor came into the world screaming.

Elizabeth lay in the bed and stared at the sleeping child as Sean climbed on the bed. He plopped down next to her and investigated what Elizabeth had wrapped in a receiving blanket.

"He got a little nose," three-year-old Sean said as he snuggled into Elizabeth's side.

"He does, but so did you when you were a baby, and you still have a button nose." Elizabeth kissed Sean's chubby cheek.

"I'm his big brudder," Sean said proudly.

"Yes, you are." Jack lifted Sean into his arms as he sat next to Elizabeth and the baby.

"I'm not cleaning poopy diapers." Sean cringed and plugged his nose.

"We'll leave that to Mommy and Daddy, okay?" Jack kissed the top of Sean's head.

"I love the name you chose." Charlie stood next to Elizabeth as he gently touched the baby's cheek.

"I think your brother would burst a button or two over that." Her mother smiled.

"Me too." Elizabeth laughed.

Jack's mother wasn't happy about the baby's name, but his father thought it was a beautiful tribute to Elizabeth's brother and father. Jack suggested the name shortly before the baby was born. She would have liked to add Billy's name too, but three names were way too much for a baby.

"Do you want us to take Sean for the night?" Geraldine asked.

"I no wanna go. I wanna stay and help Mommy with baby Kurt." Sean started to get extremely upset.

"Okay, buddy." Jack chuckled as Sean clung to him.

"Oh, I guess I'll have to make those cookies all by myself." Geraldine sighed dramatically.

Sean looked utterly torn. He loved his new little brother, but cookies were his weakness. He glanced from Elizabeth to Jack, then back to the baby, before he turned back to Geraldine. After a minute, he made his decision.

"I'll come help tomorrow, Mommy. Aunt Geraldine needs me." Sean kissed Elizabeth and hugged Jack before he hopped off the bed and launched himself into Charlie's arms.

"I guess cookies are a notch higher on the ladder." Charlie chuckled.

"Do you need me to stay with you tonight?" Her mother slowly got to her feet.

"We'll be fine, Isabelle." Jack allowed her mother to link into him as he walked her out of the room.

Her mother seemed more feeble with each passing year. She was only fifty-one years old, but the loss of her husband had taken its toll. It worried Elizabeth, especially since all her mother's siblings, except Jean, died before the age of fifty. Not to mention, both her parents hadn't seen their sixtieth birthday.

"I'm scared for her," Elizabeth whispered after her mother left.

"She does look ill," Jack agreed.

"I should probably talk to Dr. Connolly." Elizabeth glanced down at baby Kurt in her arms and smiled as he squirmed.

"I don't know if he'll tell you anything, Betty, but you can certainly ask him." Jack got into the bed next to her and the baby. "Right now, let's enjoy this new little miracle."

Jack was right, she was holding a little angel in her arms, and Elizabeth knew that someday both her sons would be a force of good in the world. She'd raise them to be good, decent men, just like their father.

By the end of the week, the family's little bit of joy turned to sadness when they received word that Elizabeth's Aunt Jean passed away. They'd expected it, but her mother struggled with the loss.

Jean had been living in a nursing home for the last year, and Geraldine took Elizabeth's mother back and forth to see Jean at least once a week. Geraldine had told Elizabeth that Jean didn't recognize anyone in the last few months.

"She's with my mudder and fadder now," her mother said as they stood next to the gravesite.

"She'll always be looking down on us." Elizabeth wrapped her arm around her mother's shoulders, and they stood for several minutes in silence.

Saying goodbye was never easy.

Elizabeth sighed as her brother brought the last of the boxes out of Jean's house. Since Elizabeth's mother had no other family, Jean's estate went to her. Her mother didn't want the house, and it went up on the market

Her mother split everything in the house between Elizabeth and Charlie. Considering the way her mother's health had deteriorated, the money they received from the home sale could come in handy for medical costs.

"Why does it feel like every time I turn around, we're losing someone?" Charlie placed the box in the back of his truck.

"It does seem that way." Elizabeth sighed as she climbed into the truck.

Elizabeth's mother sat in the rocking chair on the front porch with Sean and Kurt in her arms. She was humming to the boys an old Irish song that Elizabeth heard more times than she could count. She even found herself singing the same song to the boys when she was putting them to bed.

"How were they?" Elizabeth asked as she sat in the other chair on the porch.

"Angels, as usual." Her mother smiled down at baby Kurt.

Elizabeth chuckled because she was sure that the boys could have been screaming bloody murder all day long, but her mother would still say they were angels. Her mom was that grandmother who would give the grandchildren anything they wanted.

She was glad her children were able to spend time with their grandparents. It was something she and her brothers never got to do. Elizabeth's grandparents either died before she was born or when she was young.

"Let's hope they stay angels." Elizabeth smiled.

"They certainly have lots of angels watching them," her mother's smile faded.

Elizabeth saw her mother's eyes fill with tears. It had to be tough to realize she was the only one left of her family. The only thing Elizabeth could do was to make sure she didn't let her mother slip into depression. At least the boys could put a smile on her mom's face, and hopefully, they could keep it there for a long while.

Chapter 17

"This is impossible." Elizabeth panted as she turned back to the toilet to vomit again.

"Nothing's impossible, ducky." Geraldine laughed.

"Kurt isn't even seven months old. How can I be pregnant again?" Elizabeth groaned.

"If you don't know the answer to that question, then it's no wonder you have number three on the way." Geraldine snickered.

"I'm not ready for another baby so soon." Elizabeth wiped her mouth.

When the upset stomach subsided, she brushed her teeth and left the bathroom. Elizabeth didn't have to see Dr. Connolly to know for sure that she was pregnant. Over the last two weeks, she'd noticed her breasts were sore, and she was always tired.

"You better get ready," Geraldine told her.

Elizabeth gazed down in the crib where baby Kurt lay sound asleep. By the time the next baby was born, Kurt would still be in

160

diapers. Sean was four and wouldn't be in school until the following year.

Was she ready for another baby? She knew Jack would be happy, and she wanted more children, but she would have liked to have more time between them. As angry as she was with God, maybe it was his way of showing her she was ready.

"Maybe this one will be a girl," Geraldine whispered as they made their way out of the bedroom.

"What one will be a girl?" Louise appeared at the top of the stairs.

Elizabeth cringed at the sight of her mother-in-law. The last thing she needed was for Louise to know about the baby before Jack. Her mother-in-law already kept her distance from Kurt, but maybe if the baby was a boy, Elizabeth could redeem herself and name the baby after Billy.

"Betty, you aren't pregnant again?" Louise said with a hint of disgust.

"I'm not talking about this until I get a chance to talk to Jack first." Elizabeth tried to step around Louise to go down the stairs.

"Betty, it isn't decent to have another baby so soon." Louise followed Elizabeth down to the kitchen.

"Mrs. O'Connor, this is between Jack and me." Elizabeth tried to keep her tone respectful.

"Is it? I mean, you've been going into town a lot lately." Louise crossed her arms and gave Elizabeth an accusatory glare.

"Just what are you insinuating?" Elizabeth snapped.

"I'm not insinuating anything. I'm just saying people are talking about how often you go into St. John's." Louise picked a none-existent piece of thread off her dress.

"People, or Maureen and Anne?" Elizabeth returned.

"There are rumors that the farm boy is back in Newfoundland and living in town." Louise sneered.

"Get out," Elizabeth said with a growl.

"I beg your pardon?" Louise gasped in shock.

"Get out of my house. Now." Elizabeth raised the volume of her voice.

"My son owns this house." Louise waved her hand around.

"And I'm his wife. Now get out of our house before I throw you out," Elizabeth shouted.

"I'll be telling Jack how you treated me," Louise replied as she quickly scurried out through the front door when Elizabeth picked up a rolling pin.

When the door slammed, Elizabeth growled in aggravation as she slammed the wooden object down on the kitchen table. She trembled with rage and wanted to scream but was afraid she'd wake the baby and scare Sean. He'd run into the kitchen when Elizabeth raised her voice.

"That was interesting," Geraldine said softly.

"Mommy, why are you upset with Nanny Louise?" Sean looked ready to burst into tears.

"It's okay, honey. Mommy and Nanny were having a little disagreement." Elizabeth picked up her son and hugged him to her.

"You sounded really angry." Sean put his head on her shoulder.

"I know, and I'm sorry I scared you." Elizabeth swallowed the lump in her throat as she glanced at Geraldine.

"Hey, I need someone to help me make some cookies for Uncle Charlie when he comes home on Friday. Do you know someone who would come to my house and help me bake some, Betty?" Geraldine asked.

"Me. Me." Sean lifted his head, and a huge grin appeared on his face.

"I didn't even think of that." Geraldine pressed her hand against her chest and feigned surprise.

"Thanks, Geraldine," Elizabeth mouthed the words as Geraldine left with Sean.

Elizabeth had herself wound up tighter than a drum by the time Jack arrived home. She didn't know how he would react to the way she'd thrown her mother-in-law out. She felt guilty, but the fact that Louise had accused her of being unfaithful had made her see red.

Jack came into the house with a huge smile, and as always, kissed her hello. When he stepped back, his smile faded at the expression on her face.

"What's wrong?" Jack asked.

"I'm going to jail," Elizabeth told him.

"I'm sorry, what?" Jack said in confusion.

"I'm going to go to jail for murder." Elizabeth began to pace.

"Betty, who did you kill?" Jack stepped in front of her and placed his hand on her shoulders.

"Oh, I haven't killed her yet, but I'm just letting you know. I'm going to strangle your mudder." Elizabeth looked up and met his eyes.

"What did she do now?" Jack sat on one of the kitchen chairs and pulled her into his lap.

"She turned something that should be a happy thing into something shameful," Elizabeth snapped.

"Talk to me, darling." Jack cupped her cheek.

Her husband always had a way of calming her when Elizabeth felt as if her head would explode. It was rare for him to get angry, and even when they disagreed, he would remain calm and cool. Sometimes it pissed her off because she would want to yell, and it was hard to do that when he wouldn't raise his voice.

"I'm pregnant, and your mother overheard me talking to Geraldine." Elizabeth sighed.

"We're having another baby?" Jack grinned.

"Yes, but I didn't want to tell you while I was in this mood. She insinuated it was a terrible thing to have a baby so soon after Kurt. Then she went on to imply that maybe this baby wasn't yours." Elizabeth blew out an exasperated breath.

"Okay, and who does she think is the father?" Jack laughed.

"Tommy." Elizabeth sighed.

Elizabeth felt him stiffen under her, and when she met his eyes, she saw something that made her stand up. She'd never seen any doubt in his eyes before, but at that very moment, it was there like a shining light in a storm.

"Jack?" Elizabeth narrowed her eyes.

"What?" He stood up and walked to the window.

"Please tell me you don't believe that I would ever be unfaithful to you." Elizabeth could barely get the words out.

"I've heard rumors that Tommy is living in St. John's." Jack didn't answer her question.

"Jack," Elizabeth shouted as she grabbed his arm and turned him around.

"Why have you been going to town so much lately?" Jack asked.

"Are you serious? I've been going in with Geraldine so she can see her husband during the week. I can't believe I need to justify that to you." Elizabeth tried to keep her voice calm, but it was hard when the man she loved looked at her with doubt.

"Okay." Jack nodded.

"Okay? Okay? That's all you're going to say. I can't believe you would even think for one second that this baby isn't yours. That I would ever do something like that to you." Elizabeth stepped back from him and shook her head. "Why don't you go run back to your mudder and let her get exactly what she wants? That woman never liked me, and this is how she's going to get what she wants. Get out, Jack. I'm going up to check on our baby, and when I come back down, you better be gone." Elizabeth stomped up the stairs fighting the tears.

She wasn't about to let him see how much he hurt her. She'd hide the tears until she was behind the bedroom door. Secretly she hoped he would come after her, but when she heard the slam of the front door, she knew that wouldn't happen.

Elizabeth lay in the bed and snuggled Kurt next to her. He'd slept through her argument with Jack. She managed to stop the tears long enough to feed and bathe the baby. She didn't want to sleep in the bed alone, which was why she had Kurt in the bed with her.

Kurt looked at her with his big blue eyes and gave her a huge smile as he kicked his legs. He resembled Jack. Both the boys were like their father, and she swallowed hard to keep the tears from starting again.

"You're going to have a little brother or sister. What do you think about that, Kurt?" Elizabeth whispered as Kurt cooed.

A tear slipped down her cheek and dripped onto the pillow below her head. She couldn't speak anymore, so she let the baby play with her fingers as she silently sobbed.

How could he even entertain the thought that she would bed with another man? Tommy was her past, and although part of her still cared about him, another part hated him for leaving her without an explanation. Even if she had run into Tommy, there wasn't a chance that she would ever betray Jack.

"We may have to raise this baby together. Me, you and your brother. Do you think you can help Mommy if Daddy doesn't come back?" Elizabeth's words cracked, but she chuckled when Kurt let out a long sigh.

She'd just placed Kurt down for the evening, and she lay in her bed. The only light in the room was the moonlight shining through the window. Jack still hadn't returned home, and she was pretty sure where he'd gone. Back to his mother's house.

Maybe he ran off to Maureen to cry on her shoulder. That would give the little witch exactly what she wanted, Jack vulnerable and in her arms. Elizabeth quickly shook that bad image off because even with how upset he was, he would never run to the one woman Elizabeth hated.

Elizabeth woke up on her side, although she had no memory of falling asleep. Kurt slept soundly as she eased out of bed. When she glanced at her watch, she swallowed the lump that formed there. Jack hadn't returned home, and it was after one in the morning.

She went to the bathroom and relieved herself before she made her way down to the kitchen. Elizabeth wouldn't get back to sleep any time soon, and she knew if she stayed in the bedroom, the tears would start again.

When she got to the kitchen, the light was on, but she wasn't sure if she'd left it on or Jack had come home. After she placed the kettle on the stove, Elizabeth wrapped her arms around herself and gazed through the kitchen window.

Outside was eerily dark since the sky was full of looming clouds. There wasn't even the light from the moon to brighten the front of the house. It's why the loud thud in the living room startled her, and she spun around. Elizabeth slowly made her way into the other room and stopped.

Jack had his back to her as he placed a book on the coffee table. When he turned around, he staggered and barely caught himself from falling over. After a muttered curse he stabled himself. Jack met her eyes as he started toward her, and the odor of his breath confirmed her suspicion. Jack had been drinking. A lot. When his eyes met hers,

Elizabeth spun around and made her way back to the kitchen without a word. She poured herself a cup of tea, and as she stirred in the sugar, she could practically feel his eyes on her.

"I guess I deserve the silent treatment." Jack's words slurred as he clumsily pulled out the kitchen chair and almost missed it when he tried to sit.

Elizabeth didn't answer as she stirred the milk into her tea and sipped it carefully. She straightened her spine and blinked back the tears forming there because she wasn't going to let him know how hurt she felt.

"I'm a stupid, foolish bastard, Betty," Jack choked out the words.

"I won't argue with that." Elizabeth had to respond to his admission.

Jack chuckled and blew out a breath as he sat back in the chair. She didn't turn to look at him, but she could see his reflection in the window. It wasn't the first time she'd seen him drunk, but it was rare and never after a disagreement.

"That's my girl." Jack struggled to kick off his boots.

"I'm your girl?" Elizabeth turned and glared at him.

"Betty, you're my life. I was a damn fool to say what I did. I know you'd never do that." Jack struggled to his feet and made his way toward her. "I'm not a jealous person. You know that. It's just I heard people talking about him being back, and I'm terrified he's going to come back here. I'm fucking scared to death he's going to take you away from me."

Jack ran a finger down her cheek as she lifted her eyes to meet his. They were glistening with tears, and she saw his Adam's apple bob up and down. Jack had never been a man who lacked confidence, or at least he never showed it, but she wasn't about to let him off the hook that easy.

"So your answer was to go out and get piss-eyed drunk, then come back, expect me to see your weepy eyes, and forget everything you said." Elizabeth pulled away from his touch and walked around him.

"I went to the pub down on the dock." Jack braced his fists on the counter.

"That's not a pub, Jack. It's a shack where all the men go drinking." Elizabeth sat at the table and placed her teacup in front of her.

"Not just men anymore," Jack whispered.

"What?" Elizabeth's stomach lurched.

"There are a few local gals who go there too." Jack dropped his head.

"Let me guess, Maureen," Elizabeth said through gritted teeth.

"Yep, she offered to give me a place to sleep off the rum." Jack turned and grabbed the edge of the counter to steady himself.

He leaned against the counter and awkwardly crossed his arms across his chest. He was waiting for a reaction. Elizabeth could tell by the way he lifted his brow and stared at her. She simply lifted her cup and sipped her tea.

"That was nice of her." Elizabeth wanted to vomit on the words.

"You know as well as I do she wasn't being nice for no reason," Jack scoffed.

"I'm assuming since you're here, you didn't take her up on her offer," Elizabeth returned.

"God damn it, Betty, I love you. Why would I go home with the likes of her? I'm sorry, and I know that's just words, but darling, I thank my lucky stars every damn day that Tommy Roberts and my ex left. They made it possible for me to be the happiest man in this fucking world." Jack staggered toward her and dropped down on his knees next to her chair.

"Stop the foul language, Jack." Elizabeth sighed.

"Betty, I'm so sorry. I would kick my own arse for what I said if I could. I know you would never cheat on me, and for the record, I would die before I'd hurt you like that." Jack turned her chair, making it hard for her to avoid his eyes.

"I love you too, Jack, and no, I would never be unfaithful to you. Never. Yes, I loved Tommy, and he'll always have a piece of my heart, just as your ex will always have a piece of yours. That's what makes us who we are." Elizabeth cupped his face in her hands. "But if you ever, ever, hint at that again, I will bury you with your mother."

Jack stared at her for a moment then laughed as she pressed her lips against his. She didn't care that he smelled like a distillery, and she did smell a hint of Maureen's perfume on his jacket. Elizabeth knew the woman well enough to know Maureen probably rubbed herself up against Jack to start trouble.

"I'll even dig the hole." Jack smiled as he pulled her into a hug.

"Now, if you're going to bed with me, you need to get a bath and wash off the smell of that woman's perfume." Elizabeth pulled back and wrinkled her nose.

"Yeah, she 'accidentally' fell against me as she was walking by my table." Jack rolled his eyes as he put air quotes around the word *accidentally*.

"Wish I'd been there to trip her," Elizabeth grumbled.

"I love you, Betty." Jack pressed his forehead against hers. "I'll also have a chat with Mudder tomorrow. I'll make sure she never says anything like that to you again."

"Thank you." Elizabeth kissed his cheek.

"Can't have you going to jail for strangling her." Jack got to his feet and held out his hand. "It's late, and you need to rest. I'll get a quick wash, and then I want to hold you all night."

"Not up for anything else, huh?" Elizabeth laughed, knowing very well that Jack was too drunk for anything but cuddling.

It was fine with her because the weight of their disagreement was off her shoulders, and she was exhausted. It was the first significant disagreement they'd had since they'd been married, and she never wanted one like it again.

Chapter 18

The months flew by, and Elizabeth was close to her due date. She couldn't be happier to see the end of her pregnancy. It had been hard for the last couple of months because the doctor had ordered her to stay in bed. Elizabeth didn't know how that was possible with a five-year-old and a one-year-old, but with the family's help, she managed to take it easy.

Louise had not been any warmer to Elizabeth, especially since Jack and his father had reprimanded the woman because of what she had said to Elizabeth. The only time her mother-in-law came by after that was when Sean didn't give her a choice.

Elizabeth was three weeks away from her due date, and she couldn't wait for the baby to be born so she could finally get out of bed. She wasn't someone who could sit around and do nothing, but it was what she'd been doing for almost two months.

The sudden urge to urinate hit her again, and she crawled out of bed. She had made it halfway across the bedroom when an excruciating pain hit like a punch in the gut. She'd never experienced such agony in her life and Elizabeth buckled over clutching her stomach. It took her several attempts before she could catch her breath and scream out to Geraldine. Elizabeth managed to make it back to the bed before a second spasm hit her, and she cried out in agony.

"Oh, God. Geraldine," Elizabeth screamed.

The bedroom door slammed open, and her sister-in-law ran into the room with Kurt in her arms. Geraldine shouted to someone downstairs and then went right to Elizabeth's side. When Elizabeth looked up, she wanted to scream again, but the pain hit harder. The fact that Louise was the only other person in the house didn't matter at that point.

"Betty, are you okay?" Louise rushed into the room.

"Do I look okay?" Elizabeth grunted through her teeth.

"Are you in labor?" Geraldine asked.

"This isn't labor. Something's wrong." Elizabeth shrieked again when it felt as if something was tearing inside her.

"I'll call Dr. Connolly." Geraldine started to leave but stopped when Louise gasped.

"Tell him to send an ambulance. Now," Louise shouted.

Elizabeth followed Louise's line of sight down. Blood pooled on the floor by Elizabeth's feet and down her legs. She knew this pregnancy was different, but she didn't think the baby was in any danger, not until that moment.

"What's happening?" Elizabeth howled.

"Don't panic, Betty. Everything will be fine." Louise helped Elizabeth sit on the bed. "Let's get you changed before the ambulance gets here, okay?"

Elizabeth nodded because she didn't know how to react to her mother-in-law at that moment. Louise was calm and kept full control of the situation. Elizabeth couldn't think about it because she had to keep herself relaxed. She glanced down at the blood as the pain hit again, and she screamed.

"Am I losing the baby?" Elizabeth sobbed as Louise helped her into a clean nightdress.

"You're not losing this baby. Do you hear me, young lady?" Louise shouted. "That's an O'Connor baby in there, and they're tough as nails. That baby is also half you, and there's no other woman I know stronger than you."

Elizabeth nodded as tears streamed down her cheeks. It was the first time since she found out she was pregnant that Louise referred to the baby as an O'Connor. It helped her feel less hysterical that Louise was going to help her.

Elizabeth didn't remember the ride to the hospital or the delivery room. She was barely conscious by the time the baby was born, which was why it was so odd to be sat in the wheelchair gazing at her beautiful baby girl.

The doctors told them Elizabeth was lucky Louise had moved so fast. She'd lost so much blood that by the time she got to the hospital they needed to give her a transfusion. The worst thing was she would be in for several days.

"She's so beautiful," Geraldine said from behind her.

"She so tiny," Elizabeth whispered.

"She's almost six pounds. That's not too bad. The doctors say she's doing well." Geraldine crouched next to Elizabeth.

"They said she'd probably be my last." Elizabeth sniffed as her eyes blurred with tears.

"Be happy you have three healthy little darlings." Geraldine wiped the tear away from Elizabeth's cheek.

"I'm so sorry." Elizabeth sometimes forgot that her sister-in-law could never have any children.

"Don't be. I'm just glad I get to be involved with your youngsters." Geraldine smiled.

Jack had made it to the hospital shortly after the baby was born. He'd been frantic by the time he arrived and wouldn't relax until he saw that Elizabeth and the baby were okay. Elizabeth also wouldn't tell anyone the little girl's name until he got there since they both got to pick one of the names.

"I love her name," Geraldine smiled.

"Me too, and I hope Mrs. O'Connor will be happy with it too." Elizabeth laughed.

"Cora Louise O'Connor. If that woman isn't satisfied with that, then nothing will make her happy." Geraldine snorted.

After seven days in the hospital, Elizabeth and the baby were finally released and able to go home with Jack and the boys. When they arrived home, Jack held Cora in his arm and carefully crouched in front of the boys so they could see their little sister.

The baby almost hypnotized Sean, but Kurt stared for a moment then ran to Elizabeth. She sat on the chair and pulled him up on her lap for a snuggle. She missed both of her sons more than she ever thought possible.

"Do you like your little sister, Sean?" Jack asked.

"I'll make sure nobody hurts her." Sean gently touched Cora's head.

"You're a great big brother." Elizabeth smiled.

"I missed you, Mommy," Sean moved next to Elizabeth and rested his head against her arm.

"I missed you too, my love." Elizabeth wrapped her arm around him and kissed the top of his head.

"Mommy." Kurt pressed his little hand against her cheek.

"I missed you too, little man." She chuckled as Kurt turned her face, so she had to look at him.

"Baby." Kurt pointed to the baby in Jack's arms.

"Do you love your baby sister?" Jack smiled at Kurt.

"No," Kurt grunted.

"He'll learn to love her." Elizabeth chuckled. "My brothers learned to love me."

"If she grows up to be anything like her mudder, she'll be easy to love." Jack kissed the baby's forehead.

This was her family. This was her life, and she didn't know where they were going, but she was happy, and the future would take care of itself. Who knew what they would have to face? All she knew was they would do it together as the O'Connor Family.

Chapter 19

"Mudder, tell her to leave me alone," Kurt shouted from the living room where he and Cora watched cartoons.

"Cora, leave your brother alone," Elizabeth called out as she placed the platter of eggs, bacon, and fried bread that they called toutons and hash browns on the table.

"I'm not touching him," seven-year-old Cora replied.

"You keep stepping in front of the television," Kurt yelled.

With only a year and a couple of months between the siblings, Elizabeth had hoped they would be less likely to bicker. That wasn't what happened. Cora seemed to feel that it was her duty to annoy Kurt at every turn. She also tried with Sean, but he was eleven years old and mostly ignored his little sister.

"Mudder," Kurt whined.

Before she could respond, Jack entered the kitchen and held up his hand. He hurried into the living room, and suddenly all was quiet. Elizabeth shook her head as she listened to Cora wrap her father around her little finger once again.

"You know you shouldn't be bugging your brother," Jack said softly as he walked into the kitchen with Cora in his arms.

"But Daddy, he bugs me," Cora replied.

"I know, brothers can be a pain, but you have to leave him alone, okay?" Jack lowered his head so he could look in Cora's eyes.

"Okay, Daddy." Cora grinned, and after a hug, Jack put her back on the floor.

"Get up to the table so we can have breakfast before we go to Grandda and Nanny O'Connor's house." Elizabeth helped her daughter into her chair.

"Nanny said she's gonna give me her music box." Cora beamed.

"That's wonderful. Now eat." Elizabeth placed a plate of food in front of Cora.

Before she had a chance to call the boys, Kurt and Sean ran into the kitchen and jumped into their chairs across from Cora. They quickly dug into their breakfast as if they hadn't eaten in weeks. Elizabeth sat down with a sigh and sipped her tea as she watched her family enjoy their usual Saturday morning breakfast.

"Fadder, can I start learning Karate at school?" Sean asked.

"Me too," Kurt mumbled with his mouth full of bacon.

"Kurt, don't talk with your mouth full," Elizabeth chastised.

"Who's teaching Karate?" Jack asked.

Elizabeth listened as the boys told Jack about the new teacher at the boys' school. He was a Karate instructor and had lived in Japan for a few years. Sean quickly ran to get the information form and gave it to his father.

When they'd asked Elizabeth, she told them they would discuss it when Jack had time to talk about it. They both knew Saturday morning was the best time to talk to Jack.

"What do you think, Betty?" Jack asked.

"Someone to teach our sons how to beat each other up, that sounds like a great idea," Elizabeth said sarcastically.

"Mudder, it's not just about fighting. Mr. Hanlon says it's about discipline and training," Sean explained.

"I think you all could use a little extra discipline." Elizabeth smirked.

"How much does this all cost?" Jack asked.

"He's not charging the students at our school," Sean explained.

"I like free." Jack grinned.

"So, can I?" Sean begged.

"Yeah, me too. Please." Kurt put his hands together and looked so adorable when he went into his full-on begging mode.

"I don't see why not, but if I see either of you hurting each other or your sister, the lessons stop," Jack warned.

Both boys shouted in excitement. Elizabeth glanced at her daughter to see her roll her eyes at her brothers. To her, they were only useful to irritate or to help her when the boys around picked on her.

Elizabeth loved their Saturday morning breakfast time. It was probably the only day of the week when it was just their tiny family. Most suppers they had either her mother, Charlie, and Geraldine, or Louise and Sean. Sometimes all of them would eat together, but Jack had deemed Saturday mornings as their family time.

While she listened to the children chatter on about what they'd done in school all week, it was interrupted by the ringing of the phone. Elizabeth made her way into the living room to answer it. Chances were it was Louise wanting to know how much longer they would be.

"Hello," Elizabeth answered pleasantly.

"Betty, it's Dr. Connolly," the caller said.

"Hi, Dr. Connolly. What can I do for you?" Elizabeth found it a little odd for him to call.

"Betty, I'm afraid I have some bad news," the doctor answered.

Elizabeth slowly lowered herself down on the chair of the telephone table. She could see Jack from where she sat. He obviously must have seen the change in her expression because he immediately went to her after he told the children to finish their breakfast.

"Is it Mudder?" Elizabeth choked out the words.

"No, I got a call from Louise this morning. I think you and Jack need to come here right away," the doctor replied.

"We'll be right there." Elizabeth hung up the phone and turned to Jack.

"What's going on?" Jack asked.

"Let me make a phone call first." Elizabeth picked up the phone again and called her brother.

Charlie and Geraldine were going to get a puppy that afternoon, and she prayed they hadn't left already. The phone rang several times before Geraldine finally answered.

"Geraldine, I need you and Charlie to take the kids with you today," Elizabeth whispered.

"What's wrong?" Geraldine sounded panicked.

"I'm not sure, but Jack and I need to go to his parents. Dr. Connolly is there." Elizabeth watched Jack's face turn pale.

"Send them over. I'm sure they'll love picking out a puppy," Geraldine replied.

After a very easy decision, the kids were out the door and running to Charlie's house. Jack and Elizabeth hurried toward his parents' house, but as they arrived, they saw Dr. Connolly come through the door, followed by two men with a gurney.

Elizabeth felt a chill skitter down her spine at the sight of the white sheet covering someone. Jack grabbed her hand as they stopped next to the funeral director's wagon.

"Jack, I'm sorry we have to see each other under these circumstances." Dr. Connolly held out his hand to Jack.

"Is it Mudder or Fadder?" Jack squeezed Elizabeth's hand as he asked the question.

"It's your fadder, Jack." Dr. Connolly placed his hand on Jack's shoulder.

Elizabeth saw Jack swallow hard, but he clenched his jaw and turned back to the doctor. It was evident from the grip he had on Elizabeth's hand that he was doing everything to keep himself composed.

"Where's Mudder?" Jack asked.

"She's inside with Anne," Dr. Connolly told him.

"You called Anne before you called me?" Jack sounded furious.

"No, she showed up when the wagon came here." Dr. Connolly assured him.

After they thanked the doctor, Jack and Elizabeth hurried inside. Elizabeth heard Louise the minute she entered the foyer. The harsh sobs echoed inside the house, and they made their way into the living room where Jack's mother sat rocking and crying into the cardigan that Sean wore all the time.

"He's gone. He's gone," Louise shrieked.

"She's been like this since I got here," Anne whispered as she stood next to Elizabeth.

"Jack, your fadder, he's gone." Louise looked up at them, her face blotchy and streaked with tears.

"I know, Mudder." Jack sat next to his mother and pulled her into his arms.

"What am I going to do without him?" Louise cried.

"She's hysterical," Anne whispered to Elizabeth.

"She lost the love of her life. Mudder went through the same thing," Elizabeth replied.

"Yes, but your mudder is a lot tougher than Louise," Anne returned.

Elizabeth didn't know if that was true, but when she thought about it, her mother had survived a lot in her life. Her mother lost her own father when she was barely out of her teens. Not only did her mother help raise her younger siblings but she cared for her ill mother and older sister. Then there was managing through life as a fisherman's wife. It was stressful to be constantly worried when the men were on the water and never knowing if they would return safely.

"It only just happened; she'll get through it," Elizabeth responded.

"I hope so, because if she doesn't, you may have to move in with her." Anne turned away before Elizabeth had a come back for that.

The only thing she was concerned with at that moment was how she would explain things to the youngsters. They adored their grandfather and loved when he would take them on boat rides around the harbor.

Jack's father always treated Elizabeth as if she was his daughter. He'd defended her several times with Louise, and when Jack worked, he'd be the first one to help Elizabeth. He stepped in when Elizabeth's father died, not only with her, but with her family too.

"He wasn't supposed to die so young." Louise choked on her words.

"Mudder, he had a heart condition. We were lucky to have him as long as we did." Jack's voice sounded strained.

Elizabeth could see him trying to hold in the emotion as he struggled to stay strong for his mother. Anne returned from the kitchen with a tray that contained a teapot and several cups. She placed it on the table in front of Jack and his mother.

"Louise, have some tea." Anne held out the cup.

"Tea, Anne? What is tea going to do? I lost my husband. I didn't lose an earring," Louise yelled at her friend.

"Mudder, she's just trying to help." Jack seemed as shocked by his mother's reaction as Anne did.

"Nothing is going to help." Louise stood up and practically ran out of the living room.

"I'm sorry about that, Anne." Jack stood up to go after his mother.

"Jack, give her a few minutes." Elizabeth stopped him.

Jack blew out a breath and leaned against the wall. Elizabeth could see he was struggling to keep the tears from falling as he swallowed several times.

Anne sat on the couch and placed her hands on her lap. She and Louise had been friends for years, and sometimes Elizabeth thought they were the start of the gossip vine in Cape Broyle. Most of the rumors that traveled around the small community seemed to start with Anne and her daughter.

"The youngsters are going to be devastated." Jack sighed as he pulled Elizabeth into his arms.

He probably needed the hug more than she did. Jack and his father were like two peas in a pod, and when Billy died, they grew even closer. It would be difficult for Louise to lose Sean, but Elizabeth had a feeling Jack would feel the loss deeply.

They held each other for several minutes and only broke apart when the telephone rang. Elizabeth glanced up at him and saw the tears in his eyes. He blinked several times as Anne stood up and made her way to the phone table.

"I'll get that," Anne told them.

A few minutes later, the front door opened, and a very pregnant Maureen waddled into the house. She'd finally gotten married a couple of years earlier to Peter Barnes and was pregnant with their second child. The rumor was she married Peter because she was pregnant.

"Jack, I'm so sorry about your fadder." Maureen touched Jack's shoulder.

"Thank you." Jack nodded as he pulled Elizabeth into his side.

"If you need me for anything, let me know." Maureen gazed up at Jack as if he was her favorite movie star.

"That's nice of you, Maureen, but we have our family." Jack wrapped his arm around Elizabeth, and they headed to Louise's room.

Elizabeth knew the next few days were going to be difficult for everyone. Especially Jack and his mother. Jack idolized his father, and it was clear in the way he spoke about the man. Jack was now the patriarch of the family, and he would be the one who everyone turned to for advice.

The last day of the wake was emotional for everyone. Sean was well-known and loved by everyone he met. The funeral home had a constant parade of mourners that came to pay their respects.

Elizabeth struggled to help the children understand what had happened to their grandfather. As expected, they were not only upset, but Cora was also confused. She cried when they told her, but Elizabeth began to think it was only because the boys did.

They sat in the room of the funeral home while everyone came in to say their final farewell to Sean. Cora wrapped her arms around Elizabeth's neck as she stood next to her. She watched everyone with a curiosity that Elizabeth didn't understand.

"Mommy, why is everyone crying?" Cora whispered.

"They're saying good-bye to Grandda," Elizabeth explained.

"They can come back to see him tomorrow." Cora shrugged.

"Cora, Grandda won't be here after today." Elizabeth stared into Cora's little face.

"Where's he going?" Cora asked.

"He's going to heaven to live with the angels, remember what we told you?" Elizabeth finally realized Cora didn't understand that her grandfather was gone.

"When will he be back?" Cora asked.

"Darling, he's not coming back. Do you remember what we told you about how our body is like a box that holds our soul?" Elizabeth asked.

"Uh-huh." Cora nodded.

"Well, that's only Grandda's body. His soul has gone to heaven to be with the angels," Elizabeth explained.

She saw the very second that Cora finally understood what happened to her grandfather. Her lip began to quiver, and huge tears started to run down her cheeks. She tucked her head into Elizabeth as she sobbed.

"She finally broke down, did she?" Charlie asked as Elizabeth carried Cora out of the viewing room.

"I don't think she realized that after today Mr. O'Connor wouldn't be here anymore," Elizabeth whispered to her brother.

Cora cried for a while once they'd stepped into the lobby of the funeral home. Elizabeth soothed her as she rocked the little girl in her arms. When Cora finally lifted her head and wiped away the tears, she looked at her mother.

"Why did God have to take Grandda?" Cora sniffled.

"Nobody knows why God needs to take special people from our lives, but I like to believe it's because he knows they'll make really good angels," Elizabeth whispered to her daughter.

"Grandda is a special angel now." Cora smiled.

"Yes, he is, and anytime you miss him, you can always feel him right here." Elizabeth pointed to Cora's heart.

"He's in my dress?" Cora's eyes opened wide.

"No, Cora, Grandda is in your heart, and he'll always be watching over you," Elizabeth assured her daughter.

"Really?" Cora smiled.

"Your mudder is right. Grandda will be keeping watch on all of us." Jack crouched in front of Elizabeth and Cora.

"Daddy, don't go to heaven yet, okay?" Cora leaped into Jack's arms.

"I'm not planning on going anywhere for a long time." Jack pressed his lips against the top of Cora's head.

"Good because this stuff is really sad." Cora lifted her head and looked at Jack very seriously.

"Yes, my darling, it certainly is." Jack smiled.

The funeral service was beautiful but heartbreaking. Louise sobbed uncontrollably through the entire ceremony and was barely able to stand up when they were ready to leave the church. Jack stood by his mother's side and tried to console her as he held in his own grief.

Little Sean tried to emulate his father as he stood next to Louise, but he couldn't control the tears. Elizabeth did her best to hand him a handkerchief discreetly, so he felt grown up. Elizabeth also had Kurt on one side crying and Cora on the other. She was still a little confused about the entire subject of death.

Elizabeth didn't like the idea of taking them to the graveyard for the burial. She was relieved when Kurt and Cora agreed to go back home while everyone else made their way to her father-in-law's burial plot.

It took both Jack and Elizabeth to carry Louise back to the car after the service. She clung to little Sean in the car, almost as if it was her only connection to her husband.

The entire drive back to the house, Sean tried to soothe his grandmother, and by the time they arrived home, Louise thanked him for being such a grown-up young man. It bothered Elizabeth that her eleven-year-old son felt like he had to be an adult in such a hard situation.

Their house was full of mourners who followed the family back from the graveyard. Geraldine and her mother had brought a ton of food for the reception and along with the stuff that Elizabeth had prepared, they had enough to feed half the town.

"I can't face everyone right now." Louise sniffed from the back seat of the car.

"If you'd like, you can go into the guest room, and I'll tell everyone you're too exhausted to join us," Elizabeth suggested.

"No, I need to go to my house." Louise glanced through the car window toward Jack's childhood home.

"Mudder, you shouldn't be alone right now." Jack turned in the driver's seat.

"Why? I'm going to have to live there for the rest of my life alone." Louise gave him a weak smile.

"Mrs. O'Connor, you don't have to. We have room." Elizabeth couldn't believe what she said, but her mother-in-law looked so forlorn.

"Absolutely not. I know what it's like to have your mother-in-law live with you, and it's never good." Louise touched Elizabeth's shoulder. "Thank you for the offer, though."

Since there was no changing Louise's mind, Jack drove his mother back to her house. When they arrived back home, they sat in the vehicle for a few minutes in silence. Sean had gone into the house, and Jack stared through the windshield. He still hadn't let his emotions go, and it concerned her.

"She just needs to be alone for a bit." Elizabeth reached over and covered his hand on the steering wheel.

"I know," Jack whispered.

"Maybe she'll change her mind about moving in with us," Elizabeth said but secretly hoped it wouldn't happen.

"Betty, I love you, but I know you wouldn't be happy with Mudder living in the house with us." Jack turned to her and cupped her cheek. "Besides, I remember when my grandmother lived with us. She and Mudder were like oil and vinegar."

"I feel for her." Elizabeth sighed.

"I can't believe he's gone." Jack choked on the words as his eyes filled with tears.

"I know, and it takes a while for it to sink in." Elizabeth still wasn't sure how she was able to survive the loss of her father.

"I should've spent more time…" Jack's tears started, and he dropped his head.

"I was wondering when you were finally going to let go." Elizabeth pulled him against her chest and let him dispel all the grief he'd been holding in for days.

Jack was so busy trying to be strong for everyone else that he'd neglected to let himself feel the sadness of losing his father. His hero. Jack might not have said it to his father all the time, but Elizabeth knew Jack idolized his dad. The same way young Sean and Kurt felt about Jack.

"He…he was a great fadder…and he loved us so much." Jack sobbed.

"I know. He's with Billy now," Elizabeth whispered as she gently stroked Jack's hair.

"He shouldn't have died," Jack whispered.

"There's a reason for everything, darling." Elizabeth bent down and kissed his temple.

As often as she said that phrase, she still wondered why people died suddenly or tragically. What could be the reason for something so senseless?

Chapter 20

It was late January and more than two years since Jack's father passed away. Louise and Jack struggled with their grief the first year after Sean passed. After the will reading, Louise had a mortgage-free house, and Jack took over all the business.

The fish plant worked like a well-oiled machine and gave work to about forty percent of the town. Sean had just turned twelve and started working part-time at the plant after school and on weekends. He told Elizabeth he was saving all his money to buy a car when he turned sixteen.

Elizabeth didn't think he'd be able to hold onto his money, but he opened a bank account and kept very little of the money to spend on himself. He'd also been taking guitar and piano lessons at school, and Elizabeth had been contacted by the music teacher to let her know how talented both Sean and Kurt were.

Kurt was obsessed with Karate, and according to the teacher, he was a natural. He'd also taken up playing guitar and sang in the church choir with Sean. Elizabeth would get goosebumps when she'd listen to them practice in the house.

Kurt had entered several Karate competitions, and although she was proud of how well he did, she found it difficult to watch him fight with other boys. Every time she went, she'd have to lie and tell Kurt she enjoyed it, but that was what mothers did.

Cora was the one who concerned Elizabeth. She had this quirk where she started playing matchmaker with people around the community. The odd thing was all of the couples she'd brought together were working out. So much so that people around Cape Broyle started to call the little girl Cupid.

Elizabeth's mother was not doing well. Her mother's back issues had become severe and walking was almost impossible for her. Jack and Charlie had built ramps on both of their homes. It made it easier to maneuver the wheelchair into each house, which meant she could still split her time between both of her children.

Elizabeth also started a business of her own to bring in extra money. She did some seamstress work for people around the community and was selling vegetables that she and the children were growing in the garden.

It was Saturday and Sean went to spend the night with a friend, Kurt was at an overnight competition with ten other boys and Cora was with Jack's mother for the night.

Elizabeth and Jack had plans to have a nice supper and go to the pub on the dock. Craig Colbert had taken over the small pub where most of the men used to drink and turned it into a friendly place where

couples could go and enjoy themselves. Craig put the money he'd saved over the years into renovating the pub.

Fishermen's Catch wasn't a huge place, but there was a small dance area and a few tables where people could sit. Craig always made everyone feel welcome and made sure nobody got out of hand.

After supper, Jack and Elizabeth strolled to the pub hand in hand, and Craig greeted them. Jack grabbed a table close to the dancefloor, and they both ordered a drink. They talked and laughed as they relaxed and started to enjoy their evening out.

It was nice to have a night with just the two of them. They didn't get to do it very often with three children, two ailing mothers, and Jack's dedication to the business.

"We should do this more often," Jack said as he brought her hand to his lips.

"Yes, we should." She smiled as he kissed her hand.

"Maybe we can make this a monthly thing." Jack grinned.

"I like that idea." Elizabeth leaned forward and placed a quick kiss on his lips.

After Jack spun her around the floor for what seemed like the hundredth time, Elizabeth begged him to sit for a few minutes. The music was great, and she enjoyed spending time out of the house with Jack.

Jack was about to say something to her when someone bumped into him from behind. Elizabeth glanced up at a very drunk Peter Barnes, Maureen's husband. She became immediately concerned with the way Peter glared at Jack with what looked like pure rage.

"Out wit da wife tonight are ya, O'Connor?" Peter slurred.

"Yeah, Peter, so if you don't mind…" Jack's words stopped when Peter violently shoved him.

"I do fucking mind, you fucking prick." Peter fisted the collar of Jack's shirt.

"Watch your language around my wife, Barnes." Jack stood up to his full height, which was a good eight inches over Peter.

"I'll use whatever language I want to use around a fucker like you. I've got a right to be pissed." Peter pushed Jack.

Jack staggered back a step but managed to stay on his feet since he wasn't nearly as intoxicated as Peter. Elizabeth stood up and grabbed Jack's arm to pull him back around the table. The last thing she wanted was their night to be ruined by a drunk like Peter.

"Let's go, Jack," Elizabeth suggested as she glanced around.

Everyone in the pub had turned their attention to the disturbance. Even the music had stopped, and several of the men had moved in front of the women. Elizabeth was scared and glanced toward the bar where Craig had stepped out from behind it.

"Before you do, Betty, maybe I should tell ya wat da wife told me today." He stepped in front of Elizabeth.

"Get away from her, Peter." Jack growled.

"Afraid the little woman will find out what a philanderer you are?" Peter sidestepped and almost fell onto the floor.

"What the hell are you talking about?" Jack threw his hands up in the air.

"Like you don't know. You think I wouldn't find out how you've been fucking my wife in your office at the plant," Peter shouted.

"You're out of your mind, Barnes." Jack glared at Peter.

"Am I? She told me all about your little sex games, you fucking piece of shit." Peter took that opportunity to swing a fist at Jack.

Jack's head snapped back, but he quickly recovered and fisted Peter's jacket. Jack slammed the man against the wall several times. When Jack pulled back his fist, she knew she had to put an end to it before someone got hurt.

"Jack, stop," Elizabeth shouted.

As if her words froze the room, everything went dead silent. The lights over them came on, and Elizabeth motioned for someone to help. Craig and another bartender pulled Jack off Peter, and another man grabbed Peter by the arm.

"Come on, Jack. This piece of dirt is not worth it," Craig said as the other man dragged Peter out of the pub.

"What the hell is he telling people?" Jack asked Craig.

"It's not just coming from him, Jack. Maureen has been telling people the two of you have been together," Craig told Jack.

Elizabeth could feel the rage rise inside her, and her hand trembled as she reached for her jacket. After she pulled it on, she stalked out of the pub with her head high. Everyone stepped aside as she passed by, and nobody spoke to her. She knew that her anger had to be written all over her face.

"Betty, wait," Jack yelled.

She barely heard Jack as she stomped out of the pub. Elizabeth knew what Peter said wasn't true, but the fact that Maureen could ruin Jack's reputation infuriated her. Not only that, she could destroy his business as well. Maureen had gone way too far this time. Elizabeth was almost to the road when Jack grabbed her hand.

"Betty, you have to believe me, none of that is true. I swear on my father in the grave…" Jack stopped when she turned to face him.

"Do you honestly think I believe what Peter said?" Elizabeth stared up at her husband.

"You left, and I thought…" Jack pointed back to the pub.

"I left because I need to go rip her face off and jump on it." Elizabeth turned and headed in the direction of Maureen and Peter's house.

"Hold it there, darling. You aren't killing anyone." Jack wrapped his arm around her waist and pulled her back against him.

"I'm not going to kill her. I'm going to rip… didn't you hear what I just said." Elizabeth struggled to get free from Jack.

"Everyone knows us. They won't believe a word that woman says. The ones who believe it aren't worth our time," Jack whispered in her ear.

"Are you going to fire her?" Elizabeth turned in his arms and glared up at him.

"Do you have to ask that question?" Jack snorted.

"I want to be there when you do," Elizabeth demanded.

She never interfered in any of Jack's business, but Elizabeth wanted to be there when Jack gave Maureen her walking papers. Maybe she could trip Maureen on the way out of the building.

"You know you can't, but I'll make sure I'm not alone with her when I do fire her." Jack pressed his lips to her forehead.

"Make sure that person trips her on the way out," Elizabeth snapped as they turned and made their way back home.

"I need to call Craig in the morning and apologize for the disturbance tonight," Jack murmured as they walked.

"Remember when you said we should do this once a month?" Elizabeth tucked herself into his side as he wrapped his arm around her.

"Yeah." Jack chuckled.

"Let's not do it exactly like this," Elizabeth sighed.

"I'll make sure the next time is nothing like tonight." Jack kissed the top of her head as they walked up the steps to their house. "Maybe we can figure out something to do in the house that would be a little more fun."

"I love checkers." Elizabeth grinned.

"Good, I'll make the first move." Jack dropped his jacket to the floor, and before she could say another word, he scooped her up in his arms and carried her to their bedroom.

Elizabeth laughed when he tossed her on the bed and practically jumped on top of her. When his face turned suddenly serious, she cupped her hands against his cheeks.

"Betty, I love you, and I'm so relieved you know I would never be unfaithful to you." Jack's eyes filled with tears.

"I love you, Jack. Let's forget all about it and show me how much you love me," she whispered against his lips, and he did.

Chapter 21

It had been a week since Jack told Maureen she could no longer work at the plant. If people asked her why Jack fired her, she would ignore the question. Elizabeth just wanted Maureen to stop the dreadful lies.

Jack's mother was furious with Maureen for spreading such lies about Jack. Louise had a huge blow-up with Anne at the grocery store over the situation. According to the cashier at the shop, Louise had practically bit Anne's head off. Elizabeth was surprised when Louise came into her house, fuming.

"Sean was right about those women. I should have listened to him," Louise grumbled.

"What do you mean?" Elizabeth didn't know what her father-in-law had said.

"Sean always told me that those two were nothing but gossips and weren't happy unless they were causing trouble for people. I guess he's up in heaven now grinning and saying *I told you so*." Louise plopped down on one of the kitchen chairs and sighed.

Elizabeth didn't care what people thought. She ignored the whispers and looks she got from some of the people who took Anne and Maureen at their word. Luckily, she didn't have to see any of them because Elizabeth didn't attend church regularly, much to Louise's dismay.

She and Jack did make the children go with Louise because she felt they needed the foundation of religion in their lives. They also required their Sunday classes to make their Confirmation. Once they became adults, they could do what they wanted, but until then, she expected them to go.

Elizabeth called the children for breakfast when Louise showed up. Her mother-in-law went to the kitchen like she did every Sunday, and Elizabeth woke the children.

"Sean, Kurt, come on. Nanny Louise is here to go to church," Elizabeth called to the boys from the bottom of the stairs.

"Coming, Mudder," Sean responded.

"Cora, are you up?" Elizabeth shouted.

"I'm up, Mom," Cora replied.

"Would you like a cup of tea while you wait, Mrs. O'Connor?" Elizabeth asked.

"Yes, that would be grand," Louise said as she slipped off her coat.

"Jack went to help Charlie fix a couple of steps on the back of his house," Elizabeth told her mother-in-law.

"I saw him head up there earlier." Louise nodded.

Over the last few years, Louise had mellowed in her snide remarks, and Elizabeth could actually tolerate her for longer than a couple of hours. Not that she wasn't relieved when Louise had refused to move in with them.

"Mudder, Kurt is still in bed," Sean informed her as he walked into the kitchen.

Every week she went through the same thing with Kurt. He hated to get out of bed, and she would have to call him a dozen times before he would finally make it to the table.

Elizabeth sighed as she made her way to the boys' bedroom and entered. Kurt snuggled in his bed with the blankets over his head. When she shook him, he grumbled.

"Kurt Patrick O'Connor, get out of bed now. Your grandmudder is waiting downstairs for you. You've got to go to church." Elizabeth placed Kurt's Sunday clothes on the foot of his bed.

"I'm not going to church today," Kurt grumbled.

"Indeed you are, young man. Now out of bed." Elizabeth placed her fists on her hips and glared at her son.

"I don't want to go," he replied.

"What you want to do and what you have to do are two different things. Get up and go to church." Elizabeth raised her voice.

"Why don't you practice what you preach, Mudder?" Kurt mumbled.

Elizabeth saw red. She grabbed the blankets and yanked them off her son. She lifted her foot and pulled off her slipper, but before she could give him a swat on the bottom, Kurt jumped out of bed and grabbed his clothes. She'd never seen him dress so fast, and he ran out of the room to get away from the wrath of his mother's slipper. Elizabeth followed him after she put her slipper back on her foot.

"I'm sorry. I'm sorry. Mudder, I'm going to church." Kurt held up his hands as he hid behind his grandmother.

"That's right. You are going to church and back home right after. That smart mouth just got you extra chores for the rest of this week," Elizabeth chastised.

Kurt was the child that tested Elizabeth's patience, and he did it well. As he got older, he tried to see how far she could be pushed, and at ten years old, Kurt thought because he was taller than his mother, that he could get away with more.

"You might be taller than me, Kurt, but I'll still swing up at you," she warned.

"Okay, I'm sorry." He sat down and shoveled his oatmeal into his mouth but kept a keen eye on Elizabeth.

"He reminds me so much of my Billy." Louise smiled.

"Great, he's a combination of my brother Kurt and Billy." Elizabeth sighed as she sat next to Sean.

"Could be worse." Kurt shrugged, and as much as she wanted to swat him on the backside, she could only shake her head and laugh.

"You're right, but remember, I'm still in charge." Elizabeth pointed at him.

Once they left, Elizabeth sat on the couch for a while to enjoy the quiet of the Sunday morning. They would only be gone an hour, and that was enough time for her to rejuvenate herself. She loved her children, but they could be overwhelming at times.

Kurt's words came back to her. It was true she never went to mass regularly, and it was kind of hypocritical to force the children to go. It was just hard for her because she'd prayed so hard for her father's boat to be found safe, and her family to come home. When they didn't, it was difficult for her to believe in it.

"Fadder, I know you're probably rolling over in your grave because I don't go to church," Elizabeth whispered to herself.

The church bells echoed through the town, which meant mass was about to start. She closed her eyes and listened to the clang of the brass bells. She hadn't realized she drifted off until she heard a thud of the front door slam against the wall. She glanced at her watch, but mass still had another ten minutes, so she assumed it was Jack coming home.

Elizabeth made her way to the kitchen to greet him, but when she saw another man stood in the middle of her kitchen, her heart started to thud in her chest. Elizabeth froze as Peter Barnes staggered toward her.

"I figured since your man and my woman are getting it on, me and you could have some fun too." Peter was drunk as usual, but it was the menacing glare in his eyes that worried her.

"Peter, Jack and Maureen are not having an affair. She's lying to you. Now get out of my house." Elizabeth tried to sound as if she wasn't scared to death.

"I thought you were smarter than that, Betty. Maureen sucks Jack off while he does the payroll." Peter shook off his coat.

"He does payroll in his office here, Peter." Elizabeth knew because she helped Jack.

"I bet that pretty mouth of yours can suck good." Peter reached down and unbuckled his belt.

"Peter, get out. Jack will be home any second," Elizabeth shouted.

Peter had her trapped. He stood in the entrance of her kitchen, blocking her exit through the front door. To get to the back door, she would have to get to the other side of the kitchen, and that required her to get within his reach. She had no way to escape.

"Do you suck good, Betty?" He sneered as he unzipped his pants.

Elizabeth took that chance to make a run for the back door. She hoped with his inebriated state and his pants undone that she could move faster than he could. She looked at the door and tried to run as fast as she could.

Elizabeth dodged to the left when he reached for her. She managed to get away from his first attempt to grab her, but before she could make it to the door, he had her. He slammed her face into the wall, and she cried out in pain. The metallic taste of blood turned her stomach as it filled her mouth, but she tried with all she had to free herself from his grasp. It didn't matter, as drunk as he was, Peter was stronger.

Elizabeth swallowed the bile that rose in her throat as he pressed his erection against her back. She squeezed her eyes shut when he reached around to unbutton her pants. Elizabeth fought to keep him from getting them undone, but he grabbed a handful of her hair and slammed her face into the wall again.

She whimpered in pain, and she was dazed, but it didn't keep her from trying to get away from her attacker. She could feel the blood run down her face and drip down to the floor, but she kept fighting against him as he reached inside the front of her pants. Elizabeth gasped as his hand slipped inside her underwear, and at that point, she hoped it was over fast, and then he would leave.

Peter started to lower her pants as he whispered vile things into her ear. Elizabeth held her breath as he told her the things he would do to her. Some she didn't think were even possible. Elizabeth bit back a sob as he bit her ear, and she continued to squeeze her eyes closed.

Elizabeth had prepared herself as much as she could for what was about to happen, but his weight was suddenly gone. She heard what sounded like grunts and shrieks of pain. Then someone grabbed her around the waist and pulled her to the side. She opened her eyes to see what had happened.

When she turned, she saw both her sons bring down the man that attacked her. When Peter fell to the floor, Sean grabbed his arm and twisted it behind his back while he shouted at Kurt to call the police.

A few seconds later, Cora ran in with Jack and Charlie behind her. Both of them looked ready to kill someone. She didn't know where they came from, but she was never so glad to see them. Louise had been the one to pull her out of the way and wrapped her in a blanket.

"I'll kill that fucking bastard." Jack tried to jump on Peter, but Kurt stepped in front of his father.

"Fadder, go take care of Mudder. We got this under control," Kurt told his father.

Elizabeth's legs shook as Louise helped her to a chair. She couldn't believe the young boy she'd yelled at for not wanting to go to church kept the situation under control. Both of her sons looked like grown men with the way they took charge of the situation.

"Sean, let me take over," Charlie growled.

"Uncle Charlie, it's better if you let me and Kurt do this. Mr. Hanlon showed us how to keep someone out of commission." Sean held up his hand.

"Who the hell are these youngsters?" Jack crouched next to Elizabeth as Louise wrapped Cora in her arms.

"They saved me." Elizabeth sobbed.

The police arrived several minutes later, and as if they were grown men, Sean and Kurt gave a detailed account of what happened and how Peter ended up face down on the ground.

"We were coming home from church because our mudder makes us go every Sunday. Sean and I raced, and I got to the house a second before he did. I opened the door, and that man was hurting Mudder." Kurt stood in the kitchen hands clasped behind his back and looking the police officer straight in the face.

"What did you do then?" the officer asked

"I told Cora to run and get Fadder at Uncle Charlie's house and yelled at Sean to come help. We take Karate at school, and our Sensei told us never to fight because it was for self-defense only. Mudder was in trouble, so I kicked out the guy's knee, and when he fell, Sean punched him." Kurt turned back to look at her before he continued. "He was... he hurt Mudder, and we needed to save her."

"You did well, young man, both of you." The police officer shook hands with both Kurt and Sean.

213

"I ran really fast to get Daddy," Cora whispered.

"Young lady, you did good too." The officer smiled at Cora.

"Thank you." Cora blushed.

"Mr. and Mrs. O'Connor, you have three courageous youngsters," the officer told them.

"They're amazing." Elizabeth choked out the words.

"Mrs. O'Connor, I think you should probably take a trip to the hospital just to make sure your nose or cheek isn't broken," the officer suggested.

She glanced at his nametag because she needed something to focus on until she could get her head around what happened. His last name was Dooley. He was probably from one of the surrounding communities since she didn't know any Dooleys in Cape Broyle.

Elizabeth couldn't look up to meet the officer's eyes. She couldn't even look at anyone else in the room. She was humiliated. She dropped her gaze and saw her opened pants and ripped blouse.

"You should see a doctor," the officer said again.

"I think she may be going into shock," Charlie whispered but not low enough that she couldn't hear him.

"I'll get her to the hospital right away," Jack said.

"No. I'm not going to any hospital. I'm fine." Elizabeth tried to stand, but the room began to spin, and Jack had to catch her.

"Betty, don't argue. Go to the hospital and get checked thoroughly. I'll stay with the kids," Louise ordered.

"I'd rather just call Dr. Connolly." Elizabeth glanced up at Jack.

"You may need x-rays, ma'am," Officer Dooley interjected.

"What's your first name?" Elizabeth looked up at the man that seemed around her age.

"It's Norman," he answered.

"Norman, please call me Betty. That lady there is Mrs. O'Connor, and I'm not old enough to be called *ma'am*." Elizabeth tried to smile, but it hurt, and she winced.

She realized she had a split lip, and it hurt to open her mouth. She could feel the blood drying under her nose and around her lips. Her eye was barely able to open, the taste of blood made her want to throw up, and she felt cold.

She glanced around at the people in her kitchen and felt ashamed of how she looked. Nobody said anything, but she could see by their expression that she looked a complete mess.

"I need to wash my face." Elizabeth turned to Jack.

"I'll get you a cloth, Mudder." Sean ran out of the kitchen and returned a few minutes later with a wet cloth.

Jack carefully wiped around her mouth and nose, obviously trying not to hurt her. It was the first time she looked into Jack's eyes since he arrived. Her husband looked completely crushed.

"I'm so sorry, darling." Jack's voice cracked.

"It's not your fault." Elizabeth touched his cheek.

"He was trying to hurt me because he believes the lies that Maureen is spewing. He knew if he hurt you, it would tear me apart." Jack cleared his throat before he glanced up at Norman.

"Want to tell me what you're talking about? I need to know everything because the more charges I can slap on this piece of dirt, the better." Norman seemed pissed as well.

Louise and the children left the kitchen while Jack and Elizabeth spoke with Norman. Elizabeth stayed quiet as Jack explained everything that had happened with Peter and Maureen.

"I have to ask this for the record. Is there any truth in what Maureen is saying?" Norman looked at Jack.

"Absolutely not. Maureen has been after me since we were teenagers, and I made it clear to her that I have no interest in pursuing a relationship with her. I would never cheat on my wife or hurt her in that way. Norman, we are happy, and I love Betty with all my heart. I don't know why Maureen continues to try and cause issues in my marriage, but we've learned to ignore it." Jack glanced up when there was a soft knock on the door.

"That's probably Dr. Connolly," Charlie said from where he'd been quietly listening in the corner of the kitchen.

"I'm assuming you want to press charges against, Mr. Barnes, but unfortunately, the only thing we can do about Mrs. Barnes is warn her to stay away from you both. I can give her a little scare and threaten her with a slander charge." Norman stood up as the doctor entered the kitchen.

"Thank you, Norman." Jack shook the officer's hand.

"You're very welcome. If you don't mind, I'd like to say goodbye to the youngsters. I'm very impressed with all of them. Especially Kurt, he gave his statement better than some adults I've interviewed. Keep them working on that Karate too. It's good for them to learn." Norman walked into the living room.

Jack helped Elizabeth to their bedroom so the doctor could examine her. She had some bruises and a chipped tooth, and the doctor suggested she go for x-rays the next day but only as a precaution. He did tell her to take it easy for a couple of days and to call him if she felt dizzy or sick to her stomach.

Elizabeth thanked him, and he left but wouldn't dare tell him she got sick to her stomach every time she thought about Peter touching her.

After the doctor left, she sat up and hugged her knees to her chest. The realization of what could have happened if Kurt and Sean hadn't stopped it hit her like a punch to the gut. She began to tremble and squeezed her eyes shut as she tried to calm the emotion that welled up inside her.

"Mudder?" Kurt's voice brought her out of her panic.

Elizabeth looked up. Kurt stood in the doorway of the bedroom, and he looked ready to burst into tears. Without a word, she held out her arms, and he ran to her. Elizabeth wrapped her arms around her son, and he rested his head on her shoulder.

"I'm sorry for being a brat this morning," Kurt whispered.

"I'm sorry for almost using my slipper on your rear." Elizabeth chuckled.

"Me too. Your slippers hurt." Kurt lifted his head and smirked.

"Then it did its job." Elizabeth smoothed her hand over his thick auburn hair.

"Mudder, can I tell you something?" Kurt looked down.

"You can tell me anything." Elizabeth cupped his chin, and his eyes lifted to meet hers.

"I was scared when I saw that man hurting you." Kurt's eyes filled with tears.

"You might have been scared, but you were so brave. You and Sean." Elizabeth held his face between her hands and kissed his forehead.

"I didn't even think about what I was doing. I just remembered what Mr. Hanlon said. He told us if you snap a man's knee, he'll drop like a stone, and that jerk did." Kurt rubbed his fists against his eyes.

"I'm so proud of you, Kurt." Elizabeth swallowed the lump in her throat.

"That police officer said Karate is a good thing and that me and Sean would make good cops." Kurt smiled.

"I think so too." Elizabeth pulled her son into another hug before she let the tears fall.

Elizabeth didn't know how she felt about her sons wanting to be in law enforcement, but no matter what they decided to do, she would support them. There was never a mother that was more proud of her children.

As the months went by, Elizabeth struggled with nightmares of what happened and would wake several times during the night. Jack would soothe her, and she'd fall asleep again in his arms.

She also didn't like to be alone in the house day or night, and she'd lock the door when she was. The area of the house where the attack happened gave her a cold chill, and when Jack noticed her aversion to the area, he and Charlie tore out the wall and put in a large window to let more light into the foyer.

It did make her feel more at ease that Peter would spend three years in prison for assault. She also didn't have to deal with Maureen anymore because when Peter went to jail, Maureen left town with her children. Elizabeth heard a rumor that she moved to the mainland, and Peter would join her after his release. Either way, Elizabeth was happy they'd left town.

Sean and Kurt also dealt with the ordeal better than she thought. They had a few nightmares, but with the help of their Karate teacher and their parish priest, the boys were able to expel their fears and deal with what happened.

Since most of the town knew the type of person Peter was, nobody was shocked or surprised by what happened. A couple of the men had even confessed to hearing Peter tell them what he was going to do, but they believed it was just drunk talk. Since they agreed to testify, it helped put Peter behind bars.

Elizabeth wanted to put it all behind her, and whenever the subject of the incident came up, she would shut it down as fast as possible. After the trial, Elizabeth asked that they move on and not give Peter anymore of their attention or time.

Chapter 22

Elizabeth sat in the auditorium of the school and smiled through the happy tears that kept blurring her vision. Her oldest son was valedictorian for his high school class and received his acceptance letter from Memorial University in St. John's.

She was so proud of him and his decision to become a doctor. Sean decided his career choice after his first Biology class and worked hard to graduate at the top of his class.

"He looks like a freak in that robe," Kurt whispered to Elizabeth.

"Stop it. You should be proud of your brother." Elizabeth gave Kurt a gentle tap on his knee.

"Mudder, I'll be working before he finishes school." Kurt rolled his eyes.

"Just because you've chosen to join the police force doesn't mean you won't be in for a lot of hard work. Besides, when he finishes school, he will be helping people as much as you will be," Elizabeth told her son.

"Can you two hush?" Cora leaned forward to glare at both Elizabeth and Kurt.

Kurt rolled his eyes, and Elizabeth smiled at her daughter for being so interested in her brother's speech. That was until she noticed she was not looking at Sean. She was looking at a boy in the front row who was graduating with Sean.

"Is that the Nightingale boy you're mooning over?" Elizabeth smirked when Cora's face flushed.

"No," Cora gasped.

"She's been writing his name all over her books," Kurt teased.

"Shut up," Cora snapped at her brother.

"Both of you be quiet." Jack pointed his finger at his children.

Kurt and Cora sat back in their seats, and for the rest of the ceremony remained quiet, at least until Sean walked across the stage to receive his diploma. Kurt and Cora jumped to their feet and clapped frantically. They were as proud of their brother as Elizabeth and Jack.

After the ceremony, everyone moved to the gym for the reception. Sean, as usual, was surrounded by girls and loving every second of it. Of course, where the girls were, that was where Kurt would be. He was next to Sean and getting as much attention as his brother.

"I swear your sons are girl crazy," Elizabeth said as she linked into Jack's arm.

"Why are they my sons because they are girl crazy?" Jack chuckled.

"I do remember the rumors about the O'Connor boys when I was growing up." Elizabeth smirked.

"That wasn't me, that was Billy." Jack tapped her nose with his finger.

"Sure it was," Elizabeth scoffed.

"It's not the girls I'm worried about. It's that boy making moon eyes at my little girl." Jack motioned to Cora.

It looked as though the interest wasn't one-sided. Young Brian gazed at Cora as if the sun was shining out of her eyes. When he reached out and tucked a piece of her hair behind her ear, Elizabeth had to hold Jack back.

"She's no longer a little girl. She's fourteen, and Brian is a nice young man." Elizabeth went to school with both Brian's parents.

"He's too old for her," Jack grumbled.

"He's seventeen, and she's fourteen. Which is three years, and you, Mr. O'Connor, are three years older than me." Elizabeth poked her husband in the chest.

"Well, when she's thirty-nine, and he's forty-two, then he can date her." Jack glared at the young man.

"It's going to be so much fun to watch you when she starts dating." Elizabeth chuckled.

"It's not my idea of fun." Jack groaned.

Before they went home, they'd stopped into a local restaurant in the city to eat. They arrived home just in time for Sean to get ready for a graduation party at a friend's house.

"Remember you're a gentleman, Sean, and I know there's no point of me telling you not to drink because I was seventeen once. If you're going to drink, be smart." Jack warned Sean as he headed out.

"I will, Fadder." Sean waved.

"I saw the woman you're going to marry at your reception," Cora said casually.

"Sure, you did." Sean rolled his eyes.

"I did, her friend graduated with you. Her name is Kathleen Squires. She's from Hopedale," Cora told Sean.

"Please tell me you didn't tell this girl that she was going to be my wife." Sean groaned.

"I told her she should get to know you." Cora shrugged.

"Mudder, this matchmaking thing with her has to stop." Sean motioned toward Cora.

"She's our little Cupid." Elizabeth chuckled.

"You're no help." Sean shook his head. "I'll see you all later."

"Talk to her," Cora shouted.

"Get help," Sean returned.

"I can't help what I see." Cora shrugged and went to her room.

Jack asked Elizabeth to sit so they could talk about something serious. It made her uneasy as she sat at the table across from him. He took her hands in his, and when he raised his eyes to meet hers, her heart started to pound in her chest.

"Should we take Cora to see a doctor?" Jack was so serious that she was confused at first.

"For what?" Elizabeth asked.

"These things she keeps saying about couples and telling people who they're going to marry. When she was younger, it was cute, but now, I'm really worried Cora thinks she can put couples together," Jack whispered.

"Jack, out of all the people she's told, how many do you know who ended up together?" Elizabeth tilted her head.

"Well, all the ones I've heard about have, but that's beside the point." Jack huffed.

"She's fine, Jack. She has a special gift, and instead of teasing her about it, we need to help her embrace it," Elizabeth replied.

She walked around the table and sat on Jack's lap. She wrapped her arms around his neck and kissed his cheek. Jack looked up at her, his brow furrowed, and his blue eyes filled with concern.

Elizabeth didn't worry about Cora's gift because she believed that it was probably inherited. When she thought about her father and certain things he would say about people not lasting or a couple that would have a long and happy life, it made her wonder if he had the gift too.

"Are you sure?" Jack whispered.

"I'm positive." Elizabeth brushed her lips against his.

Jack didn't need any coaching to continue. He cupped the back of her head and kissed her the way he did when he wanted to shut out the world. Kissed her the way he did when he showed her that she was his one and only.

Chapter 23

Elizabeth stood next to the hospital bed as a tear ran down her cheek. Her mother had fought hard to survive after her father died, and no matter how bad her health got, she fought through it. At sixty-seven years old, her mother had no fight left in her.

The doctors said it would only be a matter of days if not hours, and Elizabeth hadn't left the hospital since they told her. Charlie had gone to bring back supper, and Jack took the youngsters home to get some sleep. They were struggling with the thought of losing another grandparent, but they were older this time and understood that she was ill.

Sean had just finished his first year of university and was in the middle of finals. He swore he would get through them and promised his grandmother he wouldn't fail. He'd done well on his midterms, and Elizabeth hoped he could concentrate after the loss of his grandmother.

"She hasn't woken up all day," Charlie whispered.

"I know." Elizabeth stroked her mother's hand.

"Geraldine said Cora doesn't want to go to school tomorrow," Charlie said.

"That's okay." Elizabeth sighed.

The evening stretched into the night, and then Elizabeth was startled awake by the shrill sound of her mother's heart monitor erratically beeping. Charlie pulled her away as the doctors and nurses surrounded her mother's bed.

"She's not breathing," one of the nurses told the doctor.

Elizabeth clung to Charlie as the medical staff perform chest compressions and blew air into her mother's mouth. It was frightening to watch, and she had to force herself not to push them away from her mom.

"Still nothing," the nurse said.

After what seemed like hours, Elizabeth couldn't take it anymore. She pulled from Charlie's embrace and pushed one of the nurses out of the way as she held up her hands to the doctor.

"Stop. Please. She's had enough. Let her go in peace." Elizabeth sobbed.

"Betty, you have to let them do their job." Charlie tugged her away.

"No. She's had enough. What, are they going to buy her another day, another hour? No, let her go be with Fadder and Kurt," Elizabeth whispered.

The doctor stepped back and nodded as the nurse shut off the machines around the bed. Elizabeth breathed a sigh of relief as she sat on the chair where she'd been for more than two days. For the last time, she grasped her mother's lifeless hand between hers and leaned close to her mom's ear.

"Mudder, go be with Fadder and Aunt Jean. They're waiting for you with Kurt. I'll miss you so much, but I know you're not suffering anymore. Thanks for always being there for me when I needed you," Elizabeth choked out the words as tears streamed down her face.

"Say hi to Fadder and Kurt for us," Charlie whispered as he leaned down and kissed their mother's cheek.

The room was quiet as Elizabeth and her brother took their time to say goodbye to the woman who raised them. The mother that stood by them their entire lives. The strongest woman they ever knew.

Jack entered the room but stopped when Elizabeth shook her head and wiped the tears from her eyes. Jack pulled her into his arms and held her while she released the grief she couldn't contain anymore.

For the next few days, Elizabeth felt as if she was in a fog. In her head, she knew her mother was in a better place, but her heart ached. Her only solace was the hope that her mom reunited with all the family who passed before her.

After the service, they stood around the grave as her mother was lowered into the ground while Sean and Kurt sang "Amazing

Grace." Elizabeth couldn't hold back the tears, and as she glanced at the others who'd come to pay their respect to her mother, there wasn't a dry eye in the bunch.

The family erected a headstone as a memorial to Elizabeth's father and brother on the family burial plot. Her mother wanted to be buried there, and Elizabeth made sure to grant her mother's final wish

Kurt's and Sean's voices echoed through the small graveyard. With Jack on one side and Charlie on the other, Elizabeth said goodbye to another of her family.

Charlie stepped next to the grave and dropped the first white rose on top of the oak casket. He whispered something Elizabeth didn't hear, then he stepped back to allow everyone else their own private moment.

"We'll miss you, Nan." Sean dropped the flower and blew a kiss into the ground.

"I've got another angel on my shoulder." Kurt kissed the rose and dropped it into the hole.

"I'll miss you so much, Nan." Cora sobbed and dropped her flower as well.

Elizabeth knelt beside the hole and gently dropped her rose down on top of the casket. She couldn't speak, and as she lowered her head, she allowed the tears to continue.

"I love you, Mudder," she whispered.

For the next few weeks, Elizabeth caught herself picking up the phone to call her mother. Once, she even left the house to have tea with her before she remembered her mother was no longer at Charlie's place.

Charlie wasn't dealing with it any better. He wouldn't allow anyone to touch their mother's things, and he kept her bedroom closed. Elizabeth knew it would take a while to go through her stuff, but she didn't push her brother.

Sean had gotten his exam results, and as expected, he did very well, despite losing his grandmother. He told Elizabeth it was because Nan sat on his shoulder while he wrote them.

Kurt was also headed in the direction to start his career as a police officer. He only had a year left of high school, but he spent a lot of time with Norman Dooley. Norman had agreed to mentor Kurt and helped him prepare for exams and what he needed to do to join the academy.

Ever since the day Kurt met the police officer, Norman had helped Kurt whenever he had questions about his decision. Norman suggested courses for Kurt to do during the summer and even taught Kurt how to use a gun properly.

Cora also decided that when she finished high school, she was going to be a nurse. She had started to volunteer at the hospital in St. John's and also spent time at one of the nursing homes reading to patients.

The children were growing up so fast, and it made Elizabeth sad sometimes. It was only a matter of time before they would leave home and start families of their own.

"Seeing them grow up is never easy," Louise told Elizabeth one evening after Sean left.

He'd started spending a lot of time with a girl he was dating, but Elizabeth and Jack had not been introduced to the young lady up to that point. Cora believed it was Kathleen, but Sean wouldn't tell his sister if she was right or not. The only thing he said about it was that he would introduce her when he was sure about the relationship.

By the end of the school year, it was clear that Sean was in love, and the family met Kathleen. She was a sweet girl and going to the community college to do a business course. She was an only child and lived with her mother in a small town about ten minutes outside St. John's. Hopedale was about forty minutes from Cape Broyle and Sean would drive there every chance he got.

With all the children out of school for the year, Elizabeth knew it was going to be a busy summer. So when Kurt came home from school the week before summer vacation asking about spending a month in Japan with Mr. Hanlon and his wife, Elizabeth didn't know what to think.

"Mr. Hanlon is going to see his old Sensei, and I can train with him for three whole weeks." Kurt was more excited than she'd ever seen him.

"That's a long way to go, Kurt," Elizabeth said, stating the obvious.

"I know that, Mudder, but when will I ever get a chance like this again?" Kurt asked.

"It's expensive too." Elizabeth knew that wasn't going to wash with him.

"Mudder, I've got enough money saved up for the plane and to do me for a month or more. I'll do without a car if I can take this trip." Kurt had to be serious if he was giving up his dream of a car.

"It does sound amazing," Sean said as they sat around the table.

"Who's going?" Jack asked.

"I told you, anyone who can pay for the plane and have enough spending money for themselves. Mrs. Hanlon said they have a huge house over there, and we can stay with them." Kurt started to dig into his plate of roast and potatoes.

"If I wanted to go, I can go too?" Sean sat up straight.

"Yeah, actually Mr. Hanlon said to ask you," Kurt told his brother.

"Both of you gone the entire summer." Cora sounded way too excited. "Mom, let them go, please."

"You'll miss us." Kurt poked his sister in the shoulder.

"Yeah, like I missed the chickenpox." Cora rolled her eyes.

"I promise we'll call every week, and I'll write every day," Kurt begged.

"When would you leave, and when would you get back home?" Jack asked.

When Kurt pulled out a piece of paper and handed it to his father, Elizabeth knew what the answer would be. She couldn't allow her sons to miss out on such a fantastic opportunity. They would remember it for the rest of their lives.

Jack held the paper in his hand, and for several minutes he didn't lift his head. When he did, he glanced at Elizabeth as if to ask for her opinion. She could see the smile he tried to hide until he got her nod of approval. When Elizabeth nodded once, then he turned to the boys.

"We'll say yes but with conditions," Jack said.

"Anything," Kurt and Sean said together.

"You act like the gentlemen we raised you to be, and you call every Sunday. Letters are up to you, but I'm sure your mudder would love to get letters from you while you're gone," Jack told them.

"Deal." Kurt ran around the table and picked her up off the chair and spun her around.

Sean practically leaped across the table and hugged Jack as he thanked them for the opportunity. Cora grinned from ear to ear with the realization they would be out of her hair for a few weeks.

"Kurt Patrick, put me down, you bloody fool," Elizabeth shrieked.

"Thank you so much." Kurt kissed her cheek and then hugged his father.

"What is Kathleen going to do while you're gone?" Cora teased Sean.

"She'll be happy for me." Sean ruffled his sister's long hair.

"Or find a new man." Cora giggled.

"I thought you told me she was the one I was going to marry," Sean reminded his sister.

"She is, but I never said you were the only man she'd ever date," Cora smirked.

"You're a brat." Sean jumped up and chased his sister up to her room.

After the screaming stopped and the boys headed to their rooms, Elizabeth flopped down on the chair next to Jack. He still held the paper in his hand as if it would blow up.

"It's going to be so quiet while they're gone." Elizabeth sighed.

"I know, but I guess we should get used to it. It won't be long before they are out on their own," Jack reminded her.

"Where did the time go?" She dropped her head on Jack's shoulder.

"I don't know." Jack kissed the top of her head and sighed.

At forty years old, Elizabeth didn't feel old until she looked at her children and realized that Sean was the same age as she was when Tommy left town. A year later, she was with Jack, and her life changed forever.

"You know I saw an article in the paper yesterday about Tommy Roberts. It seems he's doing pretty well for himself on the mainland." Jack wrapped his arm around her.

"Good for him," Elizabeth replied.

"I'm happy for him. After the tragedy he lived through, it's good to see him come out of it on top." Jack propped his feet up on the coffee table.

"It is." Elizabeth sighed as she snuggled into Jack's side.

"No regrets?" Jack whispered.

"Not one." Elizabeth tipped her head back and met his eyes.

"None at all?" He ran a finger down her cheek.

"None at all. I could never wish for a better life or a better man to share it with." Elizabeth smiled as she cupped his cheek.

"I love you, Betty." Jack lowered his head and pressed his lips against hers.

How could anyone regret being married to such a wonderful, loving man?

Chapter 24

The boys left more than a week earlier, and Elizabeth missed them terribly. As promised, they called the first Sunday after they arrived in Japan, and although it wasn't a great connection, she was relieved to hear their excited voices.

The first letter arrived nine days after they left and one every day after that. Cora was excited to receive a letter from each of her brothers, and it started to show how much she missed them. Cora had started a countdown of the days up until they returned

Elizabeth found Jack in the boys' room early one morning. He sat on Kurt's bed, staring into space. Elizabeth walked into the room and joined him. It was several minutes before either of them spoke.

"You know, by the time I was Kurt's age, I'd been fishing for about five years. I used to go out with Fadder all the time. I quit school in grade ten, so I could go fishing full-time," Jack said in a quiet voice.

"Both my brothers never finished school either. I did, but only because Fadder insisted. I was a girl, and I couldn't go out on the water with him." Elizabeth linked her arm into his.

"You know, it's nineteen seventy-four, and I don't have a high school diploma," Jack went on as if he didn't hear what she said.

"Jack, you run a successful business, and most all your employees look up to you. School wasn't important to our generation, remember." Elizabeth kissed his cheek.

"I know, but I want my kids to be proud of me. How can they be proud of someone who quit school and was handed a business?" Jack folded his hands together in front of him.

"They're extremely proud of you and so am I. Jack, you're a wonderful husband and father. When the kids were little, I saw you sit with them to help with their homework when they were struggling. If it was something you or I didn't understand, you made sure to find someone who could help them." Elizabeth cupped his cheek and forced him to look at her.

"I want to be a high school graduate." Jack smiled.

"You want to go back to school?" Elizabeth asked.

"Yes. I was talking to Mr. Hanlon before the boys left, and he teaches night school two days a week. He said I could probably finish next summer with my diploma." Jack smiled.

"What about the plant and the boats?" Elizabeth asked.

"I wouldn't start until September, and it's only two nights a week," Jack told her.

"Then I'll support you. I can probably help out with the plant." Elizabeth shrugged.

"You're okay with this?" Jack asked.

"I'm more than okay." Elizabeth kissed his lips.

When the day came for the boys to return home, Elizabeth was so excited that she hadn't slept the night before. They'd called her when they were getting ready to leave Tokyo. They would be traveling for more than a day, and she wouldn't hear from them until they were back home in Newfoundland. Jack was going to pick them up, and she couldn't wait for them to get back to Cape Broyle.

Jack walked in through the door with a huge grin, and a second later, her two boys clomped into the house. She'd never been so glad to see anyone in her life, but before she could take a step toward them, they were across the kitchen and wrapping her up in their huge arms.

Even after only three weeks, they seemed to have grown taller and filled out considerably. Kurt was about an inch taller than Sean, and his hair was much longer than he usually kept it.

"Mudder, did ya miss us?" Sean grinned.

"Not at all, it was so quiet here," Elizabeth teased.

"Yeah, right. Fadder told us you've been awake since we called yesterday. Wait, no… the other day? No, yesterday." Kurt shook his head. "Hell, I don't know. I'm completely fooled up with the time difference."

"I don't care. I'm just happy to have my boys back home safe and sound." Elizabeth hugged them again and sighed.

As the boys told them about some of their adventures in Japan, Cora came home from her job at the local grocery store. She saw her brothers and practically leaped into their arms.

"Thought you wouldn't miss us?" Sean laughed.

"Yeah, didn't you say it would be peaceful with us gone?" Kurt ruffled her hair.

"Shut up. I want to know what you brought me." Cora punched Kurt in the arm.

"Just us, I figured that was better than any present." Sean sighed.

"Yeah, right. Souvenir. Now." Cora held out her hand.

Elizabeth sat back in the kitchen chair and smiled as she watched her children talk and tease each other. Although they were all practically adults now, they'd always be her babies.

After supper, Sean had made several calls to Kathleen, but he couldn't seem to get in touch with her. He'd mentioned that he wasn't able to reach her since his second week in Japan. The phone would only ring, and nobody would answer.

It was obvious he was upset and didn't seem to know what he should do. He sat on the couch, tapping his fingers against his legs while the family watched television. Elizabeth reached over and covered his hand with hers.

"Why don't you go to Hopedale and see what's going on?" Elizabeth suggested.

"She knew I was coming back today, and she hasn't even called. Maybe she wasn't as okay with me taking this trip as she said." Sean shrugged.

"Oh, for heaven's sake, Sean, she's the woman you're going to marry. Go check on her." Cora rolled her eyes.

"I'm not driving all the way to Hopedale to be told to buzz off." Sean stood up and started to pace.

"I'll go with you," Kurt offered.

"I'll go too." Cora stood up.

"No, I'll go alone." Sean started to leave the living room.

"Call when you get there and let us know you arrived safely," Elizabeth reminded him.

Hopefully, he didn't take a trip of a lifetime only to be dumped by his girlfriend after he returns. Elizabeth did have faith in Cora's gift, but when she thought about it, they hadn't seen Kathleen since the day before Sean left. Elizabeth told her to come by, but she hadn't.

An hour later the phone rang, and Elizabeth answered it. She was slightly annoyed that it took so long for Sean to call them, but he probably had a legitimate excuse.

"Hello," Elizabeth answered.

"Mudder, I'm here. Sorry about taking so long to call," Sean said.

"Is everything okay?" Elizabeth asked.

"Actually, no. Kathleen's mom passed away the week after I left," Sean told her.

"Oh no," Elizabeth gasped.

"She wouldn't answer the phone because she didn't want to ruin my trip," Sean explained.

"Heavens, she should have called me. That poor girl." Elizabeth's eyes filled with tears.

"If it's okay, I'm going to spend the night here," Sean said.

What could she say to that? He was over eighteen and an adult. Technically, he could do what he wanted, but he was respectful enough to see if it was okay with her and Jack.

"That's fine, but bring that girl here tomorrow. She shouldn't be dealing with this alone," Elizabeth demanded.

"She had her friends, but I'll tell her. She's dealing with a lot, Mudder. I want to see what I can do." Sean always wanted to fix things and make people feel better.

"If you need anything from us, let us know and give her a huge hug from us," Elizabeth told him and hung up the phone.

She explained everything to Jack, Kurt, and Cora. They felt terrible for being so close and not knowing what happened. Kathleen had no family left that Elizabeth knew about, and she couldn't imagine how hard it had to be to deal with so much at only eighteen. If Kathleen was going to be part of the family, she needed to know she wasn't alone.

Charlie and Geraldine dropped by that evening and were disappointed they'd missed Sean. They were also sympathetic to Kathleen's situation and wondered if she had anywhere to stay permanently.

"We have plenty of room in our house. If that girl needs a place to go, she is more than welcome to stay with us," Geraldine offered as they sat around the table playing cards.

"For a girl to lose both her parents so young, is tragic." Charlie shook his head.

"She's such a sweet young girl," Elizabeth said.

"And she's going to be family, according to Cora," Jack interjected.

That was it. Kathleen was family, and she wasn't going to deal with the loss by herself any longer. The next morning, they piled into Jack's truck and made their way to Hopedale. She was going to find out just how the O'Connor and Power families worked.

It was late morning by the time they arrived in the tiny town. Kathleen and Sean were at Kathleen's family home, and when she saw Elizabeth and the rest of the family, she burst into tears.

Geraldine told her she wouldn't be living alone anymore, but Kathleen declined at first. Elizabeth imagined the girl was still overwhelmed with everything and didn't know what she should do.

"Thank you so much, but I can't intrude on your lives." Kathleen shook her head as her eyes filled with tears.

"It's not intruding because we're family." Charlie smiled.

"Kathleen, you can't stay here alone," Sean interjected.

Elizabeth knew the poor girl didn't stand a chance of refusal when she faced the most stubborn bunch anyone had ever met. To her credit, Kathleen had a stubborn streak herself, but she finally gave in and agreed to stay with Geraldine and Charlie until she could have repairs done to her family home.

The following week, Kathleen settled into Charlie's and Geraldine's house. Sean was over the moon because he got to spend a lot more time with her, and they would drive back and forth to school together. It was only a matter of time before there would be wedding bells. Elizabeth could see it.

Chapter 25

"Betty, it's not proper," Louise whispered as she set the table for Sunday dinner.

"Mrs. O'Connor, the girl has no family, and Sean loves her. She's a wonderful young lady who's had a major blow to her life." Elizabeth tried to hold her temper.

"She's just going to move in with your brother and his wife?" Louise continued.

"Yes, until she finishes university." Elizabeth pulled the large turkey out of the oven.

"Doesn't she have a house left to her by her mother?" Louise pushed.

"Mrs. O'Connor, she's only eighteen years old. She just lost the only family she has left in the world, and yes, the house is hers, but it needs major repairs." Elizabeth placed the turkey back into the oven.

"What will she do then, sell the land?" Louise sat at the table as Elizabeth placed a cup of tea in front of her mother-in-law.

"Actually, no. According to Sean, she has a significant amount of money left to her, and once she turns twenty-one, she'll have access to it. The woman we thought was her aunt is only a close friend of her mother, and she's going to help Kathleen with all the legal details." Elizabeth didn't know why she was explaining it all to Louise because it was none of her business.

"Why can't she live with her mother's friend?" Louise sipped her tea.

"The woman lives in a small apartment in the city with one bedroom. Look, Charlie has the room, and he offered. It's not like she moved in with Sean." Elizabeth blew out a breath.

"Heavens, that would be out of the question." Louise looked mortified.

Elizabeth turned and rolled her eyes. She'd learned to tolerate her mother-in-law's old ways, and since she didn't speak with Anne since the incident, it seemed that Elizabeth had become her griping partner.

It was sad because Anne had managed to make it difficult for Louise to be involved in community events. Elizabeth would have to force her mother-in-law to do things because Louise didn't want to run into Anne and cause a scene.

"You have such a huge heart, Betty," Louise murmured as she placed her cup in the sink.

"I was taught to help people when they needed it." Elizabeth smiled.

An hour later, her children, Louise, Charlie, Geraldine, Kathleen, Jack, and Elizabeth, enjoyed the typical Newfoundland jigs dinner. It consisted of cabbage, turnip, carrots, and potatoes boiled in a pot with salt beef. There was also peas pudding and doughboys, which was the same as a boiled dumpling. Families served the meal with either turkey, chicken, or roast beef. It was a tradition for every Sunday dinner.

"Nobody makes jigs like Mudder." Kurt moaned.

"You should learn to cook it yourself," Elizabeth told her son.

"Why?" Kurt looked at her as if she was crazy.

"Because women love a man who can cook." Kathleen smirked.

"I'll help next Sunday, Mudder." Sean grinned.

"Me too," Kurt chimed in.

"I already know how to cook it." Cora shrugged.

"I think maybe we'll all join in next week. We'll give your mudder a break." Jack winked at Elizabeth.

"So Cora is going to be helping, right?" Kurt stopped eating as he stared at his father.

"If she wants, but don't you think we can cook this ourselves?" Jack asked.

"Fadder, have you ever cooked anything?" Sean snorted.

"As a matter of fact, I have, and I'm a damn good cook, thanks to my mudder. Just because I don't cook, doesn't mean I can't." Jack pointed a finger back and forth between the boys.

"Mudder, you'll be in the house, right?" Kurt chuckled.

"Don't you have any faith in your fadder and yourselves?" Charlie laughed.

"Don't think you're getting out of this, buddy." Jack pointed his fork at Charlie.

"Not a problem. I do know how to cook. Ask my wife." Charlie grinned.

"He does give me breakfast in bed every Saturday morning." Geraldine smiled.

"Uncle Charlie, you're hired," Kurt replied.

For the next few days, Kurt and Sean inundated Elizabeth with questions about cooking Sunday dinner. They were going to put everything they had into preparing the meal. She knew Jack could cook and he'd done it a lot during her pregnancies and when she was ill. The kids just couldn't remember that.

It had been a long time since he cooked, but she was looking forward to it. It would be interesting to see how the boys were going to do because Jack and Charlie had decided to let the boys do most of the work.

The following week, Elizabeth sat in the living room with Cora, Geraldine, Louise, and Kathleen. They could hear everything going on in the kitchen, and it was very entertaining.

"You're the one that wants to be a doctor. You can stick your hand up that turkey's arse," Kurt said.

"Watch your language, Kurt," Elizabeth shouted from the living room.

"Sorry," he replied.

"That smells disgusting." Sean gagged.

"Mom, are we ever going to have dinner by one?" Cora whispered.

"I'm hoping." Elizabeth laughed.

"I remember the first time Jack and Billy cooked jigs dinner. We didn't eat until four that evening." Louise chuckled.

"We had breakfast, so we should be okay until about two," Kathleen interjected.

For the next several hours, it took everything Elizabeth had not to go out in the kitchen and take over. Every time she heard something fall or Jack laugh, she knew the boys were struggling.

"This will be good for them," Geraldine said.

"I've got to see how it's going." Cora jumped up and was out of the living room before anyone could stop her.

A few minutes later, she returned and plopped down on the couch. It was the expression on her face that had Elizabeth ready to run to her kitchen.

"I'm not cleaning up after this." Cora shook her head.

It was a little after one when Jack called for them to come for dinner. Elizabeth followed the women out into the kitchen and was surprised to see the table set and a beautiful golden-brown turkey in the middle of the table.

"This looks promising." Kathleen giggled.

"Are you saying you didn't have faith in me?" Sean pulled out the chair for his girlfriend.

"I was cautiously optimistic." Kathleen smiled as she sat down.

"Darling, if you would sit here, and we'll take care of the rest." Jack pulled out Elizabeth's chair.

"Thank you." She chuckled.

"Nan, you can sit here." Kurt pulled out a chair for his grandmother.

"Geraldine, why don't you sit next to Elizabeth?" Charlie held the chair for his wife.

"No, it's fine, I can get my own chair," Cora grumbled.

The meal was a success, and most everything turned out great. The peas pudding had not worked out since the boys had used popcorn kernels mistakenly for split yellow peas. The potatoes were a little hard, but other than those little things, they did a great job.

"Well, what does everyone think?" Kurt asked.

"I think you shouldn't boil popcorn." Cora snorted.

"Shut it." Sean growled at his sister.

"I think it was wonderful." Elizabeth smiled.

"Even with the popcorn and the hard spuds?" Sean asked.

"Next time, you'll fix those issues," Elizabeth encouraged.

"Next time? I won't be doing that again." Kurt shook his head.

"It wasn't that bad, but I've come to appreciate how much work it takes to do this every week." Sean stood up and bowed. "Mudder, you're the queen."

Her son may think she was a queen, but Elizabeth considered both her sons princes. They had turned into amazing young men, and any woman who was lucky enough to marry them would have a wonderful life. Just like she did with Jack.

Chapter 26

Sean was a nervous wreck; he'd left that evening to propose to Kathleen, and for some reason, he was terrified. Elizabeth had hoped he would have put it off until he finished medical school, and Kathleen finished her course in business, but Sean didn't want to wait. He loved Kathleen, and how could she ever deny her son's happiness?

"Has he called yet?" Jack asked when she entered the living room.

"No." Elizabeth sat next to him and tucked her feet under her.

"I'm nervous for him." Jack chuckled.

"Can you believe our son could be getting married next year?" Elizabeth rested her head on Jack's shoulder.

"I can't believe we've been married twenty-one years." Jack shook his head.

Elizabeth and Jack had celebrated their anniversary a couple of weeks earlier. They went to the family cottage where they had their honeymoon and spent a weekend there. When they came back, Sean told them he was going to propose.

Sean bought the ring himself and enlisted Cora to help him pick it out. It was a diamond solitaire on a dainty gold band. Elizabeth thought it would suit Kathleen perfectly.

Sean was such a hard-working man, he was in medical school, working at the fish plant on the weekends and the money he'd inherited from Jack's father he'd put away for a nest egg.

When Jack's father passed away, he had money put in trust for all three children. It would remain there until the executor deemed they could have access to it. With Louise as the one making the decision, all Sean had to do was ask, and Louise would release the money to him.

Their family had a lot to celebrate over the next few months. Jack had not only received his high school diploma, but he'd completed a business and accounting course. Kurt joined the police academy and was doing some university courses that Norman had suggested to him. Then there was Cora. She was graduating high school and entering nursing school the following September.

It was hard to believe they were all grown up, and Elizabeth found herself with nothing to do a lot of the time. They all still lived home, but if Sean was getting married, he wasn't going to want to live at home or with Charlie. It was only a matter of time before it would be just her and Jack.

Elizabeth started to do some volunteer work at the Cape Broyle community kitchen. It was a place where they helped out the senior citizens in the town and taught young women how to prepare meals. Elizabeth had also suggested a class for young men as well, but that met resistance from the board.

"We've had a good life so far, haven't we?" Jack cupped her cheek.

"I couldn't ask for a better life." Elizabeth smiled at her husband.

Even at forty-four years old, Jack was still as handsome as the day she met him. The little lines around his eyes only made him look more attractive to her. The flecks of grey in his hair made him look distinguished, and when he sat reading with his glasses, she thought he was the sexiest man alive.

"Still no regrets about marrying me?" Jack winked.

"Not one," Elizabeth pressed her lips against his.

"Gross," Cora interrupted their moment.

"Can we help you?" Jack grumbled.

"I was just wondering if Sean called," Cora said.

"Not yet." Elizabeth smiled.

"She's going to say yes, but I would still like confirmation that I was right again." Cora grinned and left the room.

"Are you sure she shouldn't see a doctor about that?" Jack whispered.

Elizabeth laughed and wrapped her arms around Jack's neck. She knew Cora the Cupid would be just fine. With her confidence and smart mouth, who wouldn't be okay?

They were enjoying *The Rockford Files* when they heard the front door burst open and Sean shouting. Elizabeth, Jack, and Cora jumped to their feet and hurried out of the living room as Kurt clomped down the stairs. Sean stood in the kitchen with his arm around Kathleen.

"She said yes." Sean grinned.

"I knew it." Cora hugged Kathleen.

"Congratulations." Kurt shook hands with Sean and kissed Kathleen on the cheek.

"I'm so happy for both of you." Elizabeth couldn't hold back the happy tears if she tried as she pulled the young couple into a hug.

"Looks like our little family is about to add one more. Welcome to our crazy family." Jack wrapped his arms around Kathleen.

"Your family is amazing." Kathleen smiled shyly.

"It's your family, too," Sean pressed his lips against her temple.

"Does this mean she's going to boss us around now too?" Kurt laughed.

"No, I saw your future wife at the campus the other day. I'll introduce myself to her when I go back to register," Cora informed Kurt.

"Mudder, tell her to stay out of my love life." Kurt pointed at his sister.

"I wouldn't complain, Kurt. She's the reason I'm getting married." Kathleen grinned.

"I'm not getting tied down yet. I'm only eighteen years old, and there's a lot of pretty ladies that need to experience a date with this guy." Kurt smirked and pointed to himself.

"Dear Lord, he's going to die alone." Jack shook his head.

"I'm never alone, Fadder." Kurt rested his elbow on the stair railing.

"I'm pretty sure there isn't anyone upstairs with you. So technically, you were alone a few minutes ago." Cora rolled her eyes.

"Do you ever keep your comments to yourself?" Kurt snapped.

"Nope." Cora stuck her tongue out at her brother and started to head up to her room. "Congratulations, you guys, but I'm not surprised. I knew you would end up together."

The group gathered around the table and began to make plans for the upcoming nuptials. They narrowed down a date for the wedding and a list of what both of them wanted for the ceremony.

Kurt wanted to throw the bachelor party since by the time Sean and Kathleen got married, he would be of legal age to drink. As they chatted, Elizabeth noticed Kathleen was quiet. There was a sadness in her eyes even though she smiled.

"Kathleen, are you okay?" Elizabeth asked.

"Oh. Yes. I'm fine," Kathleen said softly.

"No, you're not. What's wrong? Don't you want to marry me?" Sean's voice quivered.

"Of course, I want to marry you. It's just…" Kathleen closed her eyes.

"Your fadder and mudder won't be there." Jack reached across the table and covered the girl's hand with his.

"Yes. I won't have my dad to give me away or my mom to help me get ready," Kathleen whispered as a single tear ran down her cheek.

Kurt disappeared from the kitchen and returned with a handkerchief. He handed it to Kathleen and sat back down next to Sean. Everyone waited for Kathleen to compose herself before they continued.

"I know I'm not your fadder, and Betty isn't your mudder, but we'll be here for you. I'm sure Charlie and Geraldine will be as well," Jack said softly.

"You're all so wonderful, and I would like to ask Charlie to give me away. Do you think he would?" Kathleen looked so hopeful.

"You'd have to ask him, but let me get him and Geraldine over here." Elizabeth jumped up and made the call to her brother.

A few minutes later, the couple arrived, appearing extremely concerned. Elizabeth probably should have told them why she needed them so urgently, but she wanted them to be surprised. Charlie looked ready to jump out of his skin, and Geraldine didn't look any more relaxed.

"What's wrong?" Charlie pulled out the chair for Geraldine then sat next to her.

"Nothing. Sean and Kathleen are engaged." Elizabeth smiled.

"Jesus Christ, Betty. You could have told me it was a good thing." Charlie sat back in the chair and blew out a breath.

"I wanted to ask you both something." Kathleen smiled.

"Anything you need," Geraldine replied.

"Both my parents have passed, and I have no other family. You both have taken me in and helped me after I lost my only family, and I'm so thankful. Charlie, if you wouldn't mind, I'd like you to give me away." Kathleen folded her hands in front of her.

"Me?" Charlie whispered.

"Yes." Kathleen smiled.

Charlie glanced around the table as if he was waiting for the punch line of a joke. When nobody laughed, he went back to Kathleen. There were tears in his eyes, and he swallowed several times before he finally spoke.

"I'd be honored to walk you down the aisle." Charlie choked out the words.

"Thank you." Kathleen immediately went to Charlie and gave him a huge hug.

"You don't know what this means to me," Charlie whispered.

"Geraldine, I'd like you to help me get ready. My mom won't be here to do that, and you've been the closest thing I've had next to Sean's mom." Kathleen reached over and took Geraldine's hand.

"See, now I'm going to cry." Geraldine sniffed. "Of course, I will. I'll be happy to help you with anything you need."

Elizabeth could see her brother and his wife were elated to be involved in the wedding. They probably never expected to be since they were never able to have children. Charlie had even admitted that he had regrets over not looking into adoption when he and Geraldine were younger.

Elizabeth always felt blessed to have the children that she did, and she had always been glad that Charlie and Geraldine could be involved with all the important occasions in her children's lives. Besides Jack and the kids, Charlie was the only family she had left.

"Nan is going to be so excited," Sean said.

"She's the only grandparent any of us have left." Cora's smile faded, and she glanced down at her hands.

"All your grandparents will be there in spirit." Geraldine smiled.

Elizabeth liked to believe that the family that passed was always all around them. There were times she was sure she could feel her mother's presence, and when she went to the shelter on the cliff, she could feel her father there. Hopefully, they would be there for Sean's wedding day.

Chapter 27

Elizabeth was exhausted as she tried to follow Cora around the Memorial University campus. It was September, and Cora was registering for her first year of nursing school. Kurt was also getting more annoyed by the minute because he was ready to go home.

Kurt didn't want to spend his time strolling around the campus, and the longer they were there, the more annoyed he became. He just turned nineteen and had spent the summer dating more girls than Elizabeth could count. Cora continuously told him he didn't have the right girl, but he would roll his eyes. The only reason he'd gone to the campus that day was so Cora could show him the girl she said was his future

"This is ridiculous. How can she know that I'd like some girl she hasn't even talked to yet? That girl might be taken or married already," Kurt complained.

"She was right about Kathleen and Sean, not to mention all the couples she brought together around Cape Broyle," Elizabeth reminded her cynical son.

"Mudder, I love you, but I'm starting to worry about you. Cora doesn't have some magical gift that brings couples together." Kurt shook his head.

"We'll see." Elizabeth smiled when she saw Cora wave them over to where she stood with two young women.

Elizabeth linked into Kurt and dragged him toward the girls. Cora was grinning from ear to ear, and Kurt grumbled about needing to get home to prepare for something at the academy.

"Mom, Kurt, this is Sophia Nelson and Alice White." Cora stepped back to where she partially blocked Alice.

Elizabeth glanced at her son, and the minute she saw his reaction, she knew Cora had made another match. Alice's eyes sparkled, and her cheeks flushed. Kurt was a handsome young man, and he tended to turn heads, but the way Alice gazed at him, it was obvious she was smitten.

"It's nice to meet both of you." Elizabeth nodded to both girls.

"You too, Mrs. O'Connor," Alice said.

"Call me Betty. Mrs. O'Connor is my mother-in-law, and don't get me started on her." Elizabeth laughed.

"Mom, Nan isn't that bad." Cora chuckled.

"What are you ladies doing in school?" Elizabeth asked.

"I'm going to be a nurse," Sophia answered.

"I'm not sure what I want to do. My mother thinks I should have some sort of degree." Alice shrugged.

"Kurt has joined the police academy." Cora motioned to her brother.

"That sounds exciting. Have you always wanted to be a police officer?" Alice asked.

It was the first time since he'd learned to talk that Kurt was speechless. He swallowed several times as he shoved his hands into his pockets before he answered.

"Yeah, since I was ten," Kurt replied finally.

"I envy you knowing what you want to do at such a young age. I honestly always wanted to be a stay-at-home mom." Alice shrugged.

"Mom, is it all it's cracked up to be?" Cora asked with a giggle.

"It's the best job in the world." Elizabeth smiled.

"Would you like to go to a movie?" Kurt blurted out as if he wasn't paying attention to anything going on around him.

"Me?" Alice seemed surprised.

"Yes, you." Kurt smiled, and at that point, Elizabeth knew the girl didn't have a chance to resist.

"I'd love to," Alice responded.

"Another match in my books." Cora grinned proudly.

While Kurt and Alice exchanged phone numbers and talked a little more, Elizabeth and Cora strolled around the campus. Cora talked about her excitement of starting university and how much she was looking forward to Sean and Kathleen getting married the following July.

"Do you think I should ask Brian?" Cora asked her mother.

"I didn't know you were still in contact with him." Elizabeth was surprised because Cora hadn't mentioned him in a long time.

"He just finished an accounting and business course at the community college. He called me the other day and asked if I'd be interested in going to supper." Cora smiled.

"He's a little older than you, Cora," Elizabeth reminded her daughter.

"I know, but I like him a lot," Cora admitted.

"Is he your match?" Elizabeth asked.

"You know I see it for others, but nothing flashes for me." Cora sighed.

"Explain how you see it again." Elizabeth sat on one of the benches.

"When I look at someone, it's like a cloud around them, and suddenly I see flashes of the person they are meant to be with. It's weird, and sometimes I hate it because people always think I'm weird." Cora slumped on the bench.

"Cora, you're not weird. You've got a special gift, and I honestly think you may have gotten it from my father. He told me once that the minute he met your fadder that he knew I would marry him." Elizabeth smoothed her hand over Cora's head.

"Really?" Cora smiled.

"Really." Elizabeth pulled her daughter into a hug.

"I'll never doubt you again, Cora." Kurt dropped down on the bench and kissed his sister on the cheek.

"Eww. Save your kisses for Alice." Cora wiped her cheek.

"She'll get her share." Kurt grinned.

"Don't forget you're a gentleman, young man," Elizabeth warned her son.

"I know, Mudder." Kurt nodded.

Elizabeth knew Kurt would treat his new lady friend with respect because that was the way she and Jack raised him. She just liked to be that little voice he would always hear in his head when he needed to make the right choice. She wouldn't be around forever, and although her children were good people, sometimes mistakes could be made.

Over the next few months, Kurt had fallen hard for Alice. Elizabeth liked the young girl, and the fact that she didn't allow Kurt to walk all over her made Elizabeth like the girl even more. Kathleen had been a little meek when Elizabeth first met her, but she quickly came out of her shell and was coming into her own.

Jack was also tied in knots because Cora had started dating Brian Nightingale. He was a little concerned about the age difference even though Elizabeth constantly had to remind him that it was the same age gap as she and Jack had.

Since they knew Brian's family, it made Jack a little less hostile when Brian would come to pick Cora up, but it didn't stop her brothers from trying to intimidate the boy. To his credit, he didn't seem to be worried about Kurt or Sean, and he was respectful to everyone.

One evening after supper, all the children were out for the evening, Elizabeth and Jack sat in the living room. Jack was watching something on television, and she was working on a dress for Cora.

Jack was unusually quiet, and she'd glanced at him several times. She had been with him long enough to know when he was concerned about something, and after trying to start a conversation with him several times, she got frustrated and tossed the dress onto the chair next to her.

"What's wrong with you?" Elizabeth turned to him and threw her hands up in the air.

"Me? Nothing." He seemed surprised by her question.

"Jack, you never sit for more than ten minutes without talking about something. Half the time I couldn't care less what you're talking about, but it makes me uneasy when you sit so quiet." Elizabeth reached for his hand.

"Ducky, I'm fine." Jack smiled.

"Do you want a shovel?" Elizabeth asked, knowing he was not okay.

"Why would I want a shovel?" He tilted his head in confusion.

"To keep shoveling that shit you're trying to give me." Elizabeth raised an eyebrow.

Jack chuckled and pulled her closer. He wrapped his arm around her and pressed his lips against the side of her head. He kept them there for several seconds before he tilted her head up and gazed into her eyes.

"I hate that you can read me so well, but I love the hell out of you." Jack brushed his lips against hers.

"What's wrong?" She cupped his cheek as she gazed into his eyes.

"I don't want you to worry." Jack sighed.

"Now, I'm going to worry more," Elizabeth pushed.

"Fine, but this stays between you and me. Okay?" Jack insisted.

"Yes. Jack, please tell me what's after happening now?" Elizabeth's heart started to thud in her chest.

"I've had some spells lately," Jack told her.

"Spells? As in dizzy spells?" Elizabeth asked.

"Yeah, and I've been getting some bad heartburn," Jack explained.

"All right, I'm calling Dr. Connolly." Elizabeth tried to get up, but he stopped her.

"I already went to see him." Jack smiled.

"Without telling me?" Elizabeth sat up and pushed back from him.

"I didn't want to worry you." Jack sighed and sat up with his elbows on his knees.

"So are you going to tell me or do I just have to wait until the other shoe drops?" Elizabeth wasn't happy that he hadn't told her.

"I had some bloodwork done yesterday, and I've got to go to town and have some other tests done," Jack explained.

"Jack, what does he think is wrong?" Elizabeth didn't like the sound of this.

"My blood pressure is a little high. Okay, it's really high, and he's concerned I might have the same condition that Fadder had," Jack went on.

Elizabeth stared at her husband. He wasn't even fifty years old yet, and they had to be concerned about his heart. She felt sick to her stomach, but as always, she'd lift her chin and deal with whatever came their way.

"He wants me to cut out salt. Can you imagine that? How does someone live without salt?" Jack chuckled.

Before he could say another word, she hurried to the kitchen and quickly disposed of the saltshaker and the box she had in the pantry. Jack was behind her in an instant and stopping her.

"Darling, you don't have to throw it out. I won't use it." Jack pulled her into him, and she wrapped her arms around his waist.

"Jack O'Connor, don't you dare leave me." Elizabeth choked out the words and tried to hold back the tears.

"I'm not going anywhere, Betty. I'm going to do what the doctor says and go have those tests done," Jack assured her.

"You're damn right, you are." She squeezed him.

"I don't want the youngsters or Mudder to worry unless it's something they need to be worried about, okay?" He pulled back and ducked his head so he could look into her face.

"Yes, but no more hiding things from me, you got that?" Elizabeth poked him in the chest.

"I'm sorry. I won't do that again." Jack held her face between his large hands and ran a calloused thumb across her lower lip.

"I love you, Jack," she whispered as he lowered his head and kissed her.

Over the next several months, with wedding preparations and trying to keep Jack's medical tests from the kids, Elizabeth was stressed beyond belief. She didn't mind helping Geraldine and Kathleen, but she couldn't stop worrying about Jack.

One day while she was with Geraldine, Elizabeth burst into tears and sobbed so hard that she could barely explain to her sister-in-law what was going on. She made her promise to keep it quiet, but Elizabeth felt better to be able to vent her concerns about Jack to someone.

"Betty, he's under a doctor's care, and he's taking the medication, right?" Geraldine asked.

"Yes, I make sure he takes it every day, and he's also cut down on his time at the plant. He wants to take the boys out fishing this spring. Just for recreation, but I'm not sure it's a good idea." Elizabeth still had nightmares about what her father and brother must have dealt with when they disappeared.

"Charlie will probably go with them. You can't keep him in a bubble, ducky." Geraldine smiled.

"Why not?" Elizabeth chuckled.

"Because he's a man and men don't like bubbles." Geraldine laughed.

By late March all the youngsters were either writing final exams or getting ready for them. The one thing about university was they were finished school earlier, and she didn't have to harp on them to do their homework.

Kurt still had several months of training left, but by the time he graduated from the police academy, it would be time for Sean's wedding. He told them he could have a double celebration when his brother got married because he would be heading into his career as well.

Sean and Kathleen had decided to move to Hopedale for several reasons. It was closer to the university, and since Sean would be doing his internship at the hospital in town, it would make it easier for the commute. The couple started to fix up the house Kathleen grew up in and were going to live there while they built a new home.

Every weekend, the boys and their friends would go to Hopedale with Jack and Charlie to make sure the house was liveable for the couple. The last time they went out and returned, Jack told her they finished everything.

Elizabeth returned home that evening to find a furious Kurt stomping up the stairs to his room. When she asked him what was wrong, he mumbled something about women being impossible and slammed his bedroom door.

She knew better than to try and talk to Kurt when he was in that mood. She'd never get anything out of him until he calmed down. Elizabeth made her way into the kitchen, where Jack was chatting with Sean.

"Alice broke it off with Kurt," Sean said before she even asked.

"Good heavens, what happened?" Elizabeth pulled off her coat and sat at the table.

"We were in Hopedale last night, and Alice said she wouldn't mind living in the town. Kurt laughed and told her if she wanted to stay with him, she'd be living either in St. John's or Cape Broyle." Sean smirked.

"Oh, dear." Elizabeth knew that wouldn't go over well with most women, but with Alice, it would be like adding oil to a fire.

"Yeah, she told him in no uncertain terms that if he wanted to stay with her, then he would discuss where they would live," Sean went on.

"Knowing my son, that didn't go well." Elizabeth sighed.

"No, as usual, his mouth opened before his brain turned on, and he said maybe he didn't want to stay with her. She told him to... okay, I have to use a word you don't like, Mudder." Sean cringed.

"Okay," Elizabeth chuckled.

"She told him that he could go...fuck himself...then she left the soda shop. He went after her. I don't know what else was said, but she left in a cab." Sean shrugged. "I asked Kurt about it, and he said it was over."

"Stubborn O'Connor men." Elizabeth sighed.

"Excuse me?" Jack laughed. "I think he gets some of that stubbornness from his mudder too."

"Maybe a little." Elizabeth smirked.

"Either way, Kurt is not dealing with it well. He told off one of his instructors today and got reprimanded," Sean told them.

"That won't fly. He can't throw away his career because he has a broken heart and doesn't know how to deal with it." Elizabeth shook her head.

"Anyway, I'm heading to bed. That's if I'm allowed in the room. He might have locked the door." Sean kissed Elizabeth on the cheek and hugged his father.

Elizabeth waited to hear if Sean was able to get into the room, and when she didn't hear him shout out for Kurt to open the door, she turned back to Jack.

"He loves her." Jack sighed.

"I know, but she's her own woman, and he's going to have to compromise with her." Elizabeth knew that type of woman because she was one.

"They'll work it out." Cora walked into the kitchen.

"I'm sure they will." Elizabeth smiled as her daughter kissed both of them goodnight and went to bed.

Kurt spent the next several days snapping at everyone and at one point, Elizabeth pulled off her slipper and threatened to bust his arse if he didn't change his attitude. He'd come home after training and spend the majority of his time in his room. It all came to a head at the end of the week when Sean threatened to toss Kurt through the bedroom window.

"I'm starting to lose my patience with that young fella," Jack grumbled as he came in from the back yard.

He'd asked Kurt to take one of the new nets down to the dock for one of the boats, but Jack had found the net still in the back of Kurt's truck. When Jack asked Kurt about it, he told them he'd do it later.

"You're not the only one." Elizabeth sighed.

"Either he gets his head out of his arse, or I'm going to kick it," Jack said as he sat at the table.

Their discussion was interrupted when the telephone rang. Elizabeth hurried to answer it, but Sean got to it ahead of her. She was about to go back to chat with Jack, but something about the expression on Sean's face made her heart thud in her chest.

"Okay, thanks, baby. I'll tell him." Sean hung up the phone and ran out of the room.

"Sean, what's wrong?" Elizabeth hurried behind her son.

"Kurt, get your arse down here now," Sean shouted.

"Watch your mouth," Elizabeth warned.

"What do you want?" Kurt clomped down over the steps.

"We need to get to the hospital," Sean told his brother.

"What for?" Kurt furrowed his brow.

"It's Alice. She's been in a car accident." Sean was obviously trying to break the news gently.

"Wh…what?" Kurt dropped down to the step.

"Kathleen just called me. It's not good, Kurt. Her parents, brother, and Alice were in the car. Her dad died on impact." Sean dropped his hand on Kurt's shoulder.

Kurt jumped to his feet and grabbed his keys, but Jack stopped him. Elizabeth could see the panic in Kurt's expression, and it wouldn't be a good idea for him to drive to St. John's in that condition.

"We'll all go," Jack told Kurt.

"Fadder, no offense, but you drive like an old man." Kurt tried to grab his keys.

"Which means we'll get there safe and in one piece. The last thing we need is for you to end up in an accident as well. Get in my truck." Jack pointed to the door.

The hour-drive to St. John's was quiet, and Elizabeth could feel Kurt's leg shaking behind her seat. Cora had caught them as they were leaving the house and jumped in the truck with them.

"She's fine. I know she is," Cora said softly.

"Sure she is. Her fadder is dead," Kurt snapped.

"Now, my son, the last thing that girl needs is you going in with your nasty attitude. Your sister was trying to make you feel better," Jack raised his voice.

"Sorry, Cora," Kurt murmured. "I'm just worried."

Elizabeth followed her son into the emergency room. Jack, Sean, and Cora weren't far behind them. Kurt was frantically looking around, but he didn't see anyone from the family. He saw a nurse and practically shouted at the young woman.

"I'm looking for my girlfriend. She and her family were in an accident." Kurt stood over the young nurse.

"What's her name?" The nurse said shakily.

"Alice White." Kurt lowered his tone a little.

"I'm sorry, I'll have to check with the family to see…" the nurse got interrupted when Kurt slapped his hands on the desk.

"I want to see her. Now," Kurt roared.

"Kurt, that's not the way to ask for anything. You're frightening the poor girl." Elizabeth grabbed Kurt's arm and pulled him back. "Go over there and let me find out what's going on. You need to calm yourself."

Kurt stepped away, and Elizabeth turned back to the nurse. She gave the woman an apologetic smile and proceeded to explain the situation.

"I'm so sorry for his behavior. As you can expect, he's very concerned," Elizabeth said.

"I'll go check with the family." The nurse quickly disappeared through the door behind her.

It was several minutes before she returned and nodded for them to follow her. Kurt practically ran behind the nurse as the rest of them kept close. The nurse opened the door to a room and motioned for them to enter.

"Two of the family are in here." The nurse nodded to Kurt as she scurried away.

Elizabeth stepped in and realized it was a small waiting room. Alice and her mother sat close together with their arms wrapped around each other. Alice glanced up when they entered, and her tears streamed down her cheeks at the sight of Kurt.

Without a word, he immediately had her pulled into his arms and she sobbed. Elizabeth wrapped her arms around Alice's mother, Jessica. She'd only met Alice's parents twice and had liked them immediately.

"Paul is in surgery," Alice told them between sobs.

"Baby, what happened?" Kurt asked and kissed the top of her head.

"I don't know. We got a call saying that Dad and Paul were here, and when we got here, they told us…" Alice buried her face in the crook of Kurt's neck.

"You and your mother weren't in the car?" Elizabeth asked.

"No, they were coming to pick us up," Jessica whispered.

"Have the police been here?" Kurt asked.

"They said the other guy lost control of his truck and hit them." Alice lifted her head and looked at Kurt. "Dad didn't make it."

"I know, baby. Kathleen called us, but she thought you and your mom were in the car too." Kurt ran his knuckle down her cheek wiping away tears.

"I was hysterical when I called her. I'm sorry to worry all of you." Alice sniffed.

"I'm so sorry about your father," Kurt whispered. "I'm here for you. We all are."

Alice allowed Kurt to wrap her in his embrace, and Elizabeth glanced up at Jack. The thought of anything happening to him made her chest hurt. She loved him so much that she couldn't imagine life without him, and she didn't know how Jessica would go on without her husband.

"God never gives us what we can't handle," Jessica murmured. "But I honestly don't know how I'll live without Fred."

"We're here if you need us. Anything you want or need," Kurt said immediately.

"But I…we broke up." Alice lifted her head and stared into Kurt's face.

"It doesn't matter. You need me, I'm there," Kurt replied.

Alice stared at him for several minutes before she spoke. It was the words that she said that made Elizabeth realize that Cora really did have a gift.

"I love you, Kurt. I'll live anywhere you want to live." Alice held his face between her hands.

"If you want to live in Hopedale, that's where I'll go," Kurt replied

"Life is too short to let stupid things keep you away from the person you love." Alice wept.

"I love you too, and I'll help you and your family through this." Kurt pulled her into his arms and hugged her.

"You raised an amazing son." Jessica sniffed.

"We've raised three amazing people." Elizabeth swallowed the lump in her throat as she looked at each of her children.

Her children were kind, loving, and had hearts of gold. There was nothing else a parent could want. She knew over the next few days that Alice's family would need as much support as they could get. Since it was obvious that Alice was now part of their family, Elizabeth would be right next to them.

Chapter 28

Over the next several months, Elizabeth spent her days going between St. John's, Hopedale, and Cape Broyle. She'd go to St. John's to help Jessica deal with the aftermath of losing her husband and nursing her son, Paul, back to health. With Elizabeth helping, Alice could return to school.

She also spent time in Hopedale helping Kathleen get everything prepared for after she and Sean got married. They laid the foundation for the new house, but it wouldn't be ready before the wedding. Kathleen had also told her that she and Sean had talked about having children right away and hoped they would have four.

Elizabeth had been ecstatic because she was looking forward to becoming a grandmother. Her only concern was whether the young couple would be able to handle things financially. Sean had the money that his grandfather left him, and Kathleen had her inheritance, which from what Sean explained would pay for the building of the new house.

By the time she would get home most evenings, Elizabeth would have to help Louise with some housework. Her mother-in-law was getting up in age, and although she would never admit it, she was finding it challenging to do certain things.

Jack had tried to talk her into selling the house and moving in with them, but he'd received a flat-out refusal. When he tried to argue, Elizabeth had stopped him because she knew Louise wanted to keep her independence.

They did manage to convince Louise to move her bedroom to the main floor of the house so she didn't have to tackle the stairs. It also made it easier for Elizabeth because she only had to clean the main floor of the house.

By the time she would make it home, all she wanted to do was fall in bed next to her husband. Thankfully, Cora, Sean, and Kurt kept the house cleaned, and most days, Jack would prepare supper. Elizabeth felt as if she was neglecting her own family, but she hoped after the wedding, things would be less busy.

"Kathleen picked up her dress today," Cora said as they sat down to supper.

"I guess she'll show me later," Sean said casually.

Cora and Elizabeth started to laugh, and the men seemed confused by their reaction to Sean's statement. How was it possible they didn't know the groom couldn't see the dress?

"You do know it's bad luck to see the dress?" Cora chuckled.

"No, it's bad luck to see the bride in the dress," Sean returned.

"You won't be seeing the dress. Get over it." Cora rolled her eyes.

By the time July ninth arrived, Elizabeth was ready for it all to be over. The excitement of the wedding was so much that Elizabeth couldn't remember the last time she'd been able to sleep through the night without waking up. She hadn't even been like that before her own wedding.

As she and Jack walked up to the front pew, she met Sean's smiling face. He was the mirror image of his father, and dressed in a tuxedo, she was sure he would take Kathleen's breath away. She moved her gaze to where Kurt stood and chuckled at the mischievous expression. The other groomsman was Dr. Connolly's grandson. Sean had met the young man in medical school, and they became fast friends.

Alice and Cora slowly made their way up to the front as "The Trumpet Voluntary" echoed through the church. When Alice stepped next to the altar, the music change to "The Bridal Chorus," and as the doors at the back of the church opened, everyone rose to their feet.

Charlie stood proudly next to Kathleen with a smile that lit up his face. Kathleen linked into his arm, and they slowly made their way down to the front of the church. Elizabeth glanced at Sean and smiled at the look of complete awe on his face.

Kathleen was simply beautiful in her dress, and even with the veil over her face, nothing could cover the way her beauty glowed.

Elizabeth was so happy for her son, and even though they would be living further away than she liked, she knew that she wasn't losing a son, she was gaining a wonderful daughter.

Elizabeth barely saw anything that happened at the front of the church because she couldn't keep her eyes from blurring with tears. She was so happy for the young couple, but it was hard to see her firstborn leave the nest.

Kurt and Alice were headed in the same direction, although Kurt hadn't said anything about proposing. Elizabeth could tell by the way they gazed at each other. Their love was timeless.

Cora and Brian were still going strong, much to Jack's dismay. He still couldn't get his head around the fact his little girl was so serious about a boy. Brian treated Cora like a princess and would bring her little presents anytime he came to see her. It was sweet, but it irritated Jack. Elizabeth hoped someday he'd get over the fact that his little girl was grown up.

Chapter 29

Ten months after Kathleen and Sean were married, the family was in the waiting room of the hospital. Kathleen had gone into labor, and Elizabeth was anxiously awaiting her first grandchild.

She and Jack found it odd that the hospital allowed Sean into the delivery room. Dr. Connolly insisted that since Sean was going to be a doctor himself, it would be a good experience for him to see his child born.

It had been more than ten hours since she'd gone into labor, and for some reason, Elizabeth had a feeling something was different about Kathleen's pregnancy. She was large and ordered on bed rest for the last two months. Not to mention she was a month early.

"I sure hope everything is okay," Elizabeth murmured to herself.

"Me too." Geraldine sat next to Elizabeth, wringing her hands together.

"She's a little early, but that happens sometimes." Elizabeth didn't know who she was trying to convince, Geraldine, or herself.

"She's been so careful and did everything the doctor ordered." Geraldine nodded.

Kurt was working and couldn't make it to the hospital until later that evening. Cora and Alice arrived with Brian after they picked up their final exam reports from the university. They distracted everyone with their marks for a short time, but it wasn't long before everyone started to worry about Kathleen again.

"Does it always take this long?" Cora sighed.

"Aren't you studying to be a nurse?" Alice chuckled.

"Shouldn't you shut up?" Cora retorted.

Cora, Alice, and Kathleen had become more like sisters and were regularly teasing each other. Elizabeth liked to see how close they all were and hoped it continued for years.

Sean appeared in the doorway of the waiting room. He looked happy but a little pale. He motioned for everyone to follow him and led them to the nursery at the end of the maternity ward.

"What did she have a boy or a girl?" Elizabeth asked as she looked into the window of the nursery.

"She had two boys." Sean smiled as he glanced around at the group.

"What?" Cora gasped.

"Twins?" Elizabeth whispered.

"Did you know she was having twins?" Alice asked.

286

"We knew, but we wanted to surprise everyone." Sean pointed to the two babies lying in the bassinets next to the window.

"Two babies?" Geraldine choked.

"They are a little small but fully healthy." Sean grinned.

Elizabeth clung to Jack as they peered through the glass at the two baby boys. One squirmed, and the other was quietly sleeping, but both were the most beautiful things she'd ever seen.

"How's Kathleen?" Elizabeth asked.

"She's tired, but she was incredible. I knew how babies came into this world, but it's the most amazing thing I've ever seen in my life. Mudder, you have no idea how hard it was for her." Sean's eyes filled with tears.

"No, Sean. Mom has no idea because she knit all of us," Cora said sarcastically.

"Oh, right. Of course you know." Sean chuckled as he plowed his hand through his hair.

"She's going to need a lot of help with these two." Elizabeth smiled.

"Gee, do you know anyone who would be willing to help?" Sean wrapped his arms around Elizabeth and Geraldine.

"It'll be hard, but I'm sure we'll figure something out." Geraldine laughed.

An hour later, everyone was able to see Kathleen. Sean had been right, she was tired, but she looked incredibly happy. Kurt had arrived a short while later and was shocked to find out he had two nephews.

"You had to start with a bang, didn't you, bro?" Kurt laughed as Alice tucked herself under his arm.

"I just hope neither of them turns out like you, Kurt." Cora smirked.

"What are you talking about? I was an angel." Kurt feigned shock.

"Really?" Sean laughed.

"Can I please give evidence of you're not so angel-like behavior?" Cora snorted.

"So, you're going to be a lawyer now?" Kurt returned.

"Have you told Alice about that day you didn't want to go to church?" Sean asked.

"That was one incident, and I redeemed myself later that evening." Kurt met Elizabeth's eyes.

"You did." Elizabeth smiled.

"Please tell me." Alice chuckled.

"Fine, but I'm telling her." Kurt pointed his finger around the room to tell everyone to be quiet.

"As long as you tell her the truth, we won't interrupt." Cora laughed.

"I will. So, Mudder used to make us go to church with Nan every Sunday. I think I was about ten and I didn't want to go that morning. Mudder kept calling out to me, and when I didn't get up, she came up to the room." Kurt glanced at Elizabeth and then continued. "She told me to get up, and I kept refusing. After what seemed like the hundredth time she told me to get up, I told her to practice what she preached."

Alice and Kathleen looked appalled by what Kurt said. Elizabeth could understand their reaction, but they didn't know how Kurt had changed that day. They didn't know that he'd saved his mother from a terrible ordeal.

"What happened?" Brian asked.

"I went to church that day." Kurt laughed.

"I bet you did." Alice laughed.

"Mudder whacked me with her slipper from the top of the stairs to the kitchen." Kurt smirked.

"I did not. I only got you at the top of the stairs." Elizabeth laughed.

"He made up for it after church, though." Jack's face turned serious.

"Yes, he did." Elizabeth shuddered at the memory of what happened later that day.

"What happened?" Alice asked.

"I'll tell you about that another time. It's a happy day, but let's say that day I decided what I wanted to do with my life." Kurt kissed Alice's temple.

Elizabeth sat contented as she listened to the conversation. She didn't know what it was about, but as she took in every one of the smiling faces, she tensed when she glanced at Sean.

"I'm a dad. I have two sons," Sean whispered as if it had finally sunk in.

"You know that's double the diapers and sleepless nights, right?" Brian teased.

"Who let this guy in here?" Sean grumbled.

"He's not wrong." Kurt chuckled.

"You can all leave now." Kathleen sighed.

"Hey, you didn't tell us, what are you naming the boys?" Geraldine asked.

"We're naming them after people we admire." Kathleen smiled.

"You don't have to name them after me. I'll be happy to be their favorite uncle." Kurt smirked.

"Good, cause they aren't named after you." Sean shook his head.

"What are the names?" Cora asked.

"One we are calling John, after you, Jack, and he will have Sean's middle name. The other baby we are calling James, after my dad. His middle name will be Charles." Kathleen glanced toward where Charlie stood.

"They are good strong names." Elizabeth smiled.

"Yes, they are," Kurt agreed.

Elizabeth had a feeling for the next few years, her family would be having a lot more moments like they had that day. With Kurt working as a police officer and Cora almost finished nursing school, it was only a matter of time before they would be looking to the future and following in Sean's footsteps.

It was bittersweet to think about it. Elizabeth loved her children, and it made her sad to realize they'd grown up so fast. Her only solace was they gained so much more.

Chapter 30

Christmas arrived, and the family gathered around the dinner table. The twins were seven months old and growing fast. Sean had also gotten the news that he'd be doing his internship at the hospital starting the following September.

"I can't believe how fast this last year went," Cora said as she picked John up in her arms.

The two little boys weren't identical, but they tended to follow each other around. If they couldn't see each other, they would get upset. It was as if they wanted to be near each other all the time.

"I know, Johnny and Jimmy have gotten so big." Kathleen bounced James on her knee.

"Kathleen, are you okay? You look kind of pale," Louise said as she reached across the table to feel Kathleen's forehead.

"Yeah, I'm fine." Kathleen's gaze flicked to Sean.

"You might as well tell them." Sean smiled.

"Tell us what?" Elizabeth asked.

"I'm going to have another baby." Kathleen smiled.

292

"What? Oh goodness, that is way too soon." Louise gasped.

Elizabeth rolled her eyes. She remembered the same reaction when she got pregnant so soon after Kurt was born. She shook her head and ignored her mother-in-law's comment.

"That's wonderful." Elizabeth hugged Kathleen.

"It wasn't exactly planned." Sean smirked.

"You'll have what's for you, when it's for you," Elizabeth told them.

"You'll have three kids under the age of two." Cora chuckled.

For a minute, Kathleen and Sean looked confused, but the minute it hit them, Kathleen's face turned even paler, and Sean seemed as if he was about to throw up.

"How are we going to do this?" Kathleen whispered.

"You'll have lots of help, honey," Elizabeth assured her daughter-in-law.

"While we're on the subject of weddings, I wanted to let you know something," Kurt said after he cleared his throat.

"Idiot, nobody was talking about weddings." Cora slapped Kurt's arm.

"Are you going to propose?" Elizabeth practically shouted with excitement.

"Thanks for spoiling the news, Mudder." Kurt laughed.

"That will be two weddings in two years." Cora sighed.

"We'll probably wait until next year, but I'm going to ask her this weekend." Kurt reached into his pocket and pulled out a box.

The ring was beautiful and was similar to the ring that Sean gave Kathleen. She wouldn't mention it, but Cora did. Kurt explained that Sean had helped him pick it out, and since Alice had said she loved Kathleen's ring, Kurt figured he couldn't go wrong.

The ring was different in that it had a small diamond on either side of the larger one in the middle, but Elizabeth couldn't argue that it would be perfect for Alice.

"Guess we'll have to find you a man, Cora." Kurt chuckled.

"I have a man. Thank you very much." Cora pointed her fork at her brother.

"Didn't he head off to Ontario in January?" Sean took a sleeping John from Cora.

"Yes, and he'll be back in December," Cora replied.

"You're going to wait around for him. Must be love." Sean laughed.

"Go to hell," Cora snapped.

"Cora, watch your mouth," Elizabeth chastised.

"Sorry, but if they insinuate once more that Brian isn't coming back, I'm going to knock them on their arses." Cora narrowed her eyes.

"Cora, language." Elizabeth sighed.

By the time the weekend arrived, Kurt was a nervous wreck. He was worried that she would turn him down. Even though the couple was closer than ever, it was a possibility that Alice wasn't ready to think about marriage.

"If she says no, we'll still stay together. I'll ask her a year down the road," Kurt said, but it appeared to be mostly to himself.

"She's not going to say no," Kathleen assured Kurt.

"How do you know? Did you tell her?" Kurt asked frantically.

"No, I just know how much she loves you, and it's hard to resist that O'Connor charm." Kathleen winked at Sean.

"I have to agree with that." Elizabeth smiled as she met Jack's amused eyes.

"Go do it, Kurt." Sean pushed his brother toward the front door.

"I can do this." Kurt nodded as he disappeared out of the house.

"He's going to screw this up." Cora sighed.

"Great positive thinking there, Cupid." Sean chuckled.

For the next couple of hours, Elizabeth and Jack killed time by playing cards. Cora was answering a letter she'd received from Brian while Sean and Kathleen were snuggled up on the couch watching television after putting the boys down for the night.

The house was relatively quiet, and Elizabeth jumped when the front door flew open. She glanced up to see Kurt enter, but she couldn't read his expression. She also didn't see Alice with him, which made her heart sink. Kurt eased down into the chair next to Jack and placed the ring box on the table.

"Kurt, is everything okay?" Jack asked softly.

When Kurt finally lifted his eyes from where he'd been staring at the box. He folded his hands in front of him and didn't speak as Sean, Kathleen, and Cora entered the kitchen.

"What did she say?" Sean asked.

Kurt shot to his feet and turned his back to them. Elizabeth shook her head because he looked ready to burst into tears. Cora was about to say something, but Elizabeth shook her head. If Kurt was hurt, he needed a minute.

"You want to know what she said when I told her I loved her and wanted to make her my wife?" Kurt kept his back to them.

"Son, maybe she needs some time," Jack interjected.

"I poured out my heart to her and even got down on one knee. She looked at me and said…" Kurt stopped.

"She said yes." Alice ran into the house as Kurt spun around with a huge grin on his face.

At first, Elizabeth was confused. From the expressions on everyone's faces, she wasn't the only one. Kurt opened the ring box to show it was empty, and Alice held up her hand as Kurt went to her and wrapped his arm around her.

"You two buggers." Elizabeth chuckled.

"I hate you both." Cora narrowed her eyes. "I was about to cry."

"I think you should look into a career in acting, Kurt." Kathleen laughed as she hugged Alice.

"I was thinking about it." Kurt smiled smugly.

Elizabeth sat back in the chair and glanced around the table at her growing family. Jack's expression mirrored the way she felt. They were so proud of the family they raised together.

Chapter 31

More than three years after Kathleen and Sean married, their family stood in the church again to celebrate the marriage of Kurt and Alice. John and James were the cutest ring boys anyone had ever seen.

Sean's youngest child was almost a year old, and they'd named him Ian William. Everyone tended to call him Inky because when he was six months old, he got hold of a pen and chewed it until it broke in his mouth. It took Kathleen days to get it all off the chubby baby. Jack started calling the baby Inky and it stuck.

Elizabeth's gaze moved around the front of the church and stopped at her son. Kurt looked so handsome in his police dress uniform. Alice had wanted him to wear it, and Elizabeth could see why. Alice had asked her brother to walk her down the aisle, and it was the sweetest thing Elizabeth had ever seen.

Kurt and Alice purchased a portion of the land from Kathleen, and they were building their house next to Sean and Kathleen. They were living in Kathleen's old house until they finished the new home.

Elizabeth was excited for another reason as well. The week before the wedding, Brian had come to them and asked Jack for his blessing to propose to Cora. At first, Elizabeth thought her husband would say no, but Brian had grown on Jack. It was probably because he treated Cora so well.

The plan was for Brian to propose at the wedding reception, and hopefully, things would go as everyone hoped. Although Elizabeth couldn't see Cora turning down her young man. She was head-over-heels for Brian and had been since she first saw him at Sean's graduation ceremony.

Once the ceremony and reception were over, the plan was for Cora to catch the bouquet. Alice made sure all the single women knew they had to step back from Cora once the flowers were in the air.

As planned, Cora caught it easily and giggled excitedly. As she turned around, Brian dropped to his knee and proposed. Cora looked stunned, but it didn't stop her from screaming out an undeniable acceptance. It took several minutes before Brian was able to place the ring on her finger because she had her arms wrapped around him.

Once the excitement of the proposal subsided, Elizabeth turned to see her husband of twenty-five years holding out his hand. He led her to the middle of the dance floor and pulled her in close.

"Did you ever think we would be here one day?" Elizabeth smiled up at him.

"I knew the first time I saw you." Jack stared into her eyes.

"We're getting old." Elizabeth laughed.

"You're still as beautiful as the day I met you." Jack leaned down and brushed his lips against hers.

"I love you, Jack O'Connor," Elizabeth whispered against his lips.

"I love you too, Betty," Jack returned.

Elizabeth wondered what the future held for them, but she knew that the best was yet to come. Looking around the reception hall, she could see having plenty more celebrations in the future for the O'Connor family.

Over the next couple of months, everything centered around plans for Cora's wedding. By the time the end of October rolled around, they had practically everything planned.

Cora would be married the following September, and they would make final plans after the holidays. It was hard to believe that in less than a year, only she and Jack would be living in the house. Brian and Cora had started to build their house on the same land where Kathleen's childhood home had been.

The couple bought it from Kathleen. As much as her children teased each other, it seemed they wanted to remain close. All three tried to convince her and Jack to move to Hopedale as well, but Elizabeth didn't see that happening, at least not before Jack retired.

It was Sunday afternoon and everyone had just finished dinner. Kathleen and Alice were whispering in the living room when Elizabeth brought the pot of tea. Both women seemed nervous and kept glancing at Louise.

"Is something wrong?" Elizabeth asked.

"Nothing." Alice smiled as she picked up little Ian.

"Mommy, can James and me go out with Grandda?" John ran into the living room.

"It's James and I, John," Kathleen corrected her son.

"You can come too, but he's going down to look at the new boat." John jumped up and down.

"He's gonna take us on the boat." James did the same.

The boys were close but had widely different personalities. James was quiet for the most part and seemed to let John play the dominant twin. John was a little taller, and James' hair had more waves to his thick auburn hair.

"As long as you listen to Grandda and not run off," Kathleen told them

"We will," both boys shouted as they ran out of the house.

"Jack will keep an eye on them," Elizabeth assured Kathleen.

"I know." Kathleen glanced at Louise.

"Louise, did you want to lay down in the guest room for a bit? You look tired." Elizabeth glanced at her mother-in-law.

"Yes, but I'm going to go to my house. The bed in that room is not comfortable. Can you get one of the boys to take me home?" Louise stood up.

"I'll take you, Nan." Cora walked into the room and held out her arm for Louise.

"If you're not too busy, ducky, would you mind tossing a load of bedclothes into the washer? Your mudder has been too busy for it lately," Louise said as she and Cora left the room.

"I swear that woman is the reason I'm going grey." Elizabeth sighed and sat back in the chair.

"She does tend to complain a little." Alice laughed.

"You have no idea, my dear." Elizabeth shook her head as she poured tea for herself and the ladies.

"Betty, we have something to tell you," Kathleen said softly.

"I assumed something was going on with you two." Elizabeth handed a cookie to Ian, and Kathleen placed him in the playpen.

"I didn't want Mrs. O'Connor to take the joy out of it." Kathleen smirked.

"She does tend to do that." Elizabeth laughed but stopped when she realized what Kathleen had said. "Are you pregnant again?"

"I told you she'd know." Kathleen turned to Alice.

"I'm so happy for you. Maybe you'll get your girl this time." Elizabeth hugged Kathleen.

"Maybe, but if I don't, Alice might." Kathleen grinned.

Elizabeth glanced between the two women and realized what they meant. She jumped up and wrapped her arms around Alice and then pulled both women into a hug.

"We're going to have two more babies in the family." Elizabeth tried to hold back the emotion, but it was useless.

"It seems like you have very fertile sons." Alice laughed.

Cora arrived a short while later and plopped down on the chair where Louise had sat earlier. By the expression on her face, she'd probably dealt with some annoying issues at her grandmother's house.

"I love the woman, but how is it possible she raised Dad?" Cora shook her head.

"I ask myself that every day." Elizabeth chuckled.

"I'm assuming by the grin on my mother's face that you have told her the news." Cora smiled as she poured herself a cup of tea from the teapot.

"Yes, they did, and I can't believe you didn't tell me," Elizabeth chastised her daughter.

"Wasn't my news to tell, but thankfully the babies will arrive before my wedding," Cora smirked as she lifted her cup to her lips.

The news of the two new arrivals wasn't something they could keep from Louise, and as usual, she thought it was indecent for Kathleen to have another baby so soon. She didn't seem to be as appalled by Alice's pregnancy but commented on them not wasting any time.

Jack was ecstatic about more grandchildren, mostly because the three he had, thought their grandfather was a god. Especially John and James. Whenever they would come to visit, they would follow him everywhere. They were Grandda's little buddies, and they had him wrapped around their fingers.

Kurt had also taken on another venture in his life, along with being a police officer. Their former Karate instructor had opened a school for martial arts and asked both Kurt and Sean if they would be interested in teaching. Both had achieved their black belts and were qualified to be instructors.

Sean declined since he was busy with working at the hospital, and he tried to be home to help his wife with the children. Sean did enroll John and James in the school because he and Kathleen felt it was good for them.

The week before Christmas, Elizabeth was at the grocery store picking up some last-minute supplies for the family Christmas dinner. She had arrived at the cashier when she heard a familiar voice that made her body shudder.

"Well, if it isn't Jack O'Connor's little woman." Elizabeth turned around and looked up into the face of Peter Barnes.

Elizabeth turned back and thanked God that there wasn't anyone in front of her in the lineup. It was the first time she'd seen the man since that day so many years ago. She forced a smile at the young cashier as she placed her items on the counter with a shaky hand.

"No friendly greeting for an old friend?" Peter stepped closer, making Elizabeth uncomfortable.

Elizabeth ignored the comment and quickly grabbed her bags as she handed the money to the cashier. She didn't even wait for her change as she practically ran out of the store.

She was glad to see Kurt in his truck waiting for her. Elizabeth almost tripped over the steps as she ran down to the vehicle. Kurt opened the door for her, but she couldn't hide her nervousness from him.

"Mudder, what's wrong?" Kurt asked as he took the bags from her.

"Oh, nothing, I just have so much…" Elizabeth stopped when she heard Peter's voice behind her.

"Jesus, Jack, you haven't aged." Peter slapped Kurt on the shoulder.

"Get your hand off me, you piece of shit." Kurt obviously recognized Peter.

"Kurt, just get in the truck," Elizabeth begged.

"Kurt? Not little Kurt? The brat who caused me to need surgery on my knee?" Peter sneered.

"Back off, or it will be more than your knee this time." Kurt turned to walk around the truck.

"You may have grown into a large man, but I won't have my back to you this time," Peter shouted.

Thankfully, Kurt didn't say another word and got in the truck. He pulled out of the lot, and Elizabeth could tell by the way her son clenched his jaw that he was trying hard to control his anger.

"Mudder, when did he get back to Cape Broyle?" Kurt sounded calm, but there was a chill in his tone.

"I don't know. The last I heard, Peter and Maureen lived in Alberta." Elizabeth thought she'd gotten over that night, but she couldn't stop herself from shaking.

"That piece of shit should never have gotten out of jail in the first place." Kurt pulled into the driveway.

"Watch your language, Kurt," Elizabeth said, but her voice cracked.

"Mudder, did he touch you again?" Kurt turned in the seat and looked at her with such concern.

"No, he just startled me. I'm fine." Elizabeth exited the truck, but before she could get the bags, Kurt was around the vehicle and grabbed them.

Elizabeth stepped into the house and tried to shake off the fear of seeing Peter. It had been more than twelve years since that incident, and she thought she'd gotten over it. She hadn't had a nightmare about it in years, but just one look at that man and she felt as if it had just happened.

"Betty." Jack practically ran into the kitchen, and she knew Kurt had told him about what happened.

"Jack, I'm fine." Elizabeth held up her hand as she tried to place the bottle of milk in the fridge.

She pulled open the fridge, but as she tried to place the bottle on the shelf, she couldn't stop the trembling, and it tumbled to the floor. The bottle shattered, and milk spilled everywhere. Elizabeth immediately crouched to pick up the mess, but Jack pulled her away.

He tugged her into his arms, and the tears started to stream down her cheeks. He guided her upstairs to their bedroom away from where the kids could hear them. Kurt and Sean had told their wives about that night, and Brian knew as well. Elizabeth didn't want the little ones to know about it, at least not until they were much older.

Jack closed the bedroom door and guided her to their bed. For several minutes, she sobbed in his arms, and he didn't say a word. That was Jack. He never forced her to talk about anything until she was ready.

"I thought I was over this," Elizabeth whispered.

"Betty, you still have nightmares," Jack replied.

Elizabeth lifted her head and stared at him. She couldn't remember having a nightmare in a long time, and when she did, she usually didn't wake Jack. When he slept, he was like a dead man.

"What are you talking about?" Elizabeth wiped the tears from her cheeks.

"Darling, you've had a nightmare at least once a month." Jack smoothed his hand down the back of her head.

"I don't remember them." Elizabeth sighed.

"When you do, I pull you into my arms and talk to you until you settle," Jack told her.

"You should have told me," she replied.

"I thought you knew but didn't want to talk about it." Jack shrugged.

Elizabeth sighed and grabbed a couple of tissues from the night table. She still didn't understand why she'd had such a panicked reaction to seeing Peter. It wasn't like he touched her or did anything except speak to her.

"It doesn't make sense why I feel like this. I mean, he didn't actually do what he had intended." Elizabeth stood up and started to pace.

"Betty, he attacked you. He bruised your face and had your clothes ripped. He might not have done what he'd come in our house

308

to do, but that doesn't take away from the fact what his true intention was." Jack stood up and wrapped his arms around her.

"Why is he back here?" Elizabeth sighed.

"I heard Anne is going into a nursing home. Maureen is back to deal with it, but I didn't realize he was here too," Jack explained.

"Maureen is back too. That's just great." Elizabeth clung to Jack.

The last thing she needed was to deal with Maureen. If she was still the same, it meant she would probably try to cause trouble with Elizabeth and Jack again. There was no way she was letting that happen. They had so much to celebrate over the holidays, and she wasn't about to let Maureen or Peter ruin that.

Chapter 32

Elizabeth's eyes filled with tears as she watched her daughter walk down the aisle on her father's arm. Looking at Jack, it was hard to say who was crying more, him or Cora.

Cora looked so beautiful in her princess dress and lace veil that trailed behind her. The red roses she carried shook as they made it to the front of the church, and Elizabeth was sure Brian couldn't smile any bigger as he watched Cora walk toward him.

There was also the added joy of Elizabeth and Jack watching the two newest additions to the family. Kathleen gave birth in May to another boy named Keith Gregory, and Alice delivered a beautiful baby girl in June that they named Isabelle Alice.

Now it was September, and they were attending the wedding of her baby girl. It was surreal to believe that she had three married children and five grandchildren. The only downfall was they all lived more than a half-hour away. They still got together on the weekends either with her and Jack going to Hopedale or the kids coming to Cape Broyle, but she still hated not seeing them every day.

Louise's health had started to deteriorate, and Jack finally convinced his mother that she shouldn't be living alone. That meant after the wedding Elizabeth, and Jack wouldn't be alone too long. What could she do? Louise needed her, and although they clashed in the past, she wouldn't see her shoved into a nursing home.

To top things off, Maureen and Peter still hadn't left Cape Broyle, and Elizabeth had run into them more times than she wanted to. Peter had not approached her again since that time in the grocery store, but Jack still made her keep the door locked when he wasn't home.

"How did I father such a beautiful young woman?" Jack whispered as Cora and Brian kissed.

"She is lovely, isn't she?" Elizabeth smiled.

"She's the mirror image of you, my darling." Jack kissed Elizabeth's cheek.

"She has a lot of you in her too, honey." Elizabeth stood up as Father Murphy introduced the couple.

Brian's parents were a little older than Elizabeth, and she learned that they had struggled to have children, and Brian had been a long-awaited surprise to them. They also thought the world of Cora, but they were as disappointed as well that the couple would be not be living in their hometown.

As Jack constantly repeated to her, the kids needed to spread their wings and move out on their own. It was still hard to let go, but Elizabeth was adjusting to it, and so would Brian's parents.

"It's a lovely wedding," Louise said as Elizabeth placed a plate of food in front of her.

"Yes, it is," Elizabeth agreed.

"Betty looks lovely." Louise nodded at Cora.

"Mrs. O'Connor, that's Cora. I'm Betty." Elizabeth crouched down so that she was eye level with Louise.

"Oh, dear, yes. I was a little confused there for a moment." Louise reached for the fork with a shaky hand.

"I think you probably need to eat." Elizabeth motioned for Jack to come closer.

Elizabeth told Louise she and Jack were going to dance, and she'd be back. After she tugged Jack to the dancefloor, she pulled him closer so she could tell him about her concern.

"Jack, I'm worried about your mudder. She's been getting forgetful lately and confused," she explained.

"I noticed. It's why I'm glad she's coming to live with us." Jack glanced toward the table where Elizabeth had left Louise.

"We'll take care of her." Elizabeth cupped his cheek.

"What would I do without you, my beautiful darling?" Jack hugged Elizabeth tightly.

"I'm not going to let you find out." Elizabeth smiled.

Elizabeth had to be there for her family. She had a mother-in-law who needed care, children who still looked to her for advice, and grandchildren who wanted her to spoil them.

Elizabeth wished her parents were still alive to see what a wonderful family they helped create. Her father only got to see one of his grandchildren, but she liked to believe that he, her mother, and brother were watching over all of them and smiling down.

Chapter 33

Over the next week, Elizabeth and the rest of the family went through the tedious job of cleaning out Louise's house. The second floor had been completely cleared, with most of the items divided between Sean, Kurt, and Cora.

Elizabeth made her way back to Jack's childhood home and hoped that Louise finished going through the china cabinet. When she stepped inside, the first thing she heard was Louise arguing with someone.

At first, she didn't know who it was, but when she stepped into the kitchen, her body tensed. Louise was gripping a crystal pedestal cake dish to her chest. That alone would have concerned Elizabeth, but it was the tears streaming down Louise's cheeks that enraged Elizabeth.

"What the hell are you doing here?" Elizabeth said as calmly as she could to the woman trying to pry the cake dish out of Louise's hands.

"I came to get my mother's cake dish, but this crazy woman won't give it back to me." Maureen grunted as she struggled with Louise.

"You aren't taking anything out of this house. That dish belongs to Mrs. O'Connor." Elizabeth stepped in front of Louise and broke the grip Maureen had on the crystal dish.

"That is my mother's cake dish, and I'm getting it back." Maureen pointed at the dish.

"Why do you think that belongs to your mother?" Elizabeth tilted her head and narrowed her eyes.

"My mother loaned that to Louise years ago, and that woman never returned it," Maureen snapped.

"You see, I know that's a lie," Elizabeth scoffed.

"It's not a lie, and how would you know anything about what went on here before you got your hooks into Jack?" Maureen poked Elizabeth in the shoulder.

Elizabeth walked to a box she'd filled with pictures earlier that day. One of them was Louise's wedding picture. Elizabeth had sat for more than an hour listening to Louise get lost in the memory of the day she married Jack's father.

She'd also showed Elizabeth the cake dish that had displayed her wedding cake. According to Louise, it was passed from her grandmother, down to her mother, then to Louise. The dish was over a hundred years old, and Louise had plenty of pictures that showed the cake stand.

Elizabeth pulled out the wedding picture and walked back in front of Maureen. For several seconds, she glanced between the image and the cake dish. There was no mistaking, it was the same one in the picture. The rim of the disk had thick, crystal hearts around the edge.

"You see, Maureen, I know that dish doesn't belong to your mother because it was a gift passed down through Mrs. O'Connor's family for three generations." Elizabeth turned the photo around and held it up.

"You're full of shit," Maureen retorted.

"Look at the cake in front of Mrs. O'Connor on this picture." Elizabeth pointed to the photo.

"So, my mudder loaned her the dish for her wedding." Maureen snapped.

"Your mother didn't know Mrs. O'Connor back then. She didn't move here until after you were born. Remember, you were born in Wabush?" Elizabeth glared at the woman who had become a thorn in her side.

"What does that have to do with that cake dish?" Maureen tossed her hands in the air.

"Mrs. O'Connor was already married then and had Jack," Elizabeth returned.

Maureen's mouth opened and closed several times as her face turned red. Elizabeth didn't know if it was because she was angry or knew she was caught in a lie. Either way, she didn't care.

"Now, I'm going to say this once and once only. Don't you ever put your hands on Mrs. O'Connor again or you'll be dealing with me. I'm not the same person that you attacked at that dance all those years ago. I'll ram my fist right into that nose and won't hesitate to knock your teeth down your throat." Elizabeth snarled as she took steps forward while Maureen backed toward the door.

"You're crazy." Maureen reached for the door and almost fell as she yanked it open.

"You'll see how crazy if you come near her again," Elizabeth shouted as she slammed the door.

When she returned to the kitchen, Louise looked both shocked and relieved, but at least she stopped crying. She had her arms wrapped around the dish where it sat on the table.

"Are you okay, Mrs. O'Connor?" Elizabeth crouched next to her and touched her arm.

"That wasn't very ladylike, Betty. You shouldn't talk to people like that." Louise shook her head as she stared at the dish.

Elizabeth dropped her head and sighed. It didn't matter what she did. Louise was always going to have something negative to say to her. Elizabeth knew her relationship with her mother-in-law wasn't going to change, and she was okay with that.

By the end of the week, Louise's house was empty, and the *for-sale* sign placed on it. It was sad for both Louise and Jack, but it was necessary. Dr. Connolly had told Elizabeth that Louise shouldn't be on her own anymore.

Louise was seventy-six years old, and not only was she getting forgetful, but she was also diagnosed with diabetes. Elizabeth had to go with her to a special appointment to learn how to give injections. Louise didn't like it, but the doctor insisted she needed the insulin.

"You're taking on a lot with Louise," Geraldine said one evening as they sat on the front porch.

"She's my mother-in-law, and we're the only family she has." Elizabeth shrugged.

"Considering what a pain in the ass that woman has been over the years, I don't think anyone would blame you if you just shoved her in a home." Geraldine shook her head.

"That's terrible. Louise is Jack's mother and my youngsters' grandmother. She's the matriarch of our family, Geraldine. That means she should be respected and cared for when she can't do it herself," Elizabeth returned.

No matter how much Louise frustrated Elizabeth, she could never turn her back on her. That was her job as Jack's wife, and she took it seriously. It gave her someone to take care of since her children were all grown up.

Four months later, Cora had come to Elizabeth in tears. She had found out she was two months pregnant but miscarried. It was difficult for the couple, especially since Kathleen also found out she was pregnant. Cora didn't allow the loss to put a damper on the joy of another child coming into the family.

That July, Kathleen gave birth to a baby boy that they named Michael Francis. A little over a month later, Cora announced she was expecting again, and when she hit the five-month point, they figured things would be fine. The family was ecstatic, but a week later, Cora started to have severe cramping and lost the child.

Cora was heartbroken and spent several days curled up in bed, crying. Elizabeth had to sit with her and listen to her daughter sob for days over the second loss. The doctor advised her to give it a year before they tried again, but Cora told Elizabeth she didn't know if it was worth the heartache.

Six months later, both Alice and Cora announced they were pregnant. The doctors were concerned about Cora, and so was Elizabeth. She didn't know if her daughter could handle another loss. She was considered a high-risk pregnancy and was followed closely by the doctors.

Louise had become more forgetful and sometimes would get angry over the smallest thing. Elizabeth knew it was because she was frustrated, but Jack had seen it a few times and hired someone to take some of the strain off Elizabeth. Cora had told them about a nurse she went to school with who was doing home care.

Sophia Nelson was a sweet girl and engaged to a lovely young man. She came by three days a week, and it gave Elizabeth time to do errands and chores around the house. It also helped that Louise liked Sophia and didn't argue when the young girl gave her insulin injections.

Late September was unusually cold, and Elizabeth had a trying day with Louise. By the time her mother-in-law lay down for the night, Elizabeth was ready to go to bed herself. As she left Louise's room, Jack was outside, and without a word, took her hand and led her up to their bedroom.

"Jack, I'm exhausted." Elizabeth sighed.

"I know. That's why I ran a bath for you." Jack motioned to the bathroom.

"You ran a bath for me?" Elizabeth smiled.

"You've been run ragged for months. Between the youngsters and Mudder, you haven't taken any time for yourself. So, relax in the bath and after you can go to bed for the night or just read. Would you like a cup of tea, or would you rather a drink?" Jack smirked.

"A drink sounds great." Elizabeth cupped Jack's face between her hands. "Thank you, my love."

"You're the one who deserves all the thanks for everything you do. I don't know how you do it." Jack covered her hands with his.

"I love you," Elizabeth whispered and pulled him down to kiss his lips.

"I adore you, my darling." Jack smiled.

That night she managed to take an hour in the bath, and the drink that Jack had mixed for her relaxed her so much that she fell into a deep sleep.

The next morning, she woke refreshed and expecting another hectic day with Louise. At least Sophia was scheduled for the day, and she would have a buffer between her and Louise. So no matter how off Louise was during the day, Elizabeth wouldn't be alone.

Elizabeth was preparing breakfast for her mother-in-law when Sophia arrived. After a cup of coffee, Sophia went to get Louise ready for the day. Elizabeth placed the plate of breakfast on the table and turned to see Sophia stood in the kitchen.

"Sophia, are you okay?" Elizabeth asked.

"Betty, I'm afraid Mrs. O'Connor...she's umm..." Sophia looked down at the floor. "She's no longer with us."

"What?" Elizabeth gasped as she stood frozen in the middle of the kitchen.

"She's gone." Sophia lifted her head, and Elizabeth saw the tears in her eyes.

Elizabeth hurried to Louise's room and went to the side of her mother-in-law's bed. Louise looked as if she was asleep, but her face had a slight greyish appearance, and she was cold. Elizabeth couldn't stop the tears as she left the room and went immediately to call Dr. Connolly.

Within the next hour, the house filled with the family, and Louise was brought to the funeral home. Jack had been quiet, and since his mother's body had been removed from the house, he sat in his mother's room staring at the floor.

The next few days would be rough on Jack and the family. Elizabeth may not have gotten along with Louise most of the time, but now that she was gone, she knew she'd grown to love her mother-in-law no matter how insulting she was. She was going to miss her terribly.

Chapter 34

A week after the funeral on Halloween, Elizabeth received a frantic call from Brian. He had to rush Cora to the hospital because she began bleeding heavily. Elizabeth's heart sank. Cora had managed to carry this baby almost eight months, and the doctors had been optimistic she would carry the baby to term.

Elizabeth had a feeling that another loss would probably break her daughter. She barely got through the last two miscarriages. The whole way to the hospital, Elizabeth prayed that both the baby and Cora would survive.

The memory of what happened when she went into labor on Cora flashed through her mind. She'd come close to losing Cora, but she was a fighter and survived. Hopefully, the baby had the same strength as her mother.

They found Brian pacing outside the operating room looking frantic and disheveled. When he saw Elizabeth and Jack, his eyes filled with tears. He mumbled something about feeling useless and then slowly lowered himself into the chair.

"They're taking the baby out," Brian whispered.

"Brian, I'm so sorry." Jack's voice was emotional, and Elizabeth could see the tears forming in her husband's eyes.

"No, they said the baby is alive, but they have to get it out right away, but if they can't stop the bleeding…" Brian dropped his head.

"Listen to me. Cora is a fighter, and she'll make it through this. I promise." Elizabeth hugged Brian and blinked back the tears.

Sean and Kurt came running down the corridor as Elizabeth knew they would the minute they got news of their sister. After they caught up to the situation, they gathered in the small waiting room outside the operating room.

"How long does this take?" Kurt asked.

"They can get the baby out in seconds if they have to, but depending on how much bleeding and what they have to do…" Sean stopped when Elizabeth shook her head.

"They'll stop the bleeding, though, right?" Brian's eyes opened wide, and his face turned pale.

"Yes, they will, Brian. She's in the right hands right now." Elizabeth wrapped her arm around Brian's shoulders.

She wanted to believe what she told Brian, but she knew things could go wrong. Elizabeth swallowed the lump that formed in her throat as she watched Jack across the room with his hands folded in front of him. The tears in his eyes mirrored her own as he met her gaze.

"Can't you go find out something? You're a fucking doctor, aren't you?" Kurt snapped at Sean.

"Kurt Patrick, watch your language," Elizabeth chastised her son.

"I'm frustrated, Mudder." Kurt shot to his feet and started to pace the floor.

"Your mudder is right. There's no need for foul language." Jack choked out the words.

"I'm sorry." Kurt blew out a breath.

Elizabeth could see that Kurt was not only worried about his sister, but with Alice ready to deliver any day, it was giving Kurt a taste of what could happen. Their first baby came quickly and without complications, but things could turn on a dime.

Another hour passed by before the doctor entered the waiting room. Elizabeth held her breath as the doctor led them to a more private area where he could explain what had happened. Elizabeth clung to Jack's hand as the doctor closed the door and turned to the family.

"First of all, you have a healthy baby girl. She's a little early, which means she will have to be in the neonatal for a little bit." The doctor gave a faint smile.

"And my wife?" Brian said softly.

"Mrs. Nightingale had a rough time and lost a lot of blood. We came very close to losing her. We were able to stop the bleeding, but we couldn't reverse the damage to her womb," the doctor explained.

"Which means?" Kurt asked.

"They had to do a hysterectomy," Sean answered.

"A partial one, yes. It was the only way to save her life," the doctor confirmed.

"But she's going to be fine?" Brian asked.

"Yes, she'll have a longer recovery, but she'll be fine," the doctor replied.

"Thank God." Brian blew out a breath. "Can I see her?"

"Only two at a time." The doctor nodded.

"Betty, do you want to come with me?" Brian turned to Elizabeth.

"Yes." Elizabeth walked behind Brian, and they followed the doctor.

"She's probably sleeping, and she'll be groggy when she wakes up, but that's expected." The doctor pushed open the door and motioned for them to go into the room.

Elizabeth immediately went to Cora's bedside and took her hand while Brian hurried to the other. Cora was peacefully sleeping, but other than looking a little pale, she seemed fine.

Brian sat on the edge of the bed and brought Cora's hand to his lips. Elizabeth smiled. It was beautiful to see the love that he had for her daughter, and she would need that to deal with the knowledge she wouldn't have another child.

Cora slept for several hours, only waking a couple of times during the night. Brian and Elizabeth stayed while everyone else went home to get some rest. Brian didn't sleep much during the night, but Elizabeth caught a few hours on the chair in Cora's room.

Early the next morning, Cora moaned as her eyes fluttered, and then she opened them slowly. She blinked several times, and then she pulled her hand from Elizabeth's grasp and rested it against her stomach. Tears immediately started streaming down the sides of her face.

"I lost another baby." She sobbed.

"No, Cora. We have a beautiful baby girl." Brian held her hand against his chest.

"Really?" She turned to Elizabeth.

"She's in the neonatal unit. The doctor said she's as strong as her mom. She's just a little early." Elizabeth said as she smiled down at her daughter.

"So, everything is okay." Cora sighed and wiped away a tear.

"Baby, there is one thing." Brian glanced at Elizabeth.

"What?" Cora's eyes went back and forth between her mother and Brian.

"Ducky, you were bleeding a lot, and they almost lost you." Elizabeth cupped her daughter's cheek.

"What happened?" Cora whispered.

"The doctor had to do a partial hysterectomy," Elizabeth explained.

"No." Cora's eyes filled with tears, and she shook her head.

Cora turned on her side and winced. She had an incision that had to be painful, but she would heal. Elizabeth was concerned with how Cora would deal with the news. Hopefully, when she got to see her beautiful baby girl, it would help with the sadness.

"Cora, I know this is hard, but you do have a baby girl who needs you." Elizabeth ran her hand up and down Cora's back.

"Your mom is right," Brian whispered.

Elizabeth handed her daughter the box of tissues on the table next to her bed. While they waited for Cora to pull herself together, Brian went to ask the nurse if they could take Cora to see the baby.

When Brian returned, he had an enormous smile on his face as he pushed a wheelchair into the room. Cora slowly sat up in the bed and wiped her eyes. He seemed pretty proud of himself as he stepped inside the room.

"Do you want to go see her?" Brian smiled.

"Yes." Cora nodded.

"Your chariot awaits." Brian pushed the chair next to the bed.

Elizabeth helped her daughter out of bed, and she eased into the chair. Brian placed a blanket over Cora's legs and made sure she was comfortable before they headed out of the room to see their baby. Elizabeth sat in the recliner in the room and smiled as they walked through the door.

"Betty, I think your granddaughter is expecting to see you too," Brian said as he turned around in the doorway.

"Are you sure you don't want to do this with just the two of you?" Elizabeth had to hold herself back from running after them.

"Mom, I need you with me." Cora glanced over her shoulder.

Elizabeth hurried behind them and couldn't contain the excitement of seeing the baby as she followed Cora and Brian down the corridor.

The nurse led them to an incubator on the other side of the unit. The baby looked so tiny in the machine, but her full head of hair stood out. Elizabeth stood behind Cora's chair while they looked into the incubator.

"She's doing amazing." The young nurse smiled.

"She's so tiny," Cora whispered.

"She's a good size for a premature baby. She's a little over five pounds, and she's breathing on her own. We're just keeping her warm and making sure she's getting nutrition. We'll probably get you feeding her tomorrow," the nurse explained.

"Do you have a name picked out?" Elizabeth asked.

"Yeah, we're naming her Pamela Louise." Cora looked up at her mom.

"That's beautiful. Your father will be so happy, and I'm sure Brian's mother will be too." Elizabeth hugged Cora as they watched little Pamela squirm.

"You're my little miracle," Cora whispered as she touched the incubator. "I'm probably going to drive you crazy from loving you so much."

"She looks just like you when you were born." Elizabeth smiled.

As heartbreaking as it was for Cora to lose her dream of having more children, they still had Pamela. No baby would ever be loved more. Elizabeth knew that for sure.

Chapter 35

Over the next few years, they welcomed four more children into the family. A week after Pamela was born, Alice gave birth to Jessica Kathleen. A year later, Kathleen and Sean had Nicholas Sean. A little over a year later, Alice had another girl named Kristy Elizabeth, and Kathleen gave birth to Aaron Jacob nine months later.

With eleven grandchildren, Elizabeth couldn't be happier, and she spent a lot of time in Hopedale helping with the children. Most days, Jack would stay back in Cape Broyle, but on days he did come, the youngsters would be all over him. Especially John and James. They were eight years old and loved to spend time with Jack.

John had become obsessed with his Halloween costume from the previous year. He was constantly running around as Batman and Kathleen would have to let him wear it under his school uniform, or he would get upset.

"I don't know what I'm going to do with him. When I tell him I need to wash it, he sits in front of the washer and dryer until it comes out," Kathleen complained as Elizabeth fed little Aaron.

"It's a phase. He'll grow out of it," Elizabeth told her.

"I hope so, it's already getting short on him, and if he grows out of it, I don't know what he'll do." Kathleen chuckled as Nicholas, or Nicky as everyone called the toddler, started dancing to a children's show on television.

"Nanny, what does this word say?" Keith held up a children's book to her.

"That word is *caterpillar*, Keithy," Elizabeth smiled down at her almost five-year-old grandson.

He repeated the word then ran off back to the living room where he'd been sitting with a bundle of books most of the day. Keith was different from his brothers. He started reading from the age of three and could recite books after reading them once.

Kathleen and Sean found out that Keith had an eidetic memory, but most people referred to it as a photographic memory. Since he was starting school the following year, they weren't sure what would happen since he was so far advanced.

"He's reading to Mikey." Elizabeth smiled as she placed Aaron inside the bassinet.

"He does that a lot. I think it's because they're so close in age," Kathleen replied.

Elizabeth followed her daughter-in-law back into the kitchen, and they both sat with a cup of tea. Kathleen sat where she could watch the boys in the other room. Ian, John, and James were outside with Jack and Sean.

"I'm so exhausted." Kathleen sighed.

"I'm sure you are. You have seven children, boys at that." Elizabeth reached across and grasped Kathleen's hand.

"I know, but Sean's been working so much, and if it wasn't for you and Geraldine, I don't know what I would do." Kathleen's eyes filled with tears.

"Honey, why don't you go lay down for a bit?" Elizabeth suggested.

"I can't. I've got to start supper and laundry…" Kathleen began, but Elizabeth stopped her.

"I'll start supper. You go get some rest." Elizabeth stood up and ushered Kathleen to the stairs.

"Betty, seven little boys are a lot." Kathleen resisted.

"I can handle them, and if I need assistance, I'll pull Jack and Sean inside to help." Elizabeth pointed to the stairs. "Now, get upstairs."

"Thank you, Betty." Kathleen sighed.

Sean walked into the living room a short time later. Elizabeth knew she had to talk to her son about Kathleen. He was working hard, but he needed to see his wife was overwhelmed.

"Sean, can I talk to you for a minute?" Elizabeth asked.

"When you ask like that, I feel like I'm in trouble and going to be grounded." Sean chuckled.

Elizabeth motioned to the kitchen table, and Sean sat down. She settled the boys in the living room and joined Sean in the kitchen. Her son was oblivious to what was going on with Kathleen.

"Sean, you've been working a lot," Elizabeth started.

"Yes," Sean answered.

"You also have seven children all under the age of nine," Elizabeth continued.

"Stating the obvious, Mudder." Sean smirked.

"Your wife is exhausted, and she needs you," Elizabeth said bluntly.

"I try to help when I'm home, but when I try, I feel like I'm in the way." Sean folded his hands in front of him.

"You're working long hours," Elizabeth went on.

"I've been discussing opening a practice with Robert Connolly here in Hopedale. It's just going to put a dent in our savings to do it," Sean told her.

"So, do it," Elizabeth replied.

"Mudder, with seven youngsters, I don't know if I can take that chance. I need to make sure I have a guaranteed income coming in." Sean sighed.

"You can't afford not to take a chance. Kathleen needs you." Elizabeth reached across the table and placed her hands on top of Sean's folded hands.

"You think I should do this?" Sean asked.

"I do," Kathleen's voice startled Elizabeth.

Sean turned around as Kathleen entered the kitchen. She sat next to her husband and Elizabeth stood up to leave the room. The couple needed to talk, and she was happy that they were finally talking.

"Betty, stay please," Kathleen said.

"I think you need to talk alone." Elizabeth turned and made her way into the living room where the youngsters were.

Entertaining seven little boys wasn't easy, but thankfully Jack and the three older boys had come inside and were building something on the table with blocks with Keith and Ian. Nick was falling asleep on the couch, probably exhausted from everyone trying to get him to say Aaron's name correctly. For some reason, he always referred to Aaron as Aday. Sean had joked that he was probably calling him A.J. The nickname fit since it was the baby's initials.

As Elizabeth placed baby Aaron in the bassinet, Jack plopped down on the couch and blew out a breath. The grandchildren seemed to have taken all the energy out of her husband. Elizabeth felt drained as well.

"I don't know how Sean and Kathleen do it." Jack chuckled as Elizabeth sat next to him.

"It's not easy. Kathleen is overwhelmed, which is why she's talking to Sean. It seems your son doesn't realize how much is on her shoulders," Elizabeth said.

"Why is he my son when he is doing something wrong?" Jack chuckled.

"It's not that he's wrong, it's that he didn't see what Kathleen was going through," Elizabeth replied.

"They'll figure it out." Jack wrapped his arm around her shoulders and kissed her temple.

Jack was right, Sean and Kathleen were a strong couple who loved each other deeply. They just hit a little snag and would work things out. Maybe starting a practice would be the solution because he'd be home every evening with his family.

Elizabeth helped Kathleen put the children down for the night while Sean talked to his father about what it would take to start a practice in Hopedale. Since there wasn't a doctor in the small town, they would have a monopoly on patients.

By the time Jack and Elizabeth left to go home, Sean and his friend were ready to start the move to open a medical office in Hopedale. He'd also made a promise to his wife to be home more, and in turn, she would help him every way she could to get his practice up and running.

Elizabeth didn't know what would happen in the future, but she prayed that everyone would be happy. There was nothing else she and Jack wanted more than that.

Chapter 36

Elizabeth sat in the auditorium excitedly waiting for her grandson to walk out on stage and perform his first solo. Kathleen was a little worried about James since he said he wasn't feeling well when he left for school that morning.

"I hope he's okay," Kathleen said as the choir filled the bleachers on the stage.

John and James were in grade eleven, and Ian was in grade ten. All three boys were in the Holy Cross high school choir. It seemed as if all her grandsons took after their father.

Kathleen and Sean were told by the school that each of the boys could play several musical instruments and had an excellent ear for music. Every Sunday, the boys sang in the church choir and took regular music lessons in piano and guitar.

"He'll be fine, ducky," Elizabeth assured Kathleen.

The choir began to sing, and James stepped forward to the front of the stage. Elizabeth smiled as the light illuminated on her grandson, and his voice floated through the auditorium. He'd gotten through the first few lines in the song when his face turned deathly white.

The next thing anyone knew, James gagged, and he threw up over the edge of the stage. When a young girl jumped up from the front seats, she screamed. James lifted his head, and his eyes widened in horror.

"Oh dear," Kathleen jumped out of her seat and made her way to the back of the auditorium.

Elizabeth followed, and they hurried to the chorus room where the choir waited until it was their turn to go on stage. When they walked in, James was sitting on a chair with his head hung over a bucket.

"Let's get you home, Jimmy." Kathleen crouched next to her son.

"Yeah, and find me a new school," James grumbled.

"Oh, Jimmy, don't worry, you'll be okay." Kathleen rubbed her hand up and down James back.

"Mom, I just puked over one of the most popular girls from the girls' school. I'll never be able to show my face again." James stood up, grabbed the bucket, and stomped into the bathroom.

"The poor boy is so embarrassed." Kathleen sighed.

"He'll be just fine," Elizabeth returned.

"Did you see her face? That was so funny," A boy said as he walked by Kathleen and Elizabeth.

"O'Connor is not going to live that down." Another boy chuckled.

"Why don't you two shut up before I shut you up?" John appeared in front of the boys.

"Johnny, that's enough," Kathleen warned.

The other two boys looked from Elizabeth to Kathleen then immediately walked off. John looked almost as upset as James did, which wasn't unusual for the two boys.

"I'm going to go check on James." Ian walked by them and hurried into the restroom where James had gone.

Since it was late and they didn't want to drive back to Cape Broyle, Elizabeth and Jack followed Sean back to his house. According to Kathleen, the ride back to Hopedale was quiet, and James went right to his room when he got home.

Elizabeth always found it hard to sleep in a strange bed, and instead of keeping Jack awake, she went to the kitchen to have a cup of tea. The house was unusually quiet, which was why she heard James come into the kitchen.

"I didn't realize anyone was up," James said as he opened the fridge.

"Grandda is snoring like a bear," Elizabeth said, hoping it would get a smile out of her grandson.

"Mom says Dad snores too." James turned and leaned against the counter after he poured himself a glass of juice.

"Is your belly feeling better?" Elizabeth asked.

"No, I think I'm going to be sick like this for the rest of the school year." James groaned.

"Jimmy, come sit." Elizabeth pointed to the chair across from her.

"Nan, I can't go back to that school after what happened." James sighed as he sat.

"You can because you're an O'Connor. You can face anything," Elizabeth told him.

"Nan, I puked over a girl. A girl that I like. She'll never go out with me now." James sighed.

"Then you weren't meant to go out with her. What about that girl you were paling around with over the summer when you were in Cape Broyle?" Elizabeth asked as she tried to remember the girl's name.

"Are you talking about Sarah Mason?" James linked his fingers and rested them on top of his head.

"Yes, the Mason girl. You two seemed close," Elizabeth returned.

"Yeah, but she lives in Cape Broyle, and I live in Hopedale. It'll never work. Maybe when I get my driver's license, I'll ask her out." James shrugged.

"Have you asked your Aunt Cora what she thinks?" Elizabeth asked.

"Nan, please don't tell me Aunt Cora will tell me who I should be with," James scoffed.

"She's never been wrong, Jimmy." Elizabeth touched James' hand and gave it a gentle pat.

"I don't know, Nan. I'm only fifteen years old. I'm not going to be looking to settle down any time soon. I need to figure out how to convince Mom and Dad to let me transfer schools." James sighed.

"Jimmy, don't let one bad moment in your life make you forget all the good ones." Elizabeth tried to remind her grandson of all the times he'd enjoyed his performances.

"I don't think I'll ever be able to stand on stage again, Nan." James stood up and hugged her before he spoke again. "But thanks for the chat. I love you, Nan."

"I love you too, Jimmy." Elizabeth smiled as she watched him leave the room.

The years were flying by so fast, sometimes Elizabeth felt as if she would blink and a year would pass by. Of course, probably because a lot of the people she grew up with, and the older people in her community were dying off.

It was sad to think about and a little scary. Elizabeth just turned sixty years old, only seven years younger than her mother when she passed away. Elizabeth knew she was definitely in better health than her mother, but who knew what the future held?

Then there was Jack, he was slowing down, and although he tried to stick to the doctor's orders, she'd noticed he was getting short of breath quicker than he used to. He'd also turned over most of the duties for the boats and plant to managers he trusted.

Jack said it was because he wanted to spend more time with her and the grandchildren, but she had a feeling he knew he wasn't as spry as he once was. It was hard for her to see the strong, virile man she married fight against his weakening heart.

Jack still tried to stay active, and he faithfully took the medication the doctors gave him. He would still sneak something he shouldn't eat sometimes, but otherwise, he was doing well. She prayed they would have many more years together. Losing him was something she wasn't ready to do.

Chapter 37

Turning sixty-five should be an incredible milestone, but Elizabeth felt as if her heart was shattering. She stood next to the hospital bed while she watched her best friend and sister-in-law struggle to take her last few breaths.

Geraldine had been diagnosed with cancer in her liver more than a year earlier. She had gone through chemotherapy and radiation treatments, but the disease was aggressive and spread through her body.

She and Charlie had planned to travel after he retired, but only six months after his final day at work, she started getting sick. They had managed to visit Niagara Falls and Ireland, but after the trip to the Emerald Isle, she quickly went downhill.

The doctors had told the family that it was only a matter of days, maybe hours before she lost her battle. She'd slipped into a coma the day before Elizabeth's sixty-fifth birthday and only got weaker with each passing hour.

"She's so yellow," Kathleen whispered.

"The doctor said that was normal with her condition," Elizabeth replied.

"Sean finally got Charlie to go and get a bite to eat." Kathleen smoothed her hand over Geraldine's bald head.

"He's terrified he won't be here when she passes." Cora sighed from where she sat at the foot of the bed.

"Ian has been studying so hard and feels so terrible for not being here," Kathleen said.

"Geraldine wouldn't want him jeopardizing his first year of medical school," Elizabeth replied softly.

"That's what Charlie told him." Kathleen walked to the window.

It was hard to believe that some of the grandchildren already finished high school. John and James had entered the police academy and started their first year on the job. Ian was in medical school, Keith had graduated high school the previous year and was in his first year of university, but he was unsure of what he wanted to do.

Isabelle was in her last year of high school with preparations of going away to school to become a chef. Kurt wasn't happy about his daughter moving away and made it known to everyone. Thankfully, Isabelle was as stubborn as her father and didn't back down.

"You should probably go home and get some rest too, Betty," Kathleen said softly.

345

"Ducky, I'm just fine. Don't you worry about me. Maybe you should get some rest, though," Elizabeth suggested.

"I can't leave. I'm afraid I won't be here when she…" Kathleen pressed her lips together, and her eyes filled with tears.

Elizabeth understood the need to be with Geraldine in her last hours. It wasn't the best experience to be with someone when they were dying, but nobody wanted a person they loved to die alone.

It was a little after eight in the evening when the door to the room opened. Kurt barged in through the door with panic written all over his face.

"Mudder, you need to come with me," Kurt told her.

"For heaven's sake, Kurt, what's wrong?" Elizabeth asked.

"I just came to the hospital with Fadder. They think he had a heart attack." Kurt took Elizabeth's hand.

"What?" Elizabeth could barely get the word out.

"He's in the emergency room," Kurt said.

Elizabeth glanced at Kathleen and then Geraldine. She knew that her sister-in-law would demand she got to Jack's side. She gave Geraldine a kiss on the forehead, and as she walked with Kurt to the emergency department, the thought that it was the last time she'd probably see her sister-in-law alive caused a tear to slip down her cheek.

"Mudder, don't worry." Kurt wrapped his arm around her shoulder as they stepped into the room.

"Darling, don't worry, I'm fine." Jack sat propped up in the bed.

His face was pale, and he had an oxygen tube under his nose. His chest was bare, and several white stickers were stuck to his skin with wires leading to the heart monitor behind the bed. He had an IV attached to his hand, and his hair was disheveled as if he'd been running his hands through it.

"Don't worry? Are you out of your mind Jack O'Connor? Of course, I'm going to worry when I find out you might have had a heart attack." Elizabeth took his hand and held it to her chest.

"They don't know yet. The doctors have to wait for some test results." Jack glared over her shoulder at Kurt.

She knew the look because he gave it to the boys when he was upset with them. The children called it the devil's glare but would say Elizabeth's glare was more terrifying when she was angry.

"I'm sorry, Fadder. I had to tell her." Kurt shrugged.

"Don't you be sorry, Kurt and don't you be giving him a hard time," Elizabeth chastised her husband.

"No point arguing with you, is it?" Jack chuckled but cringed and grabbed his chest.

"Jack, are you okay?" Elizabeth didn't like the way his face paled, and he winced in pain.

"Just a twinge, my love." He smiled, but she knew it was forced.

"Jack, don't lie to me," Elizabeth warned.

Before he could respond, two doctors came into the room. One was about Kurt's age, and the other one looked barely old enough to be out of school.

"You must be Mrs. O'Connor," The older man held out his hand.

"Mrs. O'Connor was my mother-in-law. Call me, Betty, please." Elizabeth smiled at the doctor.

"Betty, I'm Dr. Ted Cramer. I'm the cardiologist on call. Dr. Philips asked me to come examine your husband," he told her.

"So, what's the verdict, doc?" Jack asked.

"I've examined your blood work, and it looks like you have had a heart attack," Dr. Cramer explained.

"Is he going to be okay?" Elizabeth felt Jack squeeze her hand.

"We're going to keep him here for a couple of days. I have to run a couple of more tests, but I'm leaning toward a bypass surgery." Dr. Cramer glanced at the young doctor. "Dr. Philips is my resident, and he's going to get you admitted."

Elizabeth's heart pounded in her chest. Jack would probably need surgery on his heart. She couldn't let him see how scared she was because that would only make Jack more stressed.

"I don't want to stay in this place, Betty. I can't sleep without you," Jack complained.

"I'm sure you'll sleep just fine. You have to stay here, and that's it. I'm not going home, so I'll still be here." Elizabeth glanced at Kurt. "I need you to let Sean and Cora know what's going on and check on Kathleen."

"Jesus, the last thing this family needs is me being stuck in hospital when Geraldine is dying." Jack sighed.

"My wife wouldn't want you jeopardizing your health, Jack." Elizabeth turned at the sound of Charlie's voice.

"You're as bad as your sister," Jack grumbled.

"Don't screw around with this, Jack. Let the doctors do what they have to." Charlie hugged Elizabeth. "Geraldine doesn't have much time left and you risking your life is not going to change that."

The words from Charlie seemed to settle Jack down, and Charlie gave Elizabeth a comforting hug before he left the room. She felt guilty for not being by her brother's side while he was about to lose his wife, but she had to be with Jack. The realization of what could have happened if Kurt hadn't been with his father made her body tremble.

"Betty, I'm okay. Come here." Jack tugged her toward him, and he wrapped his arms around her.

"No, you're not. You may need surgery." Elizabeth rested her head against his chest.

"I'll be fine," Jack whispered and pressed his lips against the top of her head.

It wasn't turning out to be the best birthday week, but she was going to make sure that Jack got the best care. The thought that she could have lost Jack strengthened her resolve, and she sat up straight.

"Jack O'Connor, you better get well soon. You're not leaving me alone." Elizabeth held his face between her hands and gazed into his blue eyes.

"I'm not going anywhere, darling. Only the good die young." Jack winked.

Chapter 38

Jack had gone into surgery two weeks later for a double bypass but ended up having a quadruple one. He made it through the surgery and was in intensive care for a few days. Jack woke several times during the night but didn't make sense when he did. The nurse told her that it was the pain medication, and he was doing fine.

Geraldine had passed away three days after the doctors admitted Jack. He wasn't permitted to leave the hospital for the funeral, and he'd gotten upset, but the doctor didn't feel comfortable enough to allow Jack to go.

Charlie was struggling, and Elizabeth felt horrible for not being there when her brother needed her most. He had gone to stay with Sean and Kathleen, so she was relieved he wasn't alone. It was still hard to believe that her best friend was gone. Geraldine had been there for her for so long. It was hard to think about life without her.

Elizabeth had spent more than forty-eight hours at the hospital, and she fell asleep in the chair in the family waiting room. It was quiet time in the Intensive Care Unit, and she had to leave for an hour.

She didn't know how long she'd been sleeping when she felt a hand on her shoulder. She looked up to see Dr. Cramer stood over her.

"Dr., is everything okay?" Elizabeth sat up.

"I'm sorry, I didn't mean to worry you. I just checked on your husband, and we're going to be moving him out of ICU." The doctor sat next to her and smiled.

"He's ready for that?" Elizabeth asked.

"Betty, your husband is a tough cookie. He still needs to take it easy for a while, but he's on the mend," Dr. Cramer told her.

"That's wonderful news." Elizabeth shook the doctor's hand.

By the time she called the family and told them the good news, she was able to be with Jack again. He was sitting up in the bed, and although he was a little pale, his smile lit up his face.

"You're looking wonderful." Elizabeth sat on the chair next to the bed.

"I'd feel wonderful if I could get out of this joint," Jack grumbled.

"You're moving to a new room. Does that help?" Elizabeth smiled.

"I'd like to move to my own bedroom, where I can sleep next to my wife." Jack took her hand.

"It won't be long, and you'll be home, just have some patience." Elizabeth stood up and kissed his cheek.

She wasn't wrong, because two weeks later she was in the car with her husband on the way back to Cape Broyle. Jack still had to take it easy for a while, but since Dr. Cramer was from the next community, he set up Jack's appointments for his home office.

After several weeks, Jack was back on his feet. He still had certain things he couldn't do, and he'd decided to sell the fish processing plant as well as all of his fishing boats. The only one Jack kept was the first one his father owned. He'd take the children and grandchildren fishing frequently, and Jack knew they would be disappointed to lose it.

"I feel like a burden to everyone," Jack said one evening as she brought him his medication.

"Don't be foolish. You're not a burden. We're doing this because we love you and want you to stay with us for a long time." Elizabeth crouched in front of him.

"I'm not used to sitting around like a lump on a log." Jack cupped her cheek.

"I know, darling. You'll be able to do more as the weeks go on. Please let us do this for you. I love you so much, and I can't stand the thought of going through what my brother is dealing with." Elizabeth choked out the words as a tear ran down her cheek.

"I love you too, my love. I'll try not to be a grump." Jack sighed.

When she kissed his cheek, he gave her a smile. It brightened his face and made him look even more handsome, if that was possible. They may be getting older, but to her, Jack still made her heart flutter, and her body ached for him.

The thought of a life without Jack was unthinkable to her. She was so worried about him. He survived the heart attack and surgery, but he wasn't invincible. The only thing Elizabeth could do was make sure she took care of him because she wouldn't survive the pain if she lost him.

Chapter 39

Elizabeth thanked God for every day she had with Jack. He'd had two heart attacks over the last five years, with the last one doing a great deal of damage. She didn't know how much longer she would have him, but she would make the most of every day.

Alice had decided to open a pub and diner in Hopedale. It had been her dream since the children were young to have a restaurant of her own, but since the town only had a soda shop, she knew both the pub and diner would be a hit.

The whole family helped to get things ready for the opening, but they were still not set on a name. Kurt had suggested calling it *Grub,* but Alice didn't like it since it didn't say there was a pub as well. She also kept both sections separate so that patrons could come in to eat with their families.

"How about *Grub and Pub*?" Kurt suggested as he and Sean assembled one of the tables.

"No," Alice sighed while she unboxed the utensils.

"*Alice's Diner*?" Sean interjected.

"That doesn't let anyone know there is a pub," Kathleen returned.

"*Eat and Drink?*" Charlie chuckled.

"Absolutely not." Alice laughed.

Jack was quiet as he helped Charlie fill the salt and pepper shakers. It was the only thing Elizabeth could think of for them to do. Charlie and Jack were two men that hated to feel like they were useless, and even with all the work left to do around the building, there wasn't a lot of the heavy stuff that they could do.

Her brother was seventy-five and had been confined to a wheelchair a couple of years earlier. He lost his leg after he fell off the dock and the leg slipped between a boat and the dock. Charlie had gone out fishing with Jack, Sean, Kurt, Nick, and Aaron, but when he stepped off the vessel, he didn't see the fish guts on the ground and slipped.

"How about *Jack's Place?*" Jack smirked.

Elizabeth knew he meant it as a joke, but when everyone stopped and stared at him, it hit her that it would be the perfect name. When she glanced at Alice, she could see her daughter-in-law thought the same thing.

"Oh, my God, that's perfect." Alice squealed and ran around the counter.

"I was kidding." Jack laughed as Alice wrapped her arms around his neck.

"I love it." Alice smiled at him.

Elizabeth saw tears form in Jack's eyes, and he dropped his head in an attempt to hide it. She knew the fact that Alice would call her business after him had moved him to tears.

"*Jack's Place,* it is then." Kurt grinned.

"Now, we just need to get someone to design a sign." Alice sighed.

"How's this?" Charlie held up a napkin he'd been doodling on and handed it to Alice.

Elizabeth glanced over Alice's shoulder and saw the drawing. Charlie wrote the words *Jack's Place* in cursive with *diner* and *pub* under in smaller letters. On one side of the name were two beer steins filled and foam on the top. It was perfect.

"Wow, that's it." Alice jumped up and down.

"Let's get you to the printers in St. John's before they close. Once we get the menus and the sign done, we can open this place." Kurt wrapped his arms around his wife.

"I'm so excited." Alice kissed Kurt hard on the mouth. "Thanks, Jack and Charlie."

Three months later, *Jack's Place* was open for business. It quickly became a favorite of the town, and Elizabeth would smile anytime she walked into the crowded place, and Jack would grin with pride.

"They're only here because my name is on this place," Jack teased Alice.

"Why do you think I used your name?" Alice chuckled.

"'Cause you're a smart cookie." Jack winked at her.

The only thing putting a damper on the celebrations was Charlie had passed away a week after the opening. He'd come down with pneumonia and wasn't able to fight it off. The family struggled with the loss, but they knew her brother was finally happy again. He was with the love of his life and the baby they lost so long ago.

Elizabeth did her best to stay strong but losing the only other family member that she grew up with was difficult. She and Jack were the only members of their families that were left. It was hard to believe that time passed so fast.

"Do you think it would be okay if I had a piece of Alice's blueberry pie?" Jack smirked.

"A small piece." Elizabeth narrowed her eyes but couldn't help the smile that formed on her face at his joy in having a piece of pie in front of him.

Over the next few months, the family excitedly prepared for Aaron and Kristy's graduation from high school as well as celebrating James' engagement to Sarah Mason. The couple had been seeing each other since James' last year of high school.

The rest of the grandchildren were following their own dreams. James and John were working as police officers with the

Newfoundland Police Department. Ian started his residency at the hospital in St. John's, and Mike was in his second year of university. He also was going to the University of Toronto to follow his dream of becoming a lawyer.

Nick had also decided to become a lawyer and was finishing his first year of university. Isabelle was in Ottawa and would be home for the summer. She was in chef school in Ontario and doing great.

Jess started university as well and hoping to graduate with a degree in business. She also worked part-time at a flower shop in the city, which didn't surprise anyone since the girl was a natural with horticulture.

Kristy had plans to go into nursing but wanted to take a year off school to travel. Aaron had plans to do the courses he needed at university to allow him to get into the police academy, and Pam had decided she wanted to go to design school in Ontario, much to Cora's dismay.

However, the family was excited and looking forward to the celebrations over the summer. Jack was a little quiet during supper that night, and when she asked what was wrong, he tried to brush it off. Elizabeth could tell by the paleness of his face. He wasn't okay.

"Jack, are you having pain?" Elizabeth asked.

"Nah, nothing I can't handle." Jack winked at her as he went to get up from the supper table.

When he stumbled and immediately sat down again, Elizabeth jumped up and went to him. He looked at her, and she immediately could see the fear in his eyes.

"You're having chest pain, aren't you?" Elizabeth asked.

Jack nodded.

Elizabeth called for an ambulance, and by the time it got there, Jack was having issues breathing. She didn't know if she breathed the entire way to the hospital, and her heart thudded in her chest as she waited for the medical staff to allow her to be by Jack's side.

She called Kurt, Sean, and Cora while she waited, and it gave her something to do to keep herself from thinking the worst. It was almost an hour before the doctor came to get her and tell her Jack was stable.

Elizabeth sat in the family room with her children and their spouses while the young doctor explained the situation. The words that he was saying didn't seem to sink in as Elizabeth glanced at Sean to see if he understood.

"There's nothing else we can do for him?" Sean asked as he gripped Elizabeth's hand.

"His heart has received a lot of damage with the last couple of attacks," the doctor explained.

"You're saying we're going to lose him," Cora choked.

"I'm sorry." The doctor obviously felt terrible for giving them the bad news.

"I want to see my husband." Elizabeth stood up and tugged her blouse down over her hips.

"Mudder, we need to see what to do next," Kurt interrupted.

"Is there anything you can do?" Elizabeth stared at the doctor.

"I'm sorry, no," the doctor responded.

"Well, I don't want to waste one more minute of the time we have together. I want to see Jack." Elizabeth hung her little black purse over her arm.

Nobody else said a word as the doctor opened the door to the family room. Elizabeth straightened her shoulders and followed the young man to the intensive care unit.

Elizabeth didn't want to know how much time Jack had left. All she wanted was to be with him for every precious second they had left together. Preparing herself for living without him seemed impossible, but she had to be strong for Jack and her family.

"There's the love of my life." Jack's voice was low, but his smile beamed.

"You didn't think I abandoned you, did you?" Elizabeth forced a smile.

"What's wrong?" Jack's smile disappeared, and he reached for her hand.

"Nothing." Elizabeth brought his hand up to her lips.

"Betty, darling, you're not a good liar." Jack glanced behind her as the doctor walked into the room.

Elizabeth watched him as the doctor explained everything to Jack. His expression didn't show how he felt, but the more the doctor said, the tighter he gripped Elizabeth's hand.

"I guess that's that." Jack nodded as he turned back to Elizabeth.

"Let's not dwell on that." Elizabeth smiled.

"I'm not going home again, Betty." Jack's eyes filled with tears.

"If you want to go home, we'll take you home," Elizabeth told him adamantly.

"It's better if I stay here," Jack replied.

Elizabeth spent every night at the hospital for almost three weeks. Jack was moved into a private room, and most nights, she would lay with him, holding her in his arms. They would talk about the past and how proud he was of his children and grandchildren.

One day, Aaron came to see Jack, and he looked as if he'd lost his best friend. When Jack asked Aaron how things were with his girlfriend, Aaron's jaw clenched, and he turned to look out the window.

"A.J., are you okay?" Elizabeth asked.

"Bethany went to Ontario to live with her sister." Aaron's voice sounded strained.

"Are you going to move there too?" Jack asked.

"No, Grandda. Bethany and I are over." Aaron straightened his shoulders and sat on the foot of the bed. "How about a game of crib?"

While Aaron stayed with Jack and played cards, Elizabeth took the time to go to Sean and Kathleen's house to get cleaned up. Sean was at the kitchen table when she arrived and asked her to sit before she returned to the hospital.

"Mudder, I know you don't want to talk about this right now, but Kathleen and I have been discussing this. When it's Fadder's time, we want you to come live with us," Sean said it so fast she wondered if she'd heard him right.

"Move out of Cape Broyle?" Elizabeth stared at her son.

"Mudder, your whole family lives here in Hopedale. I don't want you living alone." Sean reached across and covered her hand with his.

"Sean, I don't want to talk about this now. I got to get back to your fadder." Elizabeth stood up and quickly turned away from her son.

She didn't want him to see the tears in her eyes. It was the realization that when she did return home, it would be alone. Jack wasn't leaving the hospital, and she'd resigned herself to that, but she never thought about what would happen after.

Elizabeth was back at the hospital and barely remembered the drive. Her mind focused on getting back to Jack, and nothing else mattered.

That night while she lay next to him, Jack held her tighter than he had ever before. Elizabeth wrapped her arm around him and rested her head on his chest, listening to his heart while it was still beating.

"Betty, I don't have much time left," Jack whispered.

"Jack…" Elizabeth choked, but he stopped her.

"I want to say this before it's too late." Jack's voice was raspy.

Elizabeth lifted her head and met his gaze. His eyes were glistening with tears, and she swallowed the lump that formed in her throat at the sight of a tear slipping down the side of his face.

"I want you to know that no man has ever been as happy as I have been with you. Things weren't always easy, but we always had love. When I'm gone, I want you to promise me you'll live your life to the fullest." Jack cupped her cheek.

"Jack, I'm going to be lost without you." Elizabeth closed her eyes as she choked out the words.

"My love, I'll always be with you, but I want you to live your life when I'm gone. Don't waste the time you have left on this earth grieving over me." Jack wiped a tear from her cheek.

"You're my whole heart, Jack." Elizabeth sniffed.

"Nah, Tommy Roberts still has a piece of it." Jack smirked.

"Stop it," Elizabeth grumbled.

"Sure, sometimes I was a little jealous that he was your first love, and who knows, after I'm gone, maybe God has another love for you." Jack smiled.

"You're out of your bloody mind." Elizabeth snorted.

"Whatever happens after I'm gone, I know that I could never have loved anyone the way I love you. You gave me a better life than any man deserves," Jack whispered as he pulled her into his arms, and they lay together silently until they both fell asleep.

Three days later, Jack slipped into a coma. The family was struggling with saying goodbye, and since Jack had signed a Do Not Resuscitate order, they knew it was only a matter of time before his heart stopped.

Each of the grandchildren had entered the room to say their final farewell. It was difficult to see each of them leave the room sobbing and tears running down their faces, but Elizabeth did her best to comfort each of them.

"Mom, do you want to go get something to eat?" Cora asked on the day after Jack's coma started.

"I'm fine, ducky. You go get a bite to eat." Elizabeth sat next to Jack, running her hand up and down his arm.

"Mom, you need to eat." Cora wrapped her arms around Elizabeth from behind.

"I will when I'm hungry," Elizabeth whispered.

Elizabeth lay on the bed next to Jack and pressed her ear against his chest. She closed her eyes and listened to his labored breaths and the awkward thud of his heart.

"You know what, Jack? I think we have raised the most amazing youngsters any two people could ever have. I look at them, and I see you in each of them. I see your handsome face, your strength, your amazing kindness, and your incredible presence." Elizabeth didn't even bother to wipe away the tears that fell from her eyes.

"Our grandchildren are turning out to be another piece of you that I get to hold on to when you leave me. I know you can't stay, but I'm terrified over what life will be like without you. This world will not be the same without you, but I'll keep my promise and try to live my life to the fullest. I'll need you watching over me to give me the strength," Elizabeth whispered as she turned her head and kissed his chest. "I love you, my darling."

Less than forty hours later, Jack took his final breath with Elizabeth next to him and surrounded by the family. It was peaceful, and she knew he wouldn't suffer anymore. Elizabeth was the last to leave the room, and she whispered in his ear one last time before leaving.

"I'll see you again someday, my love." Elizabeth kissed his lips and turned to leave the room.

Jack's funeral was beautiful, and she was so happy when her grandsons joined the choir during the service. There wasn't a dry eye in the church when Aaron, Nick, and Mike stepped forward and sang "Go Rest High on that Mountain" by Vince Gill. Jack loved the song from the first time he heard it and would always have Sean's boys sing it for him.

Everyone from Cape Broyle and the surrounding communities packed the church. They came to celebrate Jack's life, and she couldn't help but feel a sense of pride. Elizabeth was relieved that it was summer because there was no way everyone from the church would fit inside the house.

"Jack was a wonderful man," one man said as he shook hands with Elizabeth.

"He was a great boss," another told her.

Everyone raved about what a great man her husband was. Not that she needed anyone to tell her because Elizabeth knew better than anyone. It was the reason when everyone was finally gone that she sat on her bed with his old sweater and finally allowed herself to let the tears flow.

"Sean wants me to move in with him and Kathleen, but I can't get rid of this house. Our whole life was here, Jack," she whispered in the silence of the room. "We were happy here and raised our family here. I could never say goodbye to that, but I can't live here without you."

She glanced around the room where everything conjured up a memory of her life with him. A chair where he would read before bed, a half bottle of Old Spice aftershave that he would slap on every morning, even a crumpled piece of paper that he'd tossed on the dresser instead of throwing it away.

"Why did you always forget to throw stuff in the garbage?" Elizabeth chuckled as she picked up the paper.

She glanced down to see the last pair of socks he'd dropped on the floor before he went to the hospital. He never put them in the hamper, and no matter how often she reminded him, he'd still forget.

"You're still here, aren't you, darling?" Elizabeth left the socks where they were and made her way out of the room.

The thought of sleeping in the bed without Jack made it hard to breathe. She wouldn't be able to sleep in their bed without him. Maybe Sean and Kurt were right. She needed to be closer to family. She'd sent them all home after the funeral, but Keith had refused to leave.

Elizabeth found him on the front porch sitting in Jack's old chair. She sat in the chair next to him. They both sat quietly for several minutes before Keith finally spoke.

"I'm going to take Grandda's advice and go to Yellowknife," Keith said softly.

"I see." Elizabeth nodded.

"I don't know what I want to do, but something is pointing me there," Keith continued.

368

"You do what's in your heart," Elizabeth told her grandson.

"Nan, can I ask you something?" Keith turned to her.

"Of course." Elizabeth gently patted his hand.

"Can I have this chair? I want something that belonged to him, and even though I'm leaving, I'll be coming back." Keith looked so hopeful.

"It's yours." Elizabeth stood up.

"Thanks, Nan." Keith rose to his full height, and she barely came to his chest.

When he wrapped his arms around her, she had to fight to keep the tears at bay. Her grandchildren dearly loved Jack, and each of them had their own special bond with him. Keith's connection was their love of reading, and he would sit with Jack discussing literature for hours sometimes. It was going to be yet another thing she missed.

"You're going to move to Hopedale, right?" Keith asked as she walked him to his Jeep.

"Don't you go starting too," Elizabeth warned.

"Nan, none of us want you here alone." Keith wrapped his arm around her.

"I'm quite capable of looking after myself." Elizabeth gently patted him on the arm.

"I don't doubt that, but we'd rather have you closer." Keith kissed her cheek.

"You're moving. I won't be closer to you." She chuckled.

"But you will be there when I come to visit." Keith smiled as he climbed into his Jeep.

"I'm still thinking about it." Elizabeth stepped back from the Jeep. "Drive safe and call when you get home."

Keith waved as he drove away, and Elizabeth kept the forced smile on her face until he was out of sight. She slowly made her way to the porch and eased down in Jack's chair.

"Maybe they're right. I have nobody left here in Cape Broyle," she murmured to herself.

She gazed out at the ocean, and for the first time in her life, it didn't make her feel at ease. It didn't give her a sense of peace like it usually did, but when a warm gust of wind blew across her face, Elizabeth felt as if an arm wrapped around her. She glanced up to see a fishing boat sail out of the harbor, bobbing up and down on the waves.

"Jack, are you trying to tell me something?" Elizabeth whispered.

She knew the answer because he wouldn't want her living alone or so far from everyone she loved. Elizabeth knew what she had to do, she was going to Hopedale, and she'd keep the home she shared with Jack for the family.

Chapter 40

The decision to move to Hopedale was the best thing she ever did. Not only did Alice and Kathleen need her help around the house and the pub, but her grandchildren were in desperate need of some guidance.

"A.J., you and Nicky can't be running around with every woman who smiles at you." Elizabeth shook her finger at her grandson as he hung up his phone after making plans for his third date of the week.

"Nan, we're young and playing the field." Aaron winked as he tossed his knapsack over his shoulder.

Aaron was in his second year of university and had become a completely different young man since Bethany broke his heart. He jumped from girl to girl without a thought of letting anyone get close again.

"What are we going to do with you?" Elizabeth shook her head as he leaned down and kissed her cheek.

"Love me like all the girls do," Aaron smirked as she gave him a swat on his backside.

"Get to school." Elizabeth shook her head as he hugged his mother and headed out.

"He's such a different person." Kathleen sighed.

"He'll get himself together. He's still young," Elizabeth told her daughter-in-law.

"I hope you're right." Kathleen placed two cups of tea on the table.

"If not, I'll give him a duff in the arse." Elizabeth nodded.

A year had passed since Jack died, but the family still felt his loss. James had married, and he and his wife had given birth to a baby boy. Elizabeth was thrilled to hold her first great-grandchild and a little sad that the little boy would never get to meet Jack.

One evening about three months after the baby was born, James and Sarah came to visit. Elizabeth sensed that there was something wrong the minute she looked at James, and Sarah's expression confirmed it.

"We have something to tell you," James said after supper.

"My goodness, you aren't pregnant again." Kathleen chuckled, but her smile faded when James and Sarah didn't laugh.

"What's wrong?" Elizabeth asked.

"I found a lump in my breast. The doctor told me today that it's cancer, and I've got to have my breast removed." Sarah swallowed.

"My God." Kathleen wrapped her arms around Sarah.

"We're all here for you, and don't you worry, we'll get you through this," Elizabeth said with as much confidence as she could.

"We'll know more after some more tests, but they don't want to waste any time," James told them as he blinked back the tears.

Elizabeth knew that there was a chance Sarah might not survive the disease. It wasn't fair to them, especially with them just starting a family and a life together. They'd bought a house in Hopedale and were in the process of landscaping.

"We wanted to know if you could watch Mason? The doctor is admitting her tomorrow," James asked.

"You don't need to ask. Of course, we'll watch him." Elizabeth didn't give Kathleen or Sean a chance to speak.

"Betty is right. You take care of Sarah, and we'll make sure Mason is well taken care of." Kathleen hugged Sarah again.

Their lives were about to be turned upside down again, and the only thing they could do was stick together like they always did. It was the O'Connor way.

Chapter 41

Elizabeth couldn't believe that she had come face to face with Tommy Roberts. Although calling a grown man Tommy seemed strange. He'd grown older, but he was still as handsome as she remembered.

Half of what was said at James' house that evening was a blur, and she did her best not to show Tommy how seeing him affected her. It was confusing because she still loved Jack so much, but as soon as she heard Tommy's voice, her heart jumped in her chest.

She didn't want to feel the way she did. He had broken her heart so long ago, and it surprised her just how much anger she still had buried deep inside.

"Elizabeth Power, well as I live and breathe," Tommy said with a huge smile.

"Tommy Roberts. Dear God, it is you." Elizabeth's heart pounded in her chest as she tried to keep her composure.

"Yes, it's me." Tommy was still so handsome, but she glared at the man who broke her heart so long ago.

"I didn't think you were ever coming back to Newfoundland for love nor money." Elizabeth crossed her arms over her chest and tried to keep her voice steady.

"I've been back in Newfoundland for about three years, Elizabeth," Tommy said, and it irritated her because nobody called her that anymore.

"It's Betty. Nobody calls me Elizabeth since my fadder died." Elizabeth turned back to the sink.

"You'll always be Elizabeth to me," Tommy said then turned to Marina. "I didn't realize you were related to her."

Marina Kelly was the sister of John's wife. She was also in love with James, and the feeling was mutual. It had been four years since Sarah passed away from breast cancer, and it had taken James a long time to move on.

"She's James' grandmother," Marina told him.

"Ah... So, Jack won the prize, did he?" Tommy chuckled. "Where is the son of a gun?"

Elizabeth swallowed the lump that formed in her throat at the sound of Jack's name. Before she turned around to tell Tommy that Jack had passed away, she straightened her spine. She wondered how he would react to the news.

"For your information, Mr. Roberts, I won the prize when I married Jack, and if you must know, we lost the love of my life six years ago," Elizabeth snapped.

"Love of your life, huh? I remember he wasn't always." Tommy raised an eyebrow.

"He always was, but I was too blind to see it at first, but thank the Lord, my mistake left the province for bigger and better things." Elizabeth stomped out of the room and didn't look back.

She was so angry, but she wasn't about to let her family see how she felt about Tommy. She didn't like the old feelings that rose to the surface, and it seemed like a betrayal to Jack.

For several weeks, she didn't allow anyone to know how much it bothered her to know her first love was so close. Elizabeth didn't know how her children and grandchildren would react if they knew the whole story.

The day that Marina and James invited her to supper and she arrived at the same time as Tommy, she thought her heart would explode in her chest. He stood on the step with a nervous smile, and she wouldn't even look him in the eye.

"Jimmy, what is the meaning of this?" Elizabeth pushed by Tommy and entered the house.

"We'll explain, Nan, but it's something you need to know, so please give us a chance," James begged.

"Why does he have to be here?" Elizabeth hitched her thumb over her shoulder toward Tommy.

"It'll all make sense soon. I promise," Marina interjected and helped Elizabeth off with her coat. "Tom, please come in. We've got a lot to tell you, too."

Elizabeth stared off into space as Marina read a letter she'd found. It concerned a daughter Tommy fathered, but he didn't know. The more Marina read, the more Elizabeth's icy exterior melted. According to Marina, she'd found journals from not only Tommy's daughter but granddaughter as well.

"I'd like to read them, if you allow me," Tom said.

"I've got them boxed up in the spare room. You can take them when you leave." Marina smiled and clasped Tom's hand.

"I'll take good care of them and make sure you get them back for Danny." Tommy sat straight up and gasped a little. "This means…"

"It means that our Danny is your great-grandson." It was the first time she spoke since they went into the living room.

Danny was Marina's son from a previous relationship. The boy's father had discovered he'd been adopted before he died and several of his family secrets had been uncovered when Marina dug into her son's heritage.

"Elizabeth, I want to explain what happened with Dorothy." Tom seemed embarrassed.

"It's none of my business." Elizabeth straightened her dress so she wouldn't show the hurt.

"I still want to tell you what happened." Tom glanced at James.

"We'll leave you two to talk," Marina offered.

"No. I want all of you to hear this, but please, Elizabeth, I'd like you to stay and listen as well," Tom begged.

"I'll stay, but if you call me Elizabeth once more, I'm going to slap you up the side of your head." Elizabeth pointed her finger in Tom's face.

"Agreed." Tom chuckled as Elizabeth sat again. "First of all, just to make it clear, I didn't know about any of this. When I went to live with the Doyles, it was after the fire. The night I got there, I was angry. I had to leave without talking to you, Betty. Mr. Doyle came to the station and picked me up. When I told him to take me to see Betty, he told me he would do no such thing, and I was to forget my life in Cape Broyle." Tom clasped his hands together and stared down at them.

"The first night, I'm ashamed to say, I stole a bottle of whiskey from Mr. Doyle's liquor cabinet, and I snuck out into the woodshed. I was about halfway through the bottle, and halfway through a letter I was writing Betty, when Dorothy came in. I won't bore you with how things happened, but it did, and I was so ashamed I tore up the letter. I figured it was better if you'd hate me rather than find out that I betrayed you." Tom reached out to touch Elizabeth's hand, but she pulled it away.

"I guess it worked because even after all these years, you still do. Anyway, for the next few weeks, I worked with the Doyles at their home. Then Mr. Doyle told me he was shipping me off to his brother's farm in Alberta because he needed the extra workers. He did agree to take me to Cape Broyle to say goodbye to you, but when I got there, your father told me you were seeing Jack O'Connor, and I was to leave you alone. I left and never came back."

Elizabeth didn't say anything for a few minutes. She couldn't believe her father would do such a thing, but she wasn't surprised because her father didn't like Tommy.

"Nan, are you okay?" James asked.

"Tommy, I'm sorry my fadder lied to you, but it was over a year after you left that I took up with Jack. My dad introduced us because Jack was on his fishing boat. He'd just ended an engagement." She stopped and glanced at James.

They didn't know about her life before Jack. They didn't know that Tommy had been the love of her life and she'd planned to marry him one day.

"But Jack was an amazing husband, father, and grandfather. I wouldn't change a second of my life with him. We had a good life." Elizabeth blinked back the tears that formed.

"I'm glad, Betty. I'm glad you were happy." Tom smiled.

"Why didn't you ever marry?" Marina asked.

"I just didn't find anyone who could hold a candle to Betty."
Tom smiled, and Elizabeth knew her cheeks had flushed.

She quickly composed herself. It was all well and good that
Tommy had appeared in front of her out of the blue, and she wondered
if it was for more than to find out that his brief affair had resulted in a
daughter. Maybe he was back for her.

"Okay, enough of this malarkey, I came here for supper, and
I'm ready to eat." She headed to the kitchen.

Elizabeth glanced back at Tommy as he stood up. He gave her
a small smile, and as if time had reversed, she saw the young man she
fell in love with all those years ago. No matter what everyone called
him, he would always be Tommy Roberts, the farmer's son who stole
her heart the first time he smiled at her. What would the future hold for
them?

Chapter 42

Elizabeth shook her head as she watched her granddaughter dance with her new husband. Pam was the last of her grandchildren to get married, and in less than a month, Elizabeth would walk down the aisle herself, again.

She still missed Jack every day and probably would until the day she died, but she promised him she would go on living after he passed. It was difficult, but it was what he wanted.

After all the danger and evil her family had endured over the last several years, they were stronger for it. She glanced around the reception hall and saw happy couples, smiling kids, and numerous friends. Elizabeth and Jack always wanted all that for their family. She could see him in every smiling face around the room.

"Are you okay, darling?" Tom asked next to her.

"I'm fine. Just happy to see all the love in this room." Elizabeth smiled at the man next to her.

"There's a lot here, and it all started with the love between you and Jack." Tom kissed her cheek.

"I love you too, Tom." Elizabeth cupped his cheek.

"I love you too, Betty, but I know part of your heart will always belong to Jack, and that's okay." Tom kissed her palm.

"He used to say the same about you," she whispered.

Elizabeth didn't know how long more she would have with Tom. They were both in their eighties, but she knew every day they had together she would cherish. Elizabeth truly believed Tom came back into her life because Jack sent him back to her again.

She truly believed things happened for a reason, and the fact that Tom came back into her life in such a random way proved it. She knew all those years ago that she and Tom were meant to be. It just took a few decades for it to come true.

Epilogue

"You look so beautiful, Nan." Jess smiled as her eyes filled with tears.

"Tom is going to flip when he sees you." Lily, Ian's daughter, grinned.

"That dress looks amazing, Nan." Kristy handed Elizabeth a bouquet of white roses.

Elizabeth turned to take one last look in the mirror before she took that walk down the aisle. She and Tom were about to join their lives together. It was surreal.

"You need to stop all your fussing. I look like an old woman." Elizabeth stared at herself.

"Nan, you are not an old woman." Isabelle wrapped her arm around Elizabeth.

"Isabelle is right. Age is just a state of mind, which would probably make you younger than all of us." Pam chuckled as she lowered herself onto one of the chairs and rested her hand on her pregnant belly.

"Are you sure you're going to make it through the day, cuz?" Jess asked Pam.

"These babies better wait until I make sure Nan is hitched." Pam rubbed her belly.

She and her husband Damon found out two months after their wedding that she was expecting. Six weeks later, she told everyone she was having twins.

Cora was over the moon, but she constantly worried about her daughter, and from what Elizabeth had seen, Cora was driving Pam a little crazy.

"I'm so glad I'm only having one." Jess gently touched her small baby bump.

"I hate you right now," Pam glared.

Elizabeth smiled as she listened to her granddaughters' conversation. It calmed the flutter in her stomach that seemed ridiculous at her age.

When the door to the diner opened, two of the men she loved most in the world walked in dressed in black suits. They were older and reminded her more of Jack every year.

"Are you ready to make an honest man out of Tom, Mudder?" Kurt winked.

"Someone has too." Elizabeth chuckled.

"Let's get this show on the road." Sean stepped next to her and held out his arm.

The girls scurried ahead of her and took their places at the end of the pub. Alice and Kathleen had turned the pub into a beautiful area for Elizabeth to marry Tom, and they would have the reception there as well.

Since Kurt was the mayor of Hopedale, he would perform the service, and Sean would walk her down the aisle. Cora was her Matron of Honor, and Tom had asked James to be his best man.

As the music started, Elizabeth peeked inside as Cora began to make her way to the archway in front of the stage. Each one of her grandchildren and great-grand-children stood on either side of the aisle, but she had no idea why.

As Cora stepped next to the stage, the music changed, and the voices of Aaron and his wife Bethany echoed through the pub singing, "I Will Always Love You."

Sean smiled down at her as they slowly walked to where Tom stood waiting for her. On her way to the man she loved, the children dropped flower petals in front of her the entire way.

Sean leaned down and kissed her cheek when they stepped next to Tom. For a moment, he stood there, and she saw him swallow several times before he spoke.

"Be happy, Mudder. I truly believe Fadder brought Tom back to you," Sean whispered next to her ear.

Elizabeth's eyes filled with tears as she wrapped her arms around Sean and hugged him. He'd struggled with the idea of Elizabeth getting remarried, but he would never say anything to her. She could tell by the way he would look at Tom, and Kathleen told her.

Kurt wasn't as apprehensive, but she truly believed that because Tom asked for their blessing, it made them realize he respected them and wanted them to be comfortable before he proposed.

"I believe that too," Elizabeth whispered into Sean's ear before she released him and stepped next to Tom.

Through the ceremony, Kurt stopped several times to compose himself, and as she glanced around, everyone seemed to have tears in their eyes, even her.

"Tom, repeat after me, I, Tom, take you, Elizabeth, to be my wife. I promise to be true to you in good times and in bad, in sickness and in health. I will love and honor you all the days of my life," Kurt said.

"I, Tom, take you, Elizabeth, to be my wife. I promise to be true to you in good times and in bad, in sickness and in health. I will love and honor you all the days of my life. Oh, and if I can add this little bit, I will always be your chauffeur when you need one." Tom grinned.

Everyone laughed because Elizabeth had stopped driving since she and Tom had been together. Whenever she needed to go anywhere, Tom would bring her. It was an ongoing joke with the family that he'd become her chauffeur.

"I forgot about that part, Tom." Kurt chuckled.

"That is an important one." Tom smiled down at her.

"This feels really strange to say, but, Elizabeth, repeat after me. I, Elizabeth, take you, Tom, to be my husband. I promise to be true to you in good times and in bad, in sickness and in health. I will love and honor you all the days of my life," Kurt said.

"I, Elizabeth, take you, Tom, to be my husband. I promise to be true to you in good times and in bad, in sickness and in health. I will love and honor you all the days of my life." Elizabeth turned to Kurt. "That will be the only time you call me anything but Mudder."

When the laughter died down, Kurt continued with the ceremony. Elizabeth and Tom exchanged rings and signed the papers that made everything legal. As they turned around, Tom took her hand, and they faced each other.

"By the power vested in me, I now pronounce you, husband and wife. Tom, you may kiss your bride." Kurt nodded.

Tom lowered his head, and his lips touched hers in a soft, tender kiss. As she was about to pull away, Tom dipped her down and gave her one long, hard kiss.

The pub erupted into applause and catcalls as Tom pulled her back up on her feet. Elizabeth felt her cheeks flush as she tried to catch her breath.

"Now, that was a kiss," Nick shouted.

"You go, Tom," Mike called out.

"Nan is blushing." Ian laughed.

"Everyone, let me introduce, for the first time, Mr. and Mrs. Thomas Roberts," Kurt shouted over the din of the crowd.

The applause became deafening as she and Tom walked to the exit of the pub and made their way into the front foyer between the pub and diner.

Jack's Place was where they were starting their life together, and most people would think that was a little odd, but to them, Jack would always be a part of their lives.

"I love you, Betty." Tom pulled her into his arms.

"I love you too." Elizabeth touched his cheek.

No matter how much time they had left together, she would make sure they lived every day to the fullest. Tom was brought back to her for a reason and she wouldn't waste a moment of it.

Elizabeth had to be the luckiest woman in the world. To have the life she had and to have two of the most wonderful men in the world to fill her heart. Tom and Jack would always share Elizabeth's heart.

The End

About the Author

What does someone say to describe themselves? You could start by saying what others say about you. Scratch that. It doesn't matter what others think about you. So here we go.

First of all, I'm a wife and mother. I'm also a grandmother. That alone would fulfill any woman's life, and to be honest, it does. But.....

I'm also a writer, someone who loves to tell stories of love, suspense, heartache, and of course, happily ever after. For most of my life, I've written those stories for myself. A type of therapy, I suppose. I love the characters I create. They become part of who I am because there's part of me in them.

So... Now that you know this about me. I hope when you read my books and fall in love with them.

You should also know that I'm a Newfoundlander. What is that you ask? We're a proud people who live on an island off the east coast of Canada. Some people believe Canada ends with Nova Scotia. It doesn't. If you keep going east, there is a beautiful island full of amazing people and magnificent scenery. That is where my stories are set because let's face it. The best stories always come from the places you know and love.

If there is anything else you would like to know about me, ask me!

Also check out

O'Connor Brothers Series

O'Connor Girls

Available on

Amazon and

Kindle Unlimited.

Rhonda Brewer

Keep up to date on all things new.

Follow me on

Facebook

Twitter

Instagram

MeWe

All Author

Bookbub

Sign up for my newsletter and never miss another release!

http://www.rhondabrewerauthor.com/talk-to-me

www.ingramcontent.com/pod-product-compliance
Lightning Source LLC
Chambersburg PA
CBHW071151250626
47159CB00001B/67